Irish Connection

BY

Keith Hoare

Irish Connection

By

Keith Hoare

All characters in this publication are fictitious and any resemblance to real persons, living or dead is purely coincidental.

The right of Keith Hoare to be identified as the author of the work has been asserted by him in accordance with the Copyright, Designs and Patent Act 1988.

II

ISBN - 978-1-908090-49-2

Published by: Ragged Cover Publishing

Chapter 1

Jack Panark was leaning against the back wall of a repair garage, smoking. In the same garage, his son Bart was shuffling around a large bolt with his foot. Aged eighteen, scrawny with tight black curly hair, Bart believed he was 'the man', and with plenty of money in his pocket, he'd little trouble attracting girls.

"Why are we in this dump, Dad, she's a fucking nuisance having us come here. I've places to go. She's nearly twenty minutes late already."

"Yes, well, just remember who pays the bills, so if Mace says we come, we come," Jack replied curtly.

At that moment the garage door opened and two men came inside, followed by a woman shuffling along behind with the help of a stick. The woman was not more than five feet two, grossly overweight, with a moon-face and red permed hair. Her clothes were tatty, the skirt less than an inch from the floor. She was also gasping, obviously struggling with her breathing.

Jack threw his cigarette away and came forward. "Mace, you shouldn't be out, we'd have come to the house."

By now she was standing in front of them both. "Sometimes it's necessary to get out, Jack." Then she looked across at Bart. "Come here," she demanded.

He walked over, hands in his pockets.

"You have a problem with what you do for me? Not happy with your pay?" she asked.

He shrugged indifferently. "It's alright, but I have expenses and could do with more."

5

She nodded her head up and down slowly. "We'd all like more. But if you think you can do better, get yourself down to the jobcentre and see if they'll give you a job that pays three hundred a week at your age."

"So, what's the point? I work for it."

Mace turned to one of the men who had come in with her. "Bring the girl."

He left the garage, minutes later he was back, grasping a girl by the arm. Her name was Bridget; she was seventeen, with black, shoulder-length hair, slim, wearing jeans and a jumper.

Bart stared at her. "Why's Bridget here?"

Mace ignored the question, already turning her attention to Bridget. "It's good of you to come, Bridget," she said with a hint of sarcasm in her voice.

"That's a laugh, didn't have a fucking choice, did I? Then, who's going to pay for my time? I'm losing money standing around here."

Mace smiled. "You're right, you are losing money." Then she shrugged with obvious indifference. "Mind you, by what returns I've seen, not so bloody much, you can't be working more than a couple of hours a day."

"Excuse me, I work at least seven hours a day, often ten, six days a week."

"Interesting," Mace commented, "in that case, are you offering an extended happy hour, or two for one deals, believing you're competing with the supermarkets?"

She sneered at Mace. "I'm not a bloody shop, I'm a prostitute, and charge what I'm told to charge. Whoever's told you differently, I'll freaking kick their head in."

Mace began to shake her head slowly in despair.

"Bridget... Bridget... I presume you've had some sort of education and can add up. Even if I meet you halfway and agree you work eight hours a day, six days a week, even with your simple mind it must add up to a grand a week. So tell me, why have I only had three hundred a week for the last month? Did you really believe I'd accept that sort of money?"

She looked down. "I don't earn a grand, more like seven hundred and I give it all to Bart as I'm told. He gives me two hundred back to live on."

"Yes she does and I pass it all on," Bart cut in.

"Then clear off, Bridget and get to work," Mace told her.

Bridget didn't delay, this woman frightened her and she was glad to be gone.

After she left, Mace turned her attention to Bart. "I had them bring Bridget so both you and I could hear just how much she was paying you, and you have agreed she was correct. That would say to me, she's not withholding. I could have brought Teresa, Stark, Billy and Gwen. But I've already had my boys talk to them. All claimed you've been taking between four and six hundred from them, every week. That on average should have been around two and half grand. So why have I only got two grand?"

Bart grinned. "I've expenses, besides, I'm entitled to more. You don't have to take the shit off them every day, whining they don't have enough to live on. I have to kick their arises when they won't go out and work, if it's raining or cold. I think two grand kickback is good money, for someone who does nothing."

Suddenly Mace raised her stick and hit Bart across

the side of his head. He screamed in pain, but she kept hitting him until he fell to the floor, rolling himself up in a ball, trying to protect his head from the blows. "You think!" she screamed at him. "You're not paid to think, yet you are prepared to steal money from the family, because you have some distorted belief you're worth more. You aren't worth shit, people like you are two a penny."

Jack just stood there watching, not lifting a hand to help his son. Bart had made a grave error in believing 'the family' would turn their back and allow him to steal from them, he had to be taught a lesson.

Mace stopped hitting Bart, her voice returning to a more normal level. "You're part of my extended family, your father has worked for me since you were in nappies. He vouched for you, said you were honest and you stood in front of me saying how much you appreciated the opportunity to join the family business. It was all lies and you not only bring shame to your father, but to us all." She looked at Jack. "You accept your son's let you down and must pay?"

"I do, Mace. Son, or not, he must be punished."

"Then get him ready," she told the men who had come in with her.

Bart was dragged up, forced face down on a large, steel table, his arms above his head, the palms of his hands flat on the table.

"Please, I beg you, I'll give back every penny I took," he shouted in desperation.

Mace smiled. "You will certainly do that, and carry the scars for the rest of your life as a reminder that you never take anything, that isn't yours, from the family again. Punish your son, Jack."

Jack picked up a lump hammer, sighing to himself. However much he'd warned Bart to never touch a penny belonging to Mace, he hadn't listened. Now, if he refused Mace's demand, Bart would be killed. To save his son's life, the punishment had to be carried out. Raising the hammer, he brought it down on his son's left hand. Bart screamed in pain as his hand was shattered, then he passed out.

Mace stood for a moment, then turned and began to shuffle out of the garage. The men who had come with her followed, leaving Jack to wrap a rag around the shattered hand. Then he began to slap Bart's face to wake him. He had to get him to hospital as quickly as he could.

Chapter 2 (Seven Weeks Later)

Odette Boyer, who five weeks earlier had come to Southern Ireland from France, to work in a bar, shuffled uneasily in the back of the car. She was wearing knickers, heeled shoes and a buttoned-up coat to hide the fact she was virtually naked. Since coming here, her life had been a nightmare. The bar job was nothing more than a front to lure girls into prostitution. She couldn't believe how stupid she'd been in coming. Even the wages were a giveaway at more than twice the going rate. But the communications with a woman who called herself Sandra, had convinced her it was a high-class bar in a hotel catering for the rich, requiring a girl with good conversational French as well as English. The very day she arrived, she realised something must be wrong. She had been taken to a dilapidated house by two men and locked in a bedroom. The following morning she'd been told in no uncertain terms there was no work in a bar, she was there to work as a prostitute. Her objections were met with a good thrashing morning and night to wear her down, leaving her with no option but to do what was asked of her. Since then she'd been locked in a room with nothing to wear, apart from her knickers and a nightdress. Her work consisted, in the day, of going through a connecting door in the cellar of the house, through to the adjoining one. There she'd be taken to a room and was expected to entertain at least five clients an hour. Late afternoon, she'd return the same way through the cellar to her own room, be given a break and food, before leaving with a minder to be taken to a hotel until the early hours, servicing up to ten clients before being brought back. There was no way of hiding anything, even her hair was down and she was not even allowed a hairgrip. When she'd finished, she'd return in her working clothes, which would be sexy underclothes, suspenders, top and a short skirt. Once in her room, she'd have to remove them all, while the minder who had taken her watched, before being allowed to put her nightdress on. He would then place the work clothes into a bag. Again, as when she was brought to the hotel, Odette had no chance of returning with anything she may have picked up in the hotel, or been given by a client.

The car turned down a narrow passage, coming out in a hotel car park. The driver, she knew as Simon Murphy. He was a man in his forties and her pimp. He turned to look at her. "Come on, move yourself, we've a busy night," he said, getting out of the car himself.

As soon as she was outside the car, with one hand carrying a bag with her work clothes inside it, he grabbed her arm, propelling her through an already open fire escape door and up two flights of stairs. Coming through the fire exit door onto the corridor, he led her to a hotel bedroom. The porter was already waiting, handing Simon the key and taking a small bundle of Euro from him, before leaving them alone.

Odette knew the routine. The room would have an interconnecting door to the next bedroom. She would be working in there until the early hours, the clients waiting in the other room. There was no escape, the door to the corridor of the bedroom she worked in would be firmly locked.

Simon slammed the door shut, following her into

the next room through the connecting door, checking its door to the corridor was locked and the telephone had been removed. By now Odette had taken the coat off, allowing him to make sure she carried nothing.

He glanced at his watch. "Your first client's in ten minutes, get yourself dressed and come through to the other room ready to welcome him."

***

Odette was bent over the side of the bed, the man behind her going at her for all he was worth. This was the sixth man of the night. Already she had begun making appropriate noises, lying to him saying she was coming and he should fuck her harder. She just wanted to get it over with.

The next moment he gave a final gasp and he pulled away. "You're a good shag, after I have a piss, I want you on top of me," he told her, as he walked through to the bathroom.

Odette sighed and picked up both his clothes and hers off the floor, throwing them onto a settee. As she turned away, she heard a dull thud. Looking back, a gun was on the floor at the side of the sofa. It must have fallen out of the man's coat. Instinctively she grabbed the gun, slipping it between the mattress and the bed base. Guns were something that Odette knew all about. She'd lived with them since she was a child. Her father had been a gunsmith and he would have her in his shop, stripping them down for cleaning. Over the years she must have handled hundreds, from regular shotguns used by farmers to illegal guns her father would take on to alter, for illegal purposes. He had no option, times were not easy and they

12

would never have survived looking after a few shotguns. She also tested most in the cellar of the shop, soundproofed and set-up for testing for the correct operation of a gun and the alignment of the sights. He'd died last year of cancer. Partly it was his own fault, chain-smoking for years. But her mother had never got over it and had closed in on herself, no longer interested in life. So bad was her mental state, she'd been taken into a special care home, leaving Odette virtually penniless after the house was sold to pay for the care. That was why she'd applied for this job, just to get out of the area and start a new life.

By now the man was back, slapping her across the head a number of times, because she wasn't ready for him. Odette just took it and worked hard to give him what he wanted, to prevent a repeat.

Now he'd finished with her and was dressing. "I'll use you again, I think," he told her as he left the room.

She on her part was virtually holding her breath hoping he'd not noticed the gun was missing. But he didn't, so she went through to the bathroom to prepare herself for the next client. Odette had no illusions, by the time the night was over, she'd have been with ten to twelve men.

***

At last the night was over. Odette was in the back of the car being taken to the house they kept her locked up in. It had been over two hours since the client who dropped the gun left. All the time she'd been expecting him to return and she'd made plans to use the gun if that happened. As it was he hadn't, now she was alone with Simon and armed.

Arriving at the house, they both climbed out the

13

car. Simon gave Odette the bag to carry, when his mobile began to ring.

"Wait," he demanded of Odette, grabbing her arm, as he answered the call. He listened all the time, watching Odette. "I'll check, I'll call you back."

Once inside the house, he slammed the door. Odette made to go to the kitchen. A sandwich was always left out for her by the woman who lived in the house who would be in bed by now.

"Just one minute," Simon shouted at her. "A client has called, tells me his gun has gone missing from his coat."

She turned to look directly at him. "So why ask me? If he's lost the bloody gun, that's his problem, not mine."

"Yes, well, to be sure, give me your bag and get yourself undressed here. Then you can collect your sandwich."

Odette threw her bag down, which contained nothing but her make-up bag and personal hygiene items.

While he went through the bag, she backed away, reaching around her back, pulling the short skirt up, grasping the gun trapped between the suspender belt and her knickers. "You'll find nothing in the bag, I'm holding the gun. Now very carefully remove your jacket, t-shirt and jeans," she told him in a matter-of-fact way. "Then I'll be sure you're carrying nothing."

He looked up from the bag, his mouth dropping slightly. "So you had it all the time. Give me the gun and I'll say no more about it."

She smiled. "You don't get it do you? This is my

get-out of jail card, so to speak. Have any sort of belief I don't know how to use a gun, think again, I do. I'll also blow your fucking brains across the floor, after what you've put me through, unless you strip."

He did as she told him. "So what now?"

"We go to your office, you open the safe and give me my passport. Also, what money there is in the safe."

He didn't argue, just went to the office and pulled open the safe. "Here's your passport, and a grand. Take any more and Mace will come after you, you'll never be safe."

"Who's this Mace?"

"Don't you know anything? She runs the Murphy gang, which I'm part of, so she owns you. They are the most notorious gang in both the Republic and Northern Ireland. Mace is not a nice person to cross."

"I'm owned by no one. Although if it was her who put me in this place, I'll look forward to meeting this woman. Where do I find her?"

He sniggered. "So you believe you can just walk into her house? Many have tried, Odette and are now dead, or so badly beaten they are crippled for life. But if you want to know, she has a place in O'Devaney Gardens. Believe me girl, that is an area you should avoid. Strangers stand out, she'd know you were there within minutes of you entering the area."

"I'll keep that in mind. But to place her on notice, empty the safe completely."

"There's over twenty-five grand in here, I can hide a grand and claim you escaped from your room. It's more than enough to get you back to France with ease, or do you really want to die that much?"

"That's big of you, you probably earned more than a grand tonight. So I take the lot, you can even tell her who took it and I'll be coming for her."

Simon shrugged indifferently, taking the money from the safe, placing it all on the desktop. At least this way, when Mace heard how a client who was part of a paramilitary group had foolishly dropped his gun and never noticed Odette had it, she'd understand he'd had no option. "There, that's the lot, enjoy it while you can, but don't take too long over spending it."

Odette took the cash, stuffing it in her bag. "I'll go now, I'll also take the car. I can't say it's been nice knowing you, it hasn't, but you owe me."

"What are you talking about? Over twenty-five grand for a month or so of your life and a few shags, that's a good deal. So piss off and watch your back."

She just smiled and fired the gun twice. The noise was shattering, her aim was good, both Simon's knees had been shattered, collapsing to the floor in agony, screaming at her that she was dead.

Odette ignored his threats and left the house, climbing into the car, she was soon leaving the house far behind.

Chapter 3

Colonel Karen Harris, commander of Unit T, an EU financed military unit, formed to help combat people trafficking, entered the camp meeting room. Already in the room were senior members of her surveillance teams, along with Stanley, who headed her intelligence unit. They all stood and came to attention as she walked to the front.

"At ease, gentlemen. I realise it's very early, I even missed my coffee this morning to be here, before I fly to Northern Ireland. Would anyone be kind enough to pour me a cup, please, while I sort my papers?"

A few minutes later she stood, and then, switching on a projector with a remote control held in her hand, a picture came up showing a large family group.

"These people, gentlemen, are the entire Murphy family. In all, there's thirty-nine of them and rising, with marriages and children." Karen changed the photo. "This is the grandmother, she's known as Mace, why we don't know, her Christian name is Doreen. But she heads the family." Karen hesitated and looked round the audience. "This eighteen stone woman, registered disabled by her obesity, is apparently no kind-hearted, sweet old lady doting over her grandchildren. She rules with a rod of iron, meeting out severe punishments to anyone who does not follow her rigid rules. That punishment is not limited to those outside her family, even members of her family are not immune."

Karen changed the photo to that of a lad. "This is Bart Panark. According to his father's statement at the hospital, he crushed his hand moving drums of oil in a garage. It's rubbish, as the injuries are consistent with a blow to the hand. He doesn't work in a garage, he looks after a number of prostitutes. We believe he's had a disagreement with Mace and this was his punishment. But I'll come back to Bart shortly."

Returning to the family photo, Karen looked around the room. "According to the British police, Mace, among other illegal operations, is now going into people trafficking. But unlike a Mafia type set-up, where they use people beyond their family, this woman doesn't, everyone is related, be it husbands, wives, sons or daughters, all of whom she affectionately calls her troops. That business, again according to the police, ranges from intimidation and extortion, even by the grandchildren in the playground. Petty crime, such as shoplifting by the teenagers of the family. The pimping of prostitutes by the older ones, besides drug dealing and organised crime. Apparently, now they are involved in the trafficking of girls from both the old Russian federation and Asia, into the brothels of Europe." Karen took a sip of her coffee. "Publicly the family is rarely out of the papers, not for their serious criminal activities, although a few of them are often in and out of prison for GBH, but because they are the original neighbours from hell. None of them own their own home, they're all in social housing, both in Northern Ireland, the Republic and the UK. Most, would you believe, claiming benefits? Then, by what I've read about the complaints against this lot, believe me, you would not want any part of this family living next door, or even in the same street as you. Your children would not be safe, your wife would be afraid of even walking along the street, you could find yourself paying them not to trash your car, beat up your kids, or a hundred and one other ways they have of giving your family a life of hell. The authorities are at a loss at what to do, with many of the officials afraid to be seen publicly opposing the family. When they have, most witnesses clam up, or change their story, often far too frightened to stand-up and be counted. Then the family plays on their need for state assistance, surrounds themselves with human rights activists, besides the do-gooders who always seem to jump out of the woodwork, believing this is a family that has lost its way and we should help not pillory them."

"May I ask what seems to me an obvious question, Colonel?" Lieutenant Calder cut in.

"What is it you want to know, Lieutenant?"

"I've known you a long time, Colonel. The way you're wording your briefing, I don't believe you're convinced in what has been said to you regarding international trafficking?"

The room remained silent, as she stood, facing them all, before leaning slightly forwards, both hands flat on the table top. "You're correct, Lieutenant. I think the very suggestion that such people could run an international trafficking operation is rubbish. Alone, they neither have the connections, nor the resources needed. Don't get me wrong, I'll accept extortion, local crime, neighbours from hell, even pimping, or snatching the odd woman. But international trafficking on the scale suggested? No. I've been in the business far too long to know if what I'm being told is correct. Large operations in people trafficking cannot be operated by a small gang like

19

this one, particularly when their base is not located on the European mainland."

Karen took a sip of her coffee and opened a file in front of her.

"Having said that, over the last months we've tracked, along with EUROPOL, representatives of the Urabeños cartel while they have been in Europe. This is a Colombian cartel that controls vast shipments of cocaine into the USA. Normally we'd not have been interested in this group, it is another department that deals with drug trafficking, if they hadn't actively been meeting with known people trafficker cartels. Such cartels, particularly the ones who have come across from South America in the past, are violent in the extreme, expect complete allegiance and will kill indiscriminately those who don't follow their dictates. Urabeños is among such cartels. Their gunmen don't even question why someone is to be killed, they just go and kill them, often openly in the street, such is their arrogance and indifference to authority. Besides other cartels, they have been observed having meetings with members of the Murphy gang." Karen hesitated for a moment, before carrying on. "The police are convinced that these meetings are not just drug related, they have intelligence that the Urabeños intend to ship women in from the Americas and they are looking for outlets. The Murphy's are strongest in the Irish Republic, mainly because prostitution is legal what isn't legal is for others, such as pimps, to gain financially. That means nothing, as most girls are paying the gangs for protection, which is another word for a pimp. Soon the law could well be changed to make paying for sex illegal, to target the men looking for sex. We know that there is a steady stream of women trafficked into the country, from traffickers we've arrested, and with the Murphy's' largest part of their extended family in the Irish Republic, they are well placed to accept such women, besides control them. In my view, to go into trafficking could be the Murphy gang's downfall, if they intend to get into bed with the Urabeños. Double-cross the Colombians in any way and they will kill you. That group does not mess around."

Again Karen stopped her briefing, allowing them to catch up with their notes while she finished her coffee.

Handing out envelopes to each of the officers, she waited until they had opened them to look at the contents. "The members of the Murphy family listed in your envelope are your targets. I want you to study your part of the operation and submit a plan for Stanley to sanction. We want tight surveillance, in fact by the end of the surveillance part of the operation, it's essential we have a complete picture of all their activities, who they deal with, the names of the prostitutes they run and any other information you can collect. You may believe we can obtain much of what you find out from the police, but as usual we don't work that way. We collect our own information, so we know it's good and is not tainted by informers. For my part, as I said earlier, I'm going to Northern Ireland. It seems like this lad Bart, who I told you had been injured, is prepared to talk about his family. He contacted my charity office in Manchester and wanted them to contact me. They often get people asking that, usually making notes for me to read when I next go. The manager of the charity thought that Bart's information

21

could be important so she emailed me his details. I've arranged a meeting with him, to see what he has to say."

"You're not going without protection are you, Colonel?" Lieutenant Calder asked, with obvious concern.

Karen smiled, glancing at Stanley then back to Lieutenant Calder. Following a number of very high risk operations, where she'd been alone and out on a limb, Stanley had insisted she always had protection from now on. Karen hadn't argued, her last operation would have been very different if she'd not had Dark Angel, the unit's strike force, with her. "No, of course not. But thank you for asking." Karen glanced at her watch. "Now I must go, the flight plan has already been logged, so I don't want to miss my slot into Derry Airport. As usual, take care. This family doesn't worry me as such, but it's essential that we treat them as a threat and proceed with caution."

Chapter 4

It was coming up to nine thirty in the morning, after a flight time of just over two hours from the Unit T base, when Karen brought her personal aircraft, a Gulfstream 450 jet, on approach into Derry airport. Onboard with her were five Unit T soldiers. Karen had managed to acquire the Gulfstream for far less than its current value, when it was sold in a sealed bid auction. To finance the purchase, Karen had sold her original Mustang, along with using some of the compensation she'd received after being abducted during a covert operation. Karen had no qualms about accepting compensation, out of the seized funds of the traffickers, as even in covert actions there were risks. This particular operation ended with her being abducted and losing contact with her surveillance team. The result of which she'd been sold and forced to work in an Algerian brothel for some time, before managing to escape. She loved the Gulfstream, usually seating thirteen in relative comfort, it had been modified by the trafficker who originally owned it, and now only seated eight, ensuring the aircraft was spacious and the height of luxury.

By the time Karen had parked up, a refuel vehicle was on its way, along with personnel to check over the aircraft. Following local airport officials coming aboard, checking the aircraft's documentation and their warrant cards, they were left alone.

"As you're all aware," Karen began, "I'm meeting Bart at a remote farmhouse close to the border later this morning. You have your locations to keep an eye on me along with eavesdropping equipment to record my conversation and transmit on to Stanley, for analysis. Vehicles are already arranged. As usual, I'll have my watch, I'll press the winder twice if we're moving location and three times if I need immediate assistance. I will also press the button once every ten minutes to keep you informed all is well. If you don't get that signal, I won't be in a position to help, so you're to proceed with caution. Let's hope that won't be necessary. Once Bart leaves, the four who are to shadow him, use your vehicles, the last soldier will return to the aircraft with me. Take care, no risks, please, we can always pick up his trail later. This is just the start of what could be a protracted operation."

***

The SUV Karen was driving approached the remote farmhouse. She had already been informed by her team that Bart had arrived and was alone. The journey had taken her down the A2 towards Londonderry, before turning off over the River Foyle and headed for the border. Then she went down a number of country roads before arriving at the farmhouse.

Pulling up outside the house, Karen climbed out of the vehicle. She was dressed in jeans, t-shirt and leather bomber jacket. Her shoes were steel capped and as usual she had her ankle knife. The last thing she did before walking to the farmhouse door was check her gun, before slipping it into the special inside pocket of her jacket.

Pushing open the door, she went inside. The sitting room, although it had a table and chairs, with two settees, was very dusty and didn't look as if it had been occupied for some years. Standing by the fireplace was Bart. He had a cigarette in his hand.

"Bart Panark? The name's Karen Harris, you wanted us to meet?"

"Can I see your ID, I've seen your picture in the papers, but I want to be sure."

Karen pulled the ID from her jackets inside pocket, passing it to him.

He glanced at the card and handed it back. "I don't suppose you're alone?"

"Would you have expected me to come here alone? Although, I assure you, as far as I'm concerned, we're not here for you, or to take you away. I'm here to listen. Maybe decide if we can use your information, or even give you help."

He smiled. "You can't help me, no one can. I was born into the Murphy gang and can never leave, alive that is. But it doesn't mean I should have allegiance to a woman who's had my hand smashed up by a lump hammer. I'll help you take her down, because I want to see that woman locked up for the rest of her life."

Karen sat down on one of the dining table chairs. "Interesting, I've known a great many with the sort of hate you have for their taskmasters. But why come to me? Why not the police?"

He sniggered. "I'd live one day if I did. Mace would know before I even left the station. Then, if the police took me to a safe house, her goons would be waiting. As for you, you can't be bought, after all, if the papers are to be believed, you're worth millions, so a few quid in your back pocket would be nothing. Apart from that you deal with large trafficker groups and believe me, Mace is going into it big time. With my help it will be her downfall."

"It's nice to know you don't believe I can be bought, but you're right, I can't. I've experienced first-hand the suffering, the terror, at times, of a victim, I'd never sell any one of them out intentionally. But it does beg the question, how can I be certain you're not setting me up, sending me in different directions to blur what she's actually doing?"

"You can't. Even if I showed you my hand and what she did to me, you can never be certain it's not all a set-up. So like I'm trusting you with my life, you will have to trust me."

He finished his cigarette and immediately pulled out the packet, taking another, after offering Karen one. She didn't smoke and just shook her head.

"I've heard you've had meetings with police from both sides of the border. They want you to sort Mace out," he said, at the same time lighting his cigarette.

"Who told you that?" Karen asked, not altogether shocked that he would know, but interested in how he did.

He smiled. "It's all round the family. After all, the great Karen Harris is taking on Mace. Already they are queuing up to take you down publicly, to show everyone the power of the Murphy's."

"Yes, I get that a lot. So which side of the border blabbed then?" Karen asked with interest.

"Both, before you'd even left the meeting, Mace's contacts were calling her, asking for money in exchange for information, in fact one offered a complete transcript of what had been said. This is partly why I decided to talk to you, after all, it seems you're another in the long line of officials that have the belief they can destroy Mace. None have, she's bulletproof and plays on her disability to shout victimisation, but with my help, you may just pull it off."

Karen sighed. "She might believe that, but this time she's up against a group that operates under street law, the same as her. But let's forget what might happen, I'm more interested in how she intends to escalate into trafficking, after all, she already operates quite a number of prostitutes, although I'm aware she's met, or other members of her family have, the Urabeños?"

"They are nothing to do with her trafficking ambitions. They met my dad and a couple of others to sort out the supply of cocaine. I know that because I heard him talking on the phone. The person she's been talking to is a Russian called Elfin Crustkin, who's involved in shipping men, women and children from Asia and Africa. They are not asylum seekers, but economic migrants after the easy life offered if they can get into the UK. Apparently Crustkin works out of St Petersburg and is looking for a partner to move not only migrants across the channel, but to take young girls from Russia for prostitution. By what I've heard most of these young girls have the impression they've a modelling job and are as young as fourteen and travelling alone. I can't believe that can be true."

Karen sighed. "It is, believe me. There any amount of agencies out there, pulling these girls in. They even run selection days when up to a hundred girls will turn up, as young as thirteen, all desperate to be chosen and come to the big fashion cities, like Paris, London and Milan. Initially, the younger ones end up in Asia, even as far away as Japan, where the age limit for models, unlike

Europe, doesn't exist. On these fashion days, there is no opportunity to show yourself off initially. The girls line-up wearing just underwear waiting to be measured and then given the opportunity to stand in front of the scouts from the fashion houses. The selection is rigorous, a centimetre too fat and they're out. If they get past that, they will move on to being photographed, besides show how they can pose. The lucky ones will get a contract from an agency, believing they are on the way to becoming a supermodel. Among the legitimate agencies are the ones looking for girls to do glamour shots and go into prostitution. Not that they make it clear to the girl, until, that is, they are a long way from home with nothing else on offer, apart from going home. Most will accept it, when they are promised stardom later. What surprises me, is how Elfin has got himself a foothold out there. It's pretty tied up with the Russian Mafia and many established agencies. Then the Mafia doesn't like Elfin, in fact, I understood they had a contract out on him."

"You've heard of him then?"

She smiled to herself. This was a man she did remember, if only for his belief that he could have bedded her. As it was she had refused his advances, but he did con her and the Americans into believing he was an agent. He was, but for himself and he very nearly got away with a ton of heroin, if she hadn't destroyed the container. "You might say that we've had a few encounters in the past. He's not to be trusted, believe me."

"Who in the trafficking business is? But, whatever you say, the photos he's shown us are of stunning looking girls. Far better than we can find in the UK and Mace wants them in exchange for bringing the migrants across the channel."

"So Mace is able to get these people across the channel is she?"

"Of course, mind you, via Ireland. You forget she has relatives on the docks, in transport and even in the customs, so time the crossing right, which she's good at, and there's no one to stop them."

"I can understand that. What about the payments? Are these girls she wants to come to Ireland?"

He grinned. "You have to be joking, they wouldn't pay the prices Mace intends to charge for them. Seven of her most experienced controllers are re-locating to London and Paris. Already she has obtained premises for the brothels. This time it's out of the council estates and into the more affluent areas. Rented of course, she never buys. I've even heard she intends to sell a number onto other operators in London and the continent with regular auction sales."

"You will be able to give me the names, maybe the addresses of these people?"

"The names yes, the addresses no way. She doesn't make such information generally available. The only way I'll know who's going will be because I'm supposed to take over their women."

"But you will know when they leave to go to London or Paris?"

"Sort of, I'll know when I'm to takeover the girls given to me."

"Then you believe she trusts you?"

He shrugged indifferently. "I've been punished for

having my hand in the till. Mace knows I'll now toe the line, because you only get punished once. The next time it's a bullet in the head."

"What about the refugees, can you give me any information on their movement?"

He shook his head. "I can't, it's just not my area. So if I began asking around, she'd soon get to hear and I'm dead. That part you'll need to pursue."

"That's fine, I can look into that side on my own. Tell me, what happens to all the money she brings in? I understand the authorities have never been able to pin that down, except there must be a great deal of wealth, if it's not in properties."

"Beats me, she lives like a tramp and even gets her rent paid by the local council, but she must be bringing in over two hundred thousand a week that I know of. Most of it will be in cash. She pays out a lot, but not that much."

"I may look into that aspect as well."

"You do that, not that I can see what you can do where others have failed to find any evidence. One other point, did you have a covert operator already working for Mace?"

Karen frowned. "That would be something I couldn't tell you, but why do you ask?"

"A French girl was pushed into prostitution against her will. Last week, according to her handler, she took a gun from one of her clients and shot her way out, not before relieving Mace of close to thirty grand and crippling her minder for life. She also made threats that she was coming for Mace. Young girls snatched off the streets don't usually have the capability of using a gun, besides threatening Mace. So rumours are circulating she was one of your covert operators."

"Why would they think that, and what's her name?"

"Odette Boyer, from Avignon. That's not far from your base, is it?"

"I can't tell you our location, but I'll look into it. Did you ever meet the girl?"

"I didn't, she was run by Simon Murphy, one of Mace's grandchildren. Mace is livid at this girl's audacity and has put a contract out on her."

"Yes, I can understand that. But there have been no police reports of such an incident happening to one of the Murphy's."

"There won't be, we sort our own problems." He glanced at his watch. "I need to go, how do I get in touch with you?"

Karen handed him a card, with only a mobile number printed on it. "This will get me day or night. If I can't answer, don't withhold and I'll come back to you. It isn't monitored, or attached to a recorder, this is personal, between you and I." In fact Karen was lying, it was not only monitored, but whoever called, their number and location would be entered into a database. She had no allegiance to informers, most were out to fill their own pockets and would use her, if necessary, to achieve this. Karen also considered when she was dealing with the lives of their victims, and it was her responsibility to assist them in any way she could; the perpetrators, even if they wanted out, were not considered.

Bart took the card and nodded, then he left saying

nothing more. Karen sat for a time, hearing his car start up and pull away over the gravel. Then she followed, picking up one of her soldiers who was waiting a short distance from the farmhouse.

"Are we going directly to the aircraft, Colonel?" he asked.

"No, I've an appointment with the chief superintendent at the Strand Road police station. My visit here must be shown to have been a fact finding mission and having discussions with the local force and what they know about the Murphy's is part of it. I'm having lunch with the superintendent, so I've arranged for you to eat in their canteen."

Chapter 5

When Karen returned to Unit T in France, normally she would drop into her camp office, but this time she drove directly home. It had been a long day and she'd had enough. The house was a short distance from the camp, set in its own grounds, which included extensive forestland surrounding the house. With five bedrooms, a guest suite and swimming pool, this was a large and very expensive house. Then, with her having so much work, Karen employed a live-in housekeeper, assisted by a daily cleaner and two gardener/handymen. A girl of twenty-two, who had no family and who Karen had known since she was sixteen, also lived there. Her name was Sherry Malloy and she was Karen's assistant. Sherry was military too, held the Silver Star for action in Afghanistan and the rank of sergeant in Unit T's special incursion group, Dark Angel. She, the same as Karen, had been abducted, except unlike Karen, who was taken at just eighteen, she had been sixteen and forced to work in a brothel, that was, until Karen rescued her. Compensation had been paid, following the seizing of the traffickers' assets, making Sherry independent financially. Sherry had been at times, like Karen, a covert operative. Neither girl had any qualms about posing as a prostitute, if it gave them an in to a trafficking operation. It was the way they lived, with neither knowing any different, both had never been able to form any sort of serious relationship with a man, although Sherry had far more opportunities than Karen, who always seemed to select the wrong men, with most of them ending up dead, or walking out on her.

The housekeeper met Karen as she entered the house.

"Good evening, Lady Harris, dinner will be in an hour, unless you prefer it earlier?"

"No, an hour's fine. Are Sherry and Ally home?"

Ally Gilroy was aged fifteen, adopted by Karen at fourteen, after her parents and younger sister were killed by traffickers. While Ally had grandparents, she couldn't relate to them and she had asked Karen if she could stay with her. Karen had doubts about having to look after a teenager, but when Stanley suggested she couldn't even look after Sherry or herself, and therefore had no chance looking after Ally, Karen had been indignant and insisted she could. In reality, Stanley was happy she had gone ahead. Karen had become far too cavalier in her operations, often putting herself at great risk, as if she was no longer interested in whether she lived or died. He hoped with her having Ally to look after, it would give Karen a reason to come home. His suspicion that it would, proved to be correct. Karen had settled, was run ragged by Ally, but had taken her responsibility seriously, now working more from her office than in the field.

"Sherry's in the lounge," the housekeeper began. "Ally's staying overnight at Charlene's. It's her birthday tomorrow, so they're both sorting everything out. She didn't think you'd mind and asked Sherry if it was alright."

"That's fine," she answered, walking through to the lounge.

"Hi, had a good trip?" Sherry asked, quickly standing and giving Karen a hug.

"Interesting, I could have done with you to share

the flying. No one on board could fly. I think I'll shower before dinner."

"Well before you go, take a look at my letter," Sherry said proudly, handing her the envelope.

Karen took it off her and pulled the letter out reading it.

"What do you think? I've got my degree, will you come with me to the presentation?" Sherry asked.

Karen smiled. "Congratulations. Of course, I'd love to. I think if your mum was still here, Sherry, she'd be so proud," she replied, handing back the paperwork.

Sherry sighed, at the same time slipping the letter back inside the envelope. "She really wouldn't, Karen. She'd just say it was a waste of time. Mum was like that, never could understand why I kept wanting more education when I could make more, like her, laid on my back. Don't get me wrong, I loved her, but to follow in her footsteps prostituting, along with the violence and drug taking that came with it, I'd rather have died than do that."

"Well, my parents were the other way around. I was never allowed to stop studying, besides spending my weekends with dad playing his stupid mock army manoeuvres, with paint guns as weapons. It took years for mum to convince dad, I wasn't a lad and preferred to be clean, and wear a dress rather than be in decidedly unfeminine army clothing at weekends and covered in mud all the time."

While Karen spoke, Sherry walked over to a side table and poured drinks for them both. Coming back, she handed one to Karen. "Looks like both of us had the wrong parents, I'd have loved to do what you did."

"Oh yes, so you're now suggesting that, following in your mums footsteps, I'd have made a good prostitute then?"

"This is getting heavy, Karen. I only suggested you'd have had a more girly life, that's all."

Karen laughed. "I know what you meant. Anyway, I'm off for a shower. After dinner, how about we go to the camp club for a change, with Ally away we can let our hair down?"

"That sounds really cool."

***

The following morning Karen was sitting with Stanley. He had a transcript of her meeting with Bart.

"The mention of Elfin Crustkin was a turn-up for the books, Karen. I never expected to hear his name again."

"Yes, but as you know, once people are into both drugs and trafficking, the returns are so high, nothing else even comes close. Although, while Elfin may have turned up dealing drugs, his involvement in people trafficking took me by surprise."

"We'll have to wait and see what happens on that side."

"I'm interested in this girl, Odette, Stanley. What have you found out?"

"A great deal. Her father had a gun shop and was renowned for his expertise. The daughter, Odette, is nineteen and had worked in the shop since she was fourteen helping out. So she's certainly comfortable around guns. The father died of cancer earlier this year, the mother is in a permanent home. Odette hasn't been seen for some time, apparently, having gone to work in Ireland, according to a local shopkeeper. But we know she took the ferry heading back to Liverpool two days ago. We have a photo of her, picked up on CCTV, which is confirmed as her by her passport photo. Again CCTV picked her up getting into a taxi outside the port terminal. We contacted the taxi office where the cab is registered. According to the driver she was taken to a hotel, the Adelphia just outside Liverpool. The hotel has confirmed a booking for three nights. Tonight was her last night, but then she added another night. The girl is foolish doing that, as if she has upset Mace, they will be watching the ports the same as us. After all, we're not sure how entrenched the gang is in Ireland's security services."

"Why is she staying in Liverpool, and not taken a flight home? There has to be a reason."

"I'm at a loss to answer that, the same as you. What do you want to do, if anything?"

"Who do we have in the area?"

"We've a surveillance team in Manchester, on a long term covert surveillance of the Ross brothers' sauna and beauty shop."

"A couple of days away from there won't make much difference, we've already enough to bring them down. Have them run over to Liverpool, check into the same hotel and keep an eye on her."

"Officially or unofficially?"

"Unofficially. I'll join them tomorrow, in the hope of talking to Odette before she moves on. I'd intended going to the Manchester office tomorrow, but I think I'll go this afternoon. Can you get me a landing slot into

Manchester and put a flight plan together?"

"I'll see to it, Karen. You believe she has value?"

"I'm not sure yet, but we can't have a gunman, or should I say girl, running around, determined to take out Mace. Apart from which she will need protection, I'm not sure she realises who she's taken on."

"I agree on that score. Away from the Murphy's, do you still intend to respond to the reply you received for the job advertised by the agency in London?"

" I do, we've already had two women come to the charity, telling us the same story, after answering an advert for a job vacancy at the agency. They found it bogus. Both of the women were then forced into prostitution, following a lot of beatings. I can't see any other way we can get close to the men running the scam."

"Well, if you insist on going in yourself, you can be sure we'll be very close to you."

"I don't really insist, but this agency has been taking women more my age, I can hardly put an eighteen-year-old in. As soon as I have the evidence, we should be able to close this operation down very quickly."

Chapter 6

Karen was in Manchester, staying in her private flat above the northern charity office of LBNF (Lost but Never Forgotten). She had showered early and after orange juice and cereal was now on the road to Liverpool.

As she drove, Karen called the surveillance unit that was watching Odette. "Frank, do you have an update?" she asked.

"Yes, Odette is currently in the breakfast room. She was not around when we arrived yesterday, but came back to the hotel at six. After going to her room, she had dinner, then stayed in the hotel bar until ten. She seemed to be waiting for someone, but whoever it was never turned up. At ten, she went directly to her room."

"Very well, if she leaves the hotel today, I want to know where she goes. Keep me informed on that please."

"You want us to liaise directly with you, Colonel, or via Stanley?"

"Me please, I'm only forty minutes away."

***

Karen turned into the hotel car park and was met by Frank. He climbed into the passenger side of her Range Rover. "Odette is still in her room, how do you want to run this?" he asked.

"There's only one way I can see, that's to confront her. Besides, it would be better seeing her in the bedroom, rather than a public space. Let's go shall we, before she decides to go out."

Odette pulled open the hotel room door when Karen knocked. She believed it was the maid coming to clean the room.

"Odette Boyer?" Karen asked, not allowing her to take control of the conversation.

"Yes, and you are?"

Karen showed Odette her warrant card. "Colonel Karen Harris of Unit T. We need to talk. Shall we use your room?" she replied curtly, still giving Odette no time to think.

Odette on her part had heard of Karen - who hadn't - except to have Karen standing there unnerved her. "Err, I suppose you had better come in," she replied meekly.

Karen followed her in, shutting the door behind her.

"So what is it you want?" Odette asked, at the same time sitting down.

"All in good time. I presume you've heard of Unit T?"

"I have, not that I can see what Unit T has to do with me."

"I understand you worked as a prostitute for the Murphy gang, but decided to bail. In fact, you injured your minder Simon and took a large amount of money?"

Her mouth dropped open. "How do you know?" she gasped.

"How I know, doesn't matter. The point is Odette, you're in great danger. Even hanging around in a hotel and not going home means they can find you, just as easily as I have. They're a very violent gang, your life would be worthless if they did get hold of you."

"That's as maybe, but for a start I didn't join them with the intention of becoming one of their prostitutes. I was offered a job in a bar. But it was a con and I ended up with a beating every day until I submitted to what they really wanted me for. But you're right, I did escape, now Mace, or whatever she likes to call herself, will pay for what she put me through. I intend to kill the bastard."

"I think perhaps you should begin at the beginning and tell me just what happened? I need to know everything, Odette. I'm not here to judge, or even arrest you. I just want to understand your position. Besides, your life may depend on what happens from now."

Odette really wanted to tell somebody what she'd been through. In her view, short of going to the police, which she didn't relish, Karen might be the better alternative. So as Karen asked, she began at the beginning, including the gun she'd pinched.

"Tell me, Odette. Why the money?"

"You mean, apart from the fact I believed I'd earned it, and I was broke, with not enough to get home?"

Karen smiled. "Yes."

"I wanted to hit this Mace woman where it hurt, in her pocket. I was thinking I also needed help, and if I was going to take her out I would have to pay for it. Dad repaired guns for many people from the criminal underworld. I helped him a great deal, especially when his eyesight was failing and he became ill. I know a few people he supplied and called one to meet me here. This is why I am in Liverpool. He lives here, but he's away and not back till tonight. We're meeting later on in a nightclub."

"Where's the gun now?"

"In my bag."

"So with your death threats towards Mace, you intend, with the help of this other person, to take her out?"

"Bloody right I do. I was a virgin, she took that away from me. She also took my dignity and my self-confidence. Now every man who gives me a second look in the street, or in a bar, I have this belief they are looking at me as a prostitute. Then maybe out of the twenty odd a day that had me, one is bound to recognise me as the girl they fucked. You have no idea what it's like."

"You believe you're alone in that? Well, you're not. Why the hell do you think I set-up my charity? I have girls who were locked up for years, servicing twenty-five a day, even I've not been immune, working thirteen hours a day at times. The point is, what am I going to do with you?"

She frowned. "You're going to do nothing. You'll not stop me from getting my revenge. I don't need you and I can pay for help."

"You really believe you know the sort of people you're going to ask help from?"

She shrugged. "Most, if not all, can be bought."

"They can, but most will take your money and walk away laughing at your naivety. Others, on finding out just how much you have, will take it all off you, maybe leave you for dead, or call Mace and deliver you to her for another fee."

"Terry's not like that. Dad's done a lot of favours for him in the past, he'll see me right. As it is, I still intend to go through with it, no matter what."

"Then you believe it's worth spending the next twenty years locked up, for a piece of shit like Mace?

Believe me, Odette, if you think a few weeks is bad, twenty years locked up in prison, for a young woman - that would really open your eyes."

Odette looked down at her clenched hands, tears trickling down her face. "You want me to walk away, after what she's done?" Then she looked up at Karen watching her. "How can you ask me to do that, when you yourself turned on your abductors?"

"For a start, don't believe all that is written about me, Odette. Yes, I've killed and yes at times it could be debatable if it was me who should have been carted off to prison, for taking the law into my own hands. But I've paid for it in more ways than you can ever imagine. The reason I'm here is not by chance, it's because I've already got Mace in my sights. I intend to take her down, you unfortunately are in my way, you could get yourself killed or maybe allow her to squirm out of what I'm setting up for her."

At that moment Karen's mobile began to ring, she looked at the caller. It was Frank and he wouldn't call for nothing. "Yes, Frank?"

"I think you may have company. You've probably got a few minutes. A car drew up outside with two men getting out. Liam was close enough to hear them at reception asking for Odette's room."

"Interesting. I may need your backup. Can both of you, find a location close enough to respond at a moment's notice, if necessary?"

"We will."

Karen cut the call and looked at Odette, at the same time taking a gun from her bag and checking it. "I think you may have more visitors, apart from me. Who they are and what they want, that's debatable. I'll wait in the bathroom, with the door slightly open, just in case."

Odette looked nervous. "I'm not expecting anyone."

"Then it's best I take these precautions. If I need to step in and confront them, hit the floor, don't let them get too close to you as they could use you as a shield."

At that moment there was a knock on her door. Karen moved to the bathroom, partly closing the door. Odette went to the room door and pulled it open a little.

"Terry, I thought you were coming tonight?"

"I came back early. Let me in and we'll talk."

Odette opened the door further to allow him in, the other man remained outside.

"Well, are you prepared to help me?" Odette asked, once they were in the room and the door was shut.

"You have the money?"

"Yes, in my bag."

"That's good. However, I've a tiny problem."

"What sort of problem?"

"It's like this, Odette. Mace has put up a reward for anyone bringing you to her. It seems you're hot property."

Odette shrugged. "It's possible, after all I pissed her off running away and taking money. I don't suppose she is used to that from a girl. But what's your problem?"

"With Mace knowing, the price has gone up, to compensate me. I want twenty-five thousand."

"What do I get for that?"

"I'll get you to the house she lives in. From there you're on your own."

"I need more than that, I could get a bloody boat over and a taxi to the estate she lives on myself. I want you to come in with me and disable the minders she has around her."

"That's a lot to ask, just for twenty-five thou." He hesitated as if in thought. "But I'll do it. Pay the money in advance and we'll leave later tonight. This time tomorrow Mace will be out of your life forever."

She smiled. "I may seem stupid, but there's no way you're walking out with all the money. You get paid half when we set off, the balance when the job's done."

Terry's attitude suddenly changed. "You're not getting it, girl. Mace has offered ten grand for you. We could take you now, pocket your money and hand you over to her. I don't need to tell you what will happen if I do that. So hand over all the money and you get to live, refuse and we take you to Mace."

Odette sighed. "I see, so this so-called help you're offering has now changed into payment to let me walk away?"

He sniggered. "Well, if you're naive enough to believe anyone is going to go up against the Murphy's, you're more stupid than I believed you to be. At least I'm letting you walk away for the twenty-five grand, I'll even forgo collecting on Mace's payment. Just go back to France, but be sure to keep your head down. Ten grand brings a lot of people out of the woodwork wanting to collect."

At that moment Karen stepped out of the bathroom. She'd heard enough, Terry was just a con man. It was time to see if his idle threats had any basis, or if he really only wanted to relieve Odette of the money. In her hand she held her gun, so Terry could clearly see it. "Interesting conversation, Terry. I hope you don't mind me calling you by your name? I'm Karen Harris, maybe you haven't heard of me, but I run a military unit called Unit T. We specialise in taking down people trafficking operations."

His mouth dropped slightly, at the same time staring down at her gun. This was a woman you didn't argue with, especially when she held the upper hand. Even so, he intended to make out he was doing the girl a favour. "I know about you, who doesn't? I'm here to save this girl's life. You of all people should know what little chance she'd have against the Murphy gang."

"It's very noble of you to try to look after Odette. I think this time your services won't be necessary, I'll save her life. I'm far cheaper, in fact, unlike you, when someone's in trouble, I don't charge."

"I have expenses, I'm not financed by the EU, or as rich as you."

"No, you're not, you're just a two-bit, low grade criminal believing he can swim among the sharks and not get eaten. I'd advise you to forget all about Odette and our meeting, otherwise I'll let it be known to Mace, how you intended to relieve Odette of Mace's money and let her leave the country. I think she'd be very interested in such information, don't you?"

Terry shrugged. "This is Liverpool, we don't take too kindly to being talked to like that, especially by a woman hiding herself behind a gun. I'd advise you not to start sticking your nose into what goes on in this city, otherwise you'll find out just what we're capable of."

Karen stood for a moment, looking at him. "Very well. Odette, hold my gun. Terry seems to believe he can take me on. Have you a knife, Terry?" she asked, reaching down and pulling hers from an ankle strap, holding it up so he could see it. "I have. So then, let's see what you're made of. One to one, beat me and you can take the twenty-five grand. Lose… well, that's academic, you'll be dead. Your throat cut by me, protecting myself from you."

He began backing away, towards the door. "You're sick, you are. I'm not taking on a psycho like you." By now his hand had touched the handle, he turned it quickly, pulling open the door, Terry ran from the room.

Karen replaced the knife. "I don't think we'll be seeing him again, Odette. Pack your case, you're coming with me. I also want the gun."

"You believe, just by him leaving, I'm giving up? I'll go back to Ireland myself and sort her out."

"Very well, go then, but you'll not take the gun. One call and you will be arrested, even before you get on the boat. I'll also impound the money as the possible proceeds of criminal activities. You can apply for it back through the courts. Not that I can see you getting anywhere, after you admit how you got it."

She glared at Karen. "You're as bad as Terry. What's the next step, put me back on the streets, destitute forcing me into prostitution just to live?"

Karen didn't reply at first, moving to the window, watching Terry, with his mate, climb into a car in the car park below, then she turned.

"You are a victim of the Murphy gang. I can register that fact and under EU law you are entitled to compensation. I'll get you that compensation, keep you safe and set you up with a new life. Decide you don't want that, go your own way, I can't stop you, or rather, I won't. It's your choice Odette, I'll be downstairs in the lounge for the next fifteen minutes."

She walked to the door, pulling it open, then turned. "Once I leave this hotel, you will never see me again. I have people here, they will make sure you leave, minus the gun and the money, don't believe for one moment I've forgotten them. You will receive a receipt for the money, try to claim it back if you want. But I advise you not to claim you had a gun, it could well be a weapon with a past. If ballistics match it up to a criminal act, life may get a little difficult for you," she said, then left the room.

**

Karen was sitting alone in the lounge of the hotel, reading, when Odette came in, carrying two bags. She came up to Karen and placed a bag in front of her.

"That's the money and the weapon. You're right, it was a stupid and naive idea that I could take such a woman on alone, relying on petty criminals to work with me. I'd like to come with you, but I have a condition."

"That is?"

"I want to help take her down, even if it means I go back on the streets in a covert operation. I can soon cut and dye my hair, they wouldn't know it was me, I'd just be another working girl for them."

"Why don't you get yourself a coffee and have mine re-filled, while I think about that?"

Karen watched her walk over to the counter. In lots of ways she could see herself in Odette. A girl who's

48

not prepared to turn her back on her persecutors, this was exactly the way she used to feel. She also liked the girl's determination, if it could be funnelled into a covert operation, she could be useful.

When Odette returned with the coffees, she sat down next to Karen. "Well, have we a deal?" Odette asked.

"Before I answer that. Operating covertly is lonely, dangerous and leaves you open to abuse. I myself, during such operations, have lap danced, offered myself willingly to men I couldn't stand the sight of, been abused, raped, beaten and drugged. I've been auctioned and sold into brothels, working under appalling conditions. You can't object, you risk a good beating resulting in injury. Once injured you're at their mercy and can't retaliate when the time comes. Your personal life is finished, boyfriends are a thing of the past, if you can even find one who wants you. Often you're sterile, caused by drugs, or even sterilized by the people who take you, so forget a family. That Odette, is the life of a female covert operator in the trafficking industry. Mace had you working for a pimp a few hours a day. Maybe she kept you away from the violent ones, who delight in giving you a good thrashing, going up your backside, and even sharing you around. Others are far more demanding working you from when you get up, to going to bed. Is that what you envisaged?"

"You think I didn't work the hours? Believe me, I may have gone to the hotel at night, but in the day, I was expected to offer quickies to a string of men, spaced fifteen minutes apart. I've also had a few good thrashings, and my share of men up my backside, so if that's what it takes, I'll take it. I've no illusions, Karen, if it means we finally get Mace and her family."

"Very well, but on one condition."

"What?"

"You spend a month, like I was forced to do, on a military training course to learn how to defend yourself, use your weapons correctly and how to operate covertly. Get through that and I'll use you. Fail and you'll be sent to a safe house until the threat to your life is eliminated."

Odette smiled. "Bring it on I won't fail, Karen."

"We'll see."

Chapter 7

Elfin Crustkin was in his early thirties, a Russian who had spent most of his time since leaving school in the military. Later he had joined Russia's diplomatic service, looking after the security of embassies. Now he was out of all that, having collected nearly forty kilos of heroin in a sting operation that included both the Russian Mafia and an Italian cartel. However, neither side was aware that he'd managed to acquire any of the heroin, they believed that Unit T had destroyed the entire shipment, with one of their Stinger missiles, launched on Karen's orders. The outcome had made Elfin very wealthy, as he was able to sell the heroin for close to twenty thousand pounds per kilo. Using this money, he had moved into trafficking, particularly displaced people from the many civil wars across the Middle East, who were looking for a new life in Europe. This had become very lucrative. He charged upwards of ten thousand pounds per person, often moving them in tens and twenties.

Tonight he was in Southern Ireland to meet Mace. He'd been met at the airport by a man who called himself Bile. In fact unknown to Elfin, Bile was Mace's brother, and he was one of her most trusted in the family.

The car they travelled in turned down a narrow opening between two hotels in Dublin, stopping in a covered car park behind one of the hotels. Following Bile, he went up a back fire escape, along a landing and into a bedroom. Mace had already arrived and was sitting on a lounge chair, her stick in one hand, its tip resting on the floor.

"Elfin, it's good to meet you at last," Mace began, "forgive me for not standing, the arthritis you know. It gets worse in the winter, making it difficult to get around."

"I understand completely, Mace," Elfin answered, at the same time kissing her on either cheek. "My mother, rest her soul, spent many years with the same condition. I'm told, on good authority, you should move to a hotter and dryer climate. It works wonders."

"Yes, so I've heard, but my work is here, I don't have time for such luxuries. Anyway, to business. My boys have told me that they have seen samples of the merchandise and it is of good quality. It now comes for us to discuss terms."

"I'm looking at a hundred thousand euro, delivered, already sterilised and ready for work."

She shrugged. "A hundred is too much, eighty is what I had in mind."

He shook his head slowly. "You can have girls at that price, but I thought you wanted the cream. They always command a premium price, less than one in thirty meets the criteria you have laid down."

Mace said nothing, preferring to look at him for a moment. "I want the best, you can have ninety, and that's top. Think you can give me shit, because you aren't getting a hundred, think again. Every girl will be vetted by Bile here. He's very experienced in assessing women to work for us and in particular what we want."

"Very well, ninety. On our other spot of business, how often can you ship the migrants and how many?"

"We can take them in batches of twenty, three times a month. The dates will vary depending on shift patterns. Will you have people to meet them once they are in the UK?"

"No way, just dump them on the roadside. My deal's to get them into the UK. What happens then is not my problem."

"Very well, two hundred and fifty per person based on twenty. If you are short that's your problem, it will still be five grand."

"I accept. Cash will be paid to whoever takes them off my hands. How will you keep in touch?"

Mace nodded to Bile, who gave Elfin a mobile telephone.

"That's pay as you go, keep it topped up. On it is one phone number, to keep in contact with us. I'll have a text sent to that phone a week in advance of the date we can take them. Closer to the time one of my men will call with the time and location where you must meet him. If for some reason you can't make it, you text us two days before, otherwise you will owe us five thousand."

"I agree."

"What about the girls for my brothel, when will they be arriving?" Mace asked.

"I can begin delivery within two months. On a more important point, you know Unit T has been asked to look into your affairs."

"I know, of course. Not that it will impact on us. We've had many investigations in the past from various government departments, none has ever come to anything."

"Perhaps, but you've not had Karen Harris on your case. While I was with the Russian embassy, I worked with her and have also been to Unit T in France to see her operation first-hand, as well as being on an operation. They are nothing like the military as I know it. Their intelligence unit is the best and holds very large databases on all aspects of trafficking and the people involved. Their allegiance is to Karen and no other. She's no fool, particularly ruthless in her execution and does not follow the laws of any country. You can be assured she will already have put her own surveillance teams in the field, maybe even covert operators. Karen relies on nothing coming from the local authorities. So I advise you to take care."

"I appreciate your advice. However, we work as a family, share nothing with outsiders and all my family are totally loyal. We will watch this woman and her activities. I am not the sort of person to bury my head in the sand, ignoring what could be a very real threat from her."

He gave a light shrug. "Very well. You of course know your business, so I'll say no more and get off. I presume I deal direct with Bile for the girls?"

"You do and no other. I don't put up with interference and will step down very hard on anyone who believes they know better than me."

***

After Bile saw Elfin to the car waiting outside, he returned to Mace.

"Elfin is correct about this Harris woman. We're entering her field of expertise, so we must take every care surrounding this new operation," Mace commented.

"I agree, this is one person we cannot buy or intimidate. Although she's apparently very wealthy, which begs the question, is she whiter than white as everyone seems to believe?"

Mace pulled a half used cigarette from her pocket, Bile leaned across and lit it for her. She took a long draw, then looked at the cigarette in deep thought. Shortly after she took her mobile telephone off the table by her side and looked down the contact numbers. Selecting one, she pressed the dial button and waited.

"Mike, its Mace," was all she said.

"It's good to hear from you Mace, is there anything I can do, or is this just a social call?"

She gave a short laugh. "I don't do social, Mike, as you know. I seem to remember you telling me, last time we met, of a freelance reporter who supplied copy to you at times, and he was investigating Karen Harris of Unit T?"

"I did and you're talking about Archie Pelar. He has this belief that an in-depth exposé of her will make him."

"Will it?"

"No, you don't go up against a woman like Karen Harris. She has very powerful friends, both in government and the EU. They cannot allow her to be taken down, even the paper's owner, beside the editor here will scrutinise, very carefully, anything being written about her before it goes to print."

"Interesting. Is this why no one seems to question why she's so wealthy?"

Mike smiled to himself. "Apparently the EU steering committee and our government know about her capital and where it came from. Both are happy no money has come from traffickers. But, if you believe she can be bought, think again, she doesn't need it, and wouldn't be interested."

"Everyone has a price, maybe not always monetary, but they do have a price. How can I contact this Archie Pelar?"

"I'll look him up and text you his number. Be warned, he has this obsession with her being a bad apple and as such holds very distorted views about her."

"Just get me the number. We know how to handle such people, believe me."

Chapter 8

A few days after talking to Mike Hancock, Bile and Mace were in London, in order for Mace to inspect the accommodation for their new venture. However, Mace had not run a successful criminal operation by ignoring what was happening around her. Mace was intelligent, understood business, never underestimated her opposition, whether it was another gang muscling in, or the authorities trying to pull her down. To this end, she had decided, while in London, to gain a further insight into Unit T and in particular Karen. She was convinced Karen really did accept money in exchange for her leaving certain operations alone. In her view, how else could Karen have amassed such wealth. Her interest in Karen wasn't out of fear of her, or even to do with the cost of keeping Karen at bay, it was more to understand an adversary, who was nothing like anyone she'd faced from a government agency before. Then there was how Karen seemed on the surface to be too good to be true, on one level a knight in shining armour, on another, a girl who would resort to subterfuge as well as violence to meet her aims. Mace was convinced Karen's operations must have produced skeletons, an Achilles heel, she could use against her.

The car Bile was driving had come to a halt in a visitor's parking spot belonging to a large block of social housing flats. Mace didn't comment when they entered the lift to take them to the eighth floor, even though it stank of urine, besides being covered in graffiti. This was the world she came from and where she was at ease.

Before the door closed, two lads, not much more

than fifteen, pushed their way in, quickly leaning back on the walls on opposite sides, looking directly at the two strangers.

"You want your car watched?" one drawled. "You could find the wheels gone, or windows smashed by druggies looking for anything of value, leaving it out there unprotected."

Mace smiled. "Then you had better get down and do just that," she came back at him, as the lift came to a halt and the doors opened.

"Five quid, in advance," he demanded, holding his hand out.

Mace nodded to Bile, who handed the lad a fiver. Just as he began to walk out, Mace raised her stick, jamming it in the corner of the lift, preventing the one who'd taken the money from leaving. "Listen and listen good," she began, the tone of her voice intimidating. "One tiny little scratch on my car, I'll break every bone in your fucking body. So make sure you're standing by it, when I come out, or I'll have Bile here come and find you. Believe me lad, you'll wish he didn't. Have we an understanding?"

The lad in reality just wanted money, and had no intention of looking after her car, except this woman made him nervous, with her heavy Irish accent and the big man stood at her side. "We'll be there lady," was all he could say.

She gave a slight nod and lowered her stick. Smiling to herself as they ran out of the lift and through the fire escape door. She used to do the same thing herself, but that was on five streets which she controlled, always choc-a-block when there was a football match and particularly lucrative then.

Bile knocked on a flat door. A man not much more than twenty-five opened it. He was around five foot three, with fair hair and wearing a tracksuit.

"You're Mace?" he asked.

"I am, this is Bile. You're Archie?"

"Yes, come in."

The flat, although it had two bedrooms, was small, with little furniture. Mace sat down in the only lounge chair, gasping a little. Bile sat on a wooden chair that was part of the small kitchen table set.

"Can I get you a drink?" Archie asked, noticing her shortage of breath.

"Just a glass of water, nothing for Bile," Mace answered.

As he filled the glass, he began speaking. "Mike called, said you were coming to talk about Karen Harris?"

"We are, I'm told this is a woman whose activities you know a great deal about?"

He turned and came back, handing her the glass. "You might say that, I've been studying her for three years now."

"Why?"

"You mean apart from how interesting her life is?" he asked, also sitting down on a wooden seat.

Mace gave a slight shrug. "Of course, unless you're a stalker with a fixation about her?"

"I'm no stalker, she's my ticket to the big time," he retorted indignantly. "Karen's an anomaly, a girl born with nothing and yet by the age of twenty she was worth

59

at least ten million. Since then, she's increased her wealth, in my estimation, to around twenty million, has a number of properties and owns a jet."

"By the tone of your voice, you don't seem to think Karen's increase in wealth is completely legitimate and yet she is very high profile. For her to hide such illicit wealth would be very difficult."

"I don't seem to think, I know, that most of her wealth is from traffickers she's taken down, with money and other items pocketed by her as the spoils of war, when she operates covertly away from prying eyes. As such, she's dirty, the same as them. I intend to show her for what she is. A woman no better than the ones she hunts. And yes, the word hunt is correct. That girl is a cold-blooded killer in every respect and probably couldn't even tell you how many have died by her hand, let alone by her aptly named unit, Dark Angel." He stood. "Let me show you."

Mace and Bile followed Archie into the second bedroom and stood there a little aghast. The room was covered in photographs, with lengths of strings attached leading to other photos. All the central photographs were of Karen, from the age of eighteen to the present day.

"This is her life story, from before the day she was abducted, her liaison with an arms dealer and her rise to power. I know more about her life than she knows herself."

Mace smiled. "Hardly."

Archie shook his head. "Initially no, but now, believe me, I do."

"Explain?"

Archie pointed to a picture of her following her parents' coffins. "It was at that point she changed. Notice her sister Sophie is missing from photos since then. Sophie was abducted by a Russian cartel and rescued, I believe, by Karen in one of her covert operations. When Sophie returned to England, she disappeared off the face of the earth. Probably, I suspect, she went into witness protection, and didn't trust Karen to look after her, besides not wanting anything to do with her sister and a world that had left their parents dead, as well as had her taken by a cartel to a brothel. All because Karen reneged on a deal."

"What sort of deal?" Mace asked with interest.

"At that time, Karen had around five million Euros in gold, diamonds and cash that belonged one of the Russian cartels, but never gave it back to them."

"How do you know about that?"

"The information came from a Russian, who was a member of the cartels European committee. She had taken the money in a drug bust. He was pissed off, lost not only money, but his status and wanted her taken down; but he was far too afraid to do it himself. Besides, he was recalled to Russia only days after talking to me. The money that she took cost Karen her parents and her sister."

"But why did she not pay it back, after all, she has plenty?"

"According to the Russian, Karen had been taken by a trafficker and subjected to a drug that destroyed her memories. After that she didn't actually know where the money had come from, or that it belonged to the Russian cartel. The funeral confirmed that. Many of her friends commented on Karen not seeming to recognise people she'd known for years. Karen was in serious trouble, caused by the drugs, then days after the funeral, she resigned as commander of Unit T." He smirked. "But that was a trick, she'd not resigned in reality, but gone covert. She became a prostitute and took on the Russian cartel trafficking women and children in Europe. The point is, why? She needed Unit T's resources and yet turned her back to go it alone."

"You found that out?" Mace asked, with interest.

"Yes and no. She wanted to find her sister, besides revenge her parents' death. To do that you don't walk in the front door of a cartel and ask politely. Karen knew how to operate under the radar and had the money to cause real problems for those she targeted. Operating covertly, she is far more dangerous, more cavalier in her operations and spends most of her time purporting to be a lap dancer, even at times a prostitute, often with a girl called Sherry Malloy at her side. If you look at her charity reports, the charity is now the richest in the world, funded not only with large donations, but by the assets of convicted traffickers. They have helped thousands of victims, own properties in various parts of the world, and if a victim needs a new identity the charity organises it, besides paying out millions in compensation. Believe me, it pays to become a victim and be looked after by Karen. Except, as I mentioned, she doesn't do it for free, often lining her own pocket."

Mace sighed. "This is all very well, but I'm more interested in how she funds her own lifestyle. Does she take bribes?"

"No one knows, neither have I been able to find that out, especially with most of the traffickers she takes on being dead. Although you could argue, why should she? Her last major operation, when she took down the psychopath Kenneth Parker, netted her legal personal compensation, I believe in the hundreds of thousands. Then a man known as Ikram stupidly abducted her and took her to Algeria. According to the official transcript of the compensation claim, he was killed by his brother. The brother, rather than hand Karen to the authorities, sold her to a brothel. It was pointless, she soon escaped. Because Ikram took her within the EU, he was classed as a trafficker and all his assets in the EU were seized including an aircraft. Karen was the only woman who came forward as being an EU victim, although there were hundreds in Algeria who couldn't claim, so she received one third of his assets located in Europe, put by to compensate victims. His assets included an aircraft which she purchased at a knock-down price. I could go on, but you get the gist in that her covert operations often leave her out on a limb and of course a victim in the eyes of the law, so she's entitled. Although, according to the papers, she pays the money she receives into her charity to help others. I, on the other hand, am after the money that does not come by way of compensation, which I know she has. Like I say, the spoils no one knows about."

Mace said nothing for a while, spending time looking at the wall and all the links back to Karen, before turning to face Archie.

"This picture of a man with a question mark stuck on top, what is that about?"

Archie came closer, looking at the picture. "He's interesting, his name is Dominick, ostensibly he was the one who found Karen's sister Sophie."

"You don't sound convinced that he did?"

He sniggered. "Dominick never found her, Karen was involved in some way. He was a night security man working at the house Sophie was in. But reading the reports in the papers and what he was saying makes me believe he played a far bigger part in the cover-up of Karen's covert battle with the Russians than what was released to the papers. It's a lead I'm still working on."

"This is important to you then, beyond just filling in another aspect of Karen's life?"

"Dominick is the key to exposing the darker, seedier part of Karen's life, in far more ways than you can imagine. If she was in Switzerland and she did rescue Sophie, then she'd have needed the assistance of Dominick to enter the house without force. For him to have helped her, they must have become very close. Well, that's the angle I'm working on."

Mace looked for a short time at the photo of Dominick, besides reading the newspaper clipping attached to the side. "I suspect all this work to help you on your way to being recognized as a super investigative journalist will not happen, unless you can get very close to Karen. This is a woman who is riding the top of the wave. I can't see her being phased by someone like you," she mocked.

He smirked. "Maybe not, but I have a plan. You see, with all her wealth, stardom, whatever, she has an Achilles heel."

"She does?" Mace asked, not outwardly showing any real interest. "What is that?"

"She wants a boyfriend. Someone who will love

and look after her. The girl is lonely most, if not all her friends are dead. Don't get me wrong, she can get any amount of casual relationships, with her looks and wealth that would be easy, except that's not what she's looking for."

"I can understand that, so I presume your plan is to get close to her via such a man? Don't you think this is no more than a pipe dream, that a man who has the sort of affection she craves would be prepared to feed you all the dirt?"

He gave a shrug. "Possibly, but you never know."

The way he reacted immediately told Mace that Archie was already in touch with such a person. However, she also suspected he wouldn't be telling anyone who this person was and what he planned. But Mace had not got where she was without the ability to read between the lines and use her instincts to assess people. She was beginning to believe Dominick was far more important than just filling in a space, and might even be Karen's downfall? Mace glanced at her watch. "It's been an interesting half-hour, Archie. Personally, I'd rip this lot up and do something else. It will consume you, both mentally and physically, jumping from situation to situation in the hope you can entrap the woman. You'd be better writing her life story, after all, it would seem you have far more information about her than anyone else." Then she changed her tone to a far more menacing one. "Take a little advice, from one who knows just what you are looking at here. Behind Karen's looks, her disarming smile, is an extremely dangerous and I suspect, both mentally and physically disturbed woman. What she has gone through has turned a naive school girl into what she is now, a killer. Karen kills not only for a living, in her official capacity, but away from that she kills to protect herself, her lifestyle, and no matter what you believe, she will squash anyone who tries to take either away from her. That means Archie, put her back against a wall, she'll kill you and think nothing of it, the same as I would, if I was her and found out how much you had been rummaging in all aspects of my life." After that comment, Mace left.

Archie stood for a time looking at the pictures on the wall. While he knew Karen was dangerous, her wrath was always directed at traffickers; in public she couldn't be a nicer person. He had believed she'd just accept being exposed meekly, but Mace had reminded him, in no uncertain terms, of the deeper, darker side of a woman who had been killing since she was eighteen. He shuddered at the very thought he could be targeted by exposing what he believed she was. Even so, he had a meeting tomorrow and intended to keep it.

***

Back at the car, the two lads were, as Mace had told them to do, standing alongside it.

"We looked after your car," one lad said.

"You did and got paid. A word of warning. If you want to make it, in any activity, legal or not, go through with what you offer. Renege on a deal, even between enemies, and you won't last long. They will come for you, the same as I would have done." Then she climbed into the car.

Bile glanced at Mace as he drove. "That Archie is a stupid man, don't you think?"

"He is, but he's managed to accumulate a large amount of interesting information on Karen. I'm beginning to feel I know Karen without coming face to face with her. He has also highlighted her weakness. Most, if not all women want security, a stable home and a loving husband. She's no different. That, Bile, opens her up to high risk."

"You're looking towards this man Dominick then?"

"Very much so. See it from her side. She needed to get into house, she suspected her sister to be in. Short of breaking in and showing her hand, what better way than to seduce the night-watchman and get inside without breaking down the door. If she found her sister, use Dominick to hide the fact that she was ever there. Why she needed to keep that quiet, would only be speculation on my side, but I think Karen considered she needed to remain in the background."

"Yes, I can understand that, but I'm still not getting it."

"You wouldn't, you're not a woman. I suspect she made a grave underestimation that she could stand back and use Dominick. He had become more than just her lover, I think she fell in love with him. This was a man that spent time with her, so she could build his trust. That trust was so high, he was even prepared to lie and claim he was the one who found her sister, which points to the fact he was also in love with her. Archie is also looking at the relationship between Karen and Dominick the same way. He knows where Dominick is and may already have been in touch with him. I want Archie watched. Let's see just what he's up to. If he leads us to this Dominick, all well and good. Once I'm satisfied we can effectively takeover, Archie needs to be shut up for good, with all the documents boxed and brought to me. He's far too obliging, in being prepared to talk to anyone wanting to know more about her. It's bound to reach her ears sooner rather than later. Knowledge is only powerful if you are the only one who hold such knowledge."

"What do you have in mind?"

"It's simple really. If she still holds some affection towards Dominick and starts the relationship again, Karen will be at her most vulnerable. She could prefer to spend her time alone with him away from her protection. At that point we can take both of them easily."

"You intend to kill her then?"

"Eventually, but I can see some mileage before that happens. She has money and could well be prepared to pay for her release, rather than earn it on her back, particularly if she is forced to watch her lover gutted in front of her. Maybe she will not want to pay at first, after all she'll be pretty annoyed with me, so she may need to be handed around to, shall we say, the more perverted of clients and both of us know the types I'm talking about. To abduct her under the noses of her unit, besides bleed her dry, will not only be very profitable, but bring a woman down who could prove to be very dangerous for us, if she's left alone." On finishing Mace began to laugh, until it turned into a bout of coughing.

Chapter 9

Karen, a week after collecting Odette and following a meeting with the EU committee that oversaw Unit T's operations in Brussels, was back in London with Sherry.

Sherry had arrived two days earlier. She had leave coming to her, and had asked Karen if she could first use the London flat as a base for shopping. Even with Karen telling Sherry she could always use the flat, she wouldn't without asking first.

"Hi, good flight?" Sherry asked, as Karen came through the flat door, dropped her case, then flopped down onto the settee.

"Stressful, I was placed in a holding pattern, because of bad weather in the US and aircraft arriving late. If that wasn't enough, the traffic into London was pretty horrendous. Would you pour me a drink, please?"

Sherry brought her a drink. "There's a lot to be said for going scheduled, like me, and taking a taxi here. I just settled down and read my book. Anyway, I've booked at our usual bistro for seven, if you're okay with that?" she told Karen after taking the seat opposite her.

"That's fine," she said, then glanced at her watch. "I think I'll have a quick run around the park to get rid of the tension, then a long soak in the bath, do you want to come?"

"Of course, I love to run."

***

By seven, both were dressed in short, flared dresses with the intention of spending the night dancing, their first stop being the bistro Sherry had booked. Following that, before the nightclub opened, they were in a bar.

"Can you get the drinks, Sherry, I've just had a text and need to make a call away from the noise," Karen told her.

"No probs, I'll get us two, it'll save us fighting this crowd later."

Sherry had just collected the drinks and was making her way to a small table she'd seen vacant.

"Sherry, it is Sherry isn't it?" a voice came from behind her.

Sherry turned and looked at the man standing there. "It is, do I know you?" she asked, genuinely not recognising him.

"We only met briefly in Switzerland. The name's Dominick, you came to see me about Amber."

Her eyes went big, now she recognised him. Except he was the last person she ever expected to meet again. This was a man Karen had used, without his knowledge, to gain a way into a house that she suspected her sister had been taken to by a Russian cartel. It would seem, from what she could piece together, that Karen liked Dominick; in fact, they were intimate a number of times, but that was on a covert operation and Karen, to keep her anonymity, had changed her hair colour and style, used contact lenses to give her brown eyes, and called herself Amber. All the same, Sherry was quite taken aback that Dominick could recognise her, after all, she'd only been with him for less than half an hour. Already alarm bells were ringing. "Sorry, I really didn't recognise you. So why are you in London?"

"I've been here a year, well nearly. A Swiss bank

took me on as a security guard. I'd been there some time when on the internal jobs listing, a senior security job came up at the bank's London branch. I applied and got it."

Sherry smiled. "I told you when we last met you'd get a job, I seem to remember you were a little down."

"I was, not just because of the job, I missed Amber. She made quite an impact on me. Did you find Amber and sort her problems out?"

"Yes, thank you. Listen Dominick, can we meet some other time, I'm a little tied up tonight. Then we will talk?"

"That's fine, I didn't intend to delay you, I just wanted to say hello."

At that moment, Karen approached Sherry, Dominick was standing with his back to her. She could see Sherry was talking to someone, but thought it was just a casual approach by a man who believed that perhaps Sherry was on her own.

"Is that my drink, Sherry, I'll take it and find a seat for us?" Karen said.

Dominick had gone cold; he'd not seen her approach, but he believed he recognised her voice immediately as Amber's.

He spun around and was just going to open his mouth, then stopped. Karen also looked at him now.

"Amber," he finally blurted out.

Karen smiled, her face showing no hint in recognition of him being right. "I'm sorry, my name's Karen," she answered.

He looked at her for a moment, then back at Sherry,

before looking again at Karen. "The name's Dominick, I apologise if I embarrassed you, it's just that your voice sounded so much like her. I shouldn't delay you both any more. Have a good night," he said, then he pulled a piece of paper from his pocket and wrote his mobile number on it. "I'd love to meet you again, Sherry. Please call, when you have some free time."

As he turned to leave them, Karen touched his arm. "Dominick, don't go, come and join us for a drink," Karen suddenly blurted out.

He hesitated, then smiled. "Thank you, where are you sitting, I'll collect my drink from the bar and join you."

They showed him the table they had selected. After he left Sherry moved closer. "What are you doing, Karen? Does he know who you really are?"

She shook her head. "Of course he doesn't. But to tell you the truth, I liked him a lot, Sherry. Well more than a lot, if it had been different, our relationship could have become more serious."

"Yes, well, you'd better forget anything like that. You're not Amber and never will be for him. She was not only a lap dancer to him, but a woman at his level. How's he going to think, when he finds out just who you really are? Relationships that begin with a lie, Karen, never survive. You of all people should know that. You should have let him walk away."

"Why, don't you want me to have some happiness in my life, Sherry?"

"I do, but this is like Sirec, a man you despised, a man who purchased you and in his eyes owned you. And yet you, being you, were willing to throw yourself at him, after he spun you some sort of story that made it all right, even though weeks before he was prepared to hand you to a trafficker, who would have sold you into a brothel. Get real, Karen, you can't ever go back, especially when you met the man while on a covert operation."

At that moment Dominick joined them. "Have you known Sherry long, Karen?" he asked.

"Since she was sixteen. So yes, we've been with each other for quite a number of years, haven't we Sherry?"

"Yes, we have. Are you alone, Dominick?" Sherry asked, not expanding the conversation that way.

"I am, it's not easy to make friends in this city. Do you both live here?"

"No, we live in France, we're here for a couple of days, then we leave," Sherry added, before Karen could say anything.

"We here a lot though," Karen added.

"Quite the travellers, what is it you both do, modelling perhaps?" Dominick asked.

Sherry sighed, the way Karen and Dominick were looking at each other said everything. "Let's not beat around the bush here. It's bloody obvious you recognise Karen as the Amber you knew, Dominick. And you Karen, it's time you told Dominick just who you are."

"You're right, Sherry," Dominick cut in. "The moment Karen spoke, I knew she was Amber, but if she chose not to admit it, I wouldn't embarrass her. I assume Karen would have her reasons."

Karen said nothing.

Except Sherry did. "You can say that again. Karen used you to rescue her sister, Dominick, didn't you Karen? It was not part of an official operation, which is why she bailed and let you take the glory. It is also why I came to see you. So are you two going to talk about it, perhaps clear the air, then move on? Because I'm not prepared to sit here watching you both making eyes at each other all night."

"I do owe you an explanation, Dominick," Karen suddenly said. "Not tonight, Sherry and I have plans. I'll take the number from Sherry and call you. If you want us to meet, we'll meet."

He picked his drink up, sipping it slowly. "I'd appreciate that, Karen. You made an impact on my life, I've never forgotten. Now I'll leave you both to get on with your night." He stood and walked away.

"Give me the paper, Sherry."

"In your dreams. This is getting like a bloody repeat of Albert off the oil rigs. Then, you nearly got him killed, besides yourself. Dominick, like Albert, will not be able to cope when he finds you're a multi-millionaire and his income wouldn't even run the aircraft. As for what you do, how do you think he'll react when he finds your work often requires you to spend time with other men, or even prostitute yourself. And don't come with the idea you'd leave it all behind for him, you wouldn't, the same as you didn't for Albert."

Karen sipped her drink, listening to Sherry. "I don't think you have the right to tell me what I should or shouldn't do as far as my private life goes. I liked Dominick, but unlike Albert, we were lovers and good

74

together. So give me the piece of paper, Sherry. I'll decide if it's at an end, not you."

Sherry gave her the paper. "I'm no longer in the mood to go dancing. I'll see you back at the flat. I'm also going home tomorrow. So you can take him back to your flat now, can't you?"

"That's a bit childish isn't it? You're not my mother, or even my sister. Unless you fancied him and feel a bit put out by him wanting to see me again."

"I'm childish, grow up, Karen. You know how it will end."

Karen shrugged indifferently. "Maybe I do, so what? But, I'll tell you this Sherry. Dominick treated me like a real boyfriend, he respected me, didn't force himself onto me. Very few men have ever done that, most preferring to put me over their knee, convinced I'd be more submissive, work harder in giving them a good time, following a hiding, often ending the session with them forcing themselves up my backside. Dominick never did that, neither did he look down on me, when as my cover, I told him I was a lap dancer. How many men would like their girlfriends stripping twenty times a night, pushing their breasts into a man's face at the same time as being sat astride them naked, pretending to have intercourse? Even you told me you had trouble with the lads in your regiment, when they found out what you'd done in the past." She looked down. "I'd give anything just for one night with a man like Dominick. The only sex life I've had since being with him, has been in brothels, forced to service twenty plus men a day, or strung up in a bizarre porn movie, being taken from both sides at once. Please

75

Sherry, give me some slack, allow me to at least dream a little, even if it is just a dream."

"You're right, I didn't look at it that way. Where are we heading, Karen? When all the time we stumble from crisis to crisis. But think about this. I saw Dominick for less than half an hour, a few years back, and yet he recognised me from behind. Come on, I'm not that recognisable, besides, I've put on a little weight and at that time was wearing jeans. In my mind, it says that he was directed towards me, what I'd like to know is by who. You should be asking yourself the same."

She was just about to comment, when two lads, both in their twenties, approached. "Hi girls, my mate Brian and I have been watching you. We decided you both look really bored and fed up, how about you come with us to a nightclub and party?"

Sherry smiled. "Why not, I've had enough in here, how about you Karen?"

She looked at the two lads, did they realise how old she was? But she also gave them a smile. "Okay, lead on."

Karen stopped Sherry for a moment, as they walked out the bar, her voice low. "I'm not a fool, Sherry. I realised he couldn't have recognised you, after all that time. But we play along and see where it leads. Also, you don't bail, I could well need you and surveillance."

Sherry didn't comment, just nodded her head. She was kicking herself, and should have known Karen would have been well ahead in her thinking. She hadn't survived this long wearing rose-tinted glasses, particularly when an old flame appeared and was as naive as Dominick.

Chapter 10

Karen, with her hair hanging loose, dressed in tight, white, hipster jeans, a silk blouse and a small two buttoned jacket, walked into Regent's Park. She had arrived by taxi to meet Dominick by the side of the lake, after calling him the day before.

Dominick was already waiting, sitting on a bench. He'd watched the ducks for a short time, nervously looking up and down the path as each person came into view. He looked at his watch for the tenth time, the hand coming up to the hour was refusing to move closer. Then he saw her coming towards him. His heart skipped a beat. With the natural swing of her hips, the way this girl moved was the Amber he had always remembered, and yet she wasn't Amber. This was a girl he believed he knew intimately, but it seemed he had never known the real girl?

He quickly stood as she approached and Karen gave him a smile before they embraced and she kissed him on each cheek.

"Thank you for coming, Karen. You don't mind me calling you Karen, do you?"

"Of course not, that's my real name, Dominick. Shall we sit down, or would you rather walk?"

"I'd rather walk a little, if you don't mind? Perhaps stop for a coffee?"

"That's fine with me," Karen answered, grasping his hand, without really thinking, as she'd done in Switzerland.

They walked slowly alongside the lake.

"Can you tell me one thing before anything else,

Karen?"

"If I can, of course, what is it you want to know?"

"Are you the Karen Harris who's often in the papers and part of a military force?"

Karen was a little taken aback. She had suspected that Dominick had turned up like he had, with perhaps someone's help, in order to set her up, but this now didn't seem to hold water, if he didn't even know who she really was.

"Yes, I am. Besides running Unit T, I run a private charity to help victims of trafficking. Is that important?"

"For me it is, in fact, it puts your life and the reason you came to Switzerland into perspective. Now I know who you are, I understand that I must have been a pawn, in what I suspect was one of your unit's operations?"

"I'll not lie, Dominick. At first, yes you were, although the operation was not run by Unit T. I was alone looking for my sister who had been taken by a trafficking cartel. It also meant I couldn't protect you once I left, that is why I wanted you to claim you found Sophie. But sometimes the best laid plans can have their problems, when the man you are with is as genuine as you. I'm sorry I never contacted you again. It wasn't that I didn't want to, I did. I liked you a great deal, often thinking about you, wondering where you were. My problem was, how could I go back as who I really am? You knew a blonde, sexy, fun loving, lap dancer called Amber, not Karen with boring brown hair, living a lifestyle that most men would walk away from. It would have really upset me to have been rejected."

"That's where you were wrong, Karen. Do you

really believe a change of hair colour, even a name would make you any less than the girl I was falling in love with? We may only have been together a short time, but you were everything I ever wanted in a woman, with your affection genuine, your smile disarming and your seemingly very real responses in wanting to get to know me as well. When you pulled a gun on me, your tone and manner changed, as if I was nothing, that really shocked and upset me. Why didn't you just tell me what you suspected, rather than let our relationship become more intimate, giving me the belief you really liked me? I'd never have condoned abduction, be it a child or an adult and would have been more than willing to help you?"

Karen came to a halt, looking at him. "Let's sit down for a moment?" she asked, walking over to an empty bench. He followed, sitting alongside her.

"I can't go into everything that has happened in my life, Dominick. Safe to say, I've been treated like shit by the majority of men since I was seventeen. Mostly, the ones I've really liked, trusted and believed wanted to be with me, have turned out to be my enemies, for a few pounds in their pocket. Even at this moment, I'm having doubts as to why you're here. So please don't think me naive enough to believe you recognised Sherry, when you'd only seen her for a few minutes."

"You are right, I didn't, or rather wouldn't have. Perhaps I should explain?"

"Yes, I'd like you to do that for me, it's very important."

"A short time back, a reporter, Archie Pelar, approached me in a pub, wanting to talk about Sophie. He

79

told me he was doing an article on trafficking and wanted to highlight Sophie's abduction, from the way she'd been transported across Europe, her being sold, to where she was kept and who by. I couldn't see a problem talking to him, after all, I'd already given her story to the papers. I'd also talked to a few local reporters in the past, mostly trying to get an angle on what had happened. After we'd talked for a while, he asked me if I knew who Sophie's sister really was. Of course I knew and said so, after all, I'd been told by most reporters she was the sister of a Karen Harris, who ran Unit T."

"So how did this Archie come around to Sherry?" Karen asked with interest.

"He pulled out two photos. One was a picture of you, the other Sherry. He asked me if I recognised one or both. When I told him who you both were, he wanted to know how I knew and if I'd met you both. Photographs shown to me in the past of you as Karen Harris by other reporters, made it easy for me to recognise you. As for meeting you, I told him I hadn't. Which was the truth, until I met you at the bar, I'd never put you and Amber together as being the same person. Thinking about it now, I should have, it's only logical, as with your skills and support, you would have been the one who'd come for Sophie. When he asked about Sherry, I told him she was a girl I'd met just after Sophie was released. He was very interested and wanted to know why had she come to see me. I told him Sherry was looking for her friend Amber. When he asked who Amber was, I couldn't tell him the truth. To admit Amber was anything to do with the finding of Sophie broke my promise to you. So I just said she was my girlfriend who had needed to return home urgently, that she had never contacted me since, and neither had Sherry. Although, I added, it would be nice to know if Sherry had found Amber."

Karen listened to his explanation, but was concerned. "No one knew we'd go into that bar, or even go out last night. Was it just by chance you saw Sherry there, maybe because you'd seen her photo a few days before?"

"No, it wasn't like that. Archie suddenly called me on my mobile, told me Sherry was in a local bar near where I lived and if I could get down there, I could ask her about Amber. You can't believe how my stomach churned, that I could actually speak to someone who would know how Amber was, or even where she was. So I virtually ran to that bar. Even then it took a great deal to approach her, I was scared she'd not remember me, or even worse tell me she had never found Amber. Then for you to join us, my entire body was shaking. You looked so different and yet, with every movement, the little quirks you pick up on about a person after spending time with them, besides when you spoke, I instinctively knew you were Amber. I'd found you again."

They both remained silent for some time, before Dominick broke the silence. "Do you still want coffee?"

"Yes, please."

He grabbed her hand, pulling her up. "Come on, I'll even buy you a cake to go with it."

Once in the coffee shop, Dominick collected coffee and cakes, joining her at a table.

"May I ask you a direct question, Karen?"

"It's important?"

"For me it is."

"Then ask anything you want and I'll answer truthfully."

"When you left, I tried to pick my life up again. I did to a degree, even though it frightened me as to who Amber really was, I missed her so much, it hurt. To see you again, safe and well, hear your voice, see your smile, left me tossing and turning all night, hoping beyond hope you would call and not walk away once more. I realise I can offer you very little, only be a man who will look after you, never let you down, work hard to give us a place we can call home, maybe even children. All I ask is for you to give me that chance and let me prove to you, that whatever you've had to do in the past, makes no difference. I love you Karen Harris, with all my heart."

Karen looked down at her coffee, cupping it with both her hands, feeling the warmth. She had waited all her life for a man to say to her what Dominick had just said. Tears were coming to her eyes, she was scared, desperately worried if she followed her heart, she'd say yes and never stop saying it. Except she knew it was too late for her. Her life had already been mapped out and no longer included her original dream of a normal family life, with a man she knew she could love. Even so, Karen didn't want to walk away. And yet, to feel him in her arms once more, wake in the morning with him at her side, would drag her into a relationship she couldn't, or more to the point wouldn't want to control.

Dominick was looking at her, he could sense her turmoil. "I really don't want to lose you again, Karen. If

I'm asking too much, maybe we could at least spend some time together? Start again, date and enjoy each other's company. Then I can prove to you, that I'm sincere in everything I say. I'm not rushing you, take as long as you want, you decide where we go next."

She looked up and smiled. "I'd like that, Dominick." At that moment her mobile, vibrated in her pocket. Karen stood, excused herself and went to the toilet. Once inside she returned Stanley's call.

"Surveillance has reported that a man in his twenties has been following you, Karen. After they sent me his photograph, we now know he's the reporter Archie Pelar. He's also taken photos of you both, using a long-range camera lens. Do you want him followed?"

"I do, he is a man I need to meet. What isn't clear is if Dominick has a part in all this."

"In what way, Karen?"

"I'm wondering if he called Archie, told him of our meeting. If that's the case, most of what he's telling me will be lies."

"I can understand that, it also leaves you vulnerable, if you're agreeing to meet him again."

"I am going to meet him again, Stanley. If I'm being set-up, it's important to know who by. Just keep surveillance going, with an extraction team close by, will you?"

"I will, you also keep your watch on, no risks Karen and don't hesitate in pressing the button to summon immediate help."

"You can be sure I won't. We'll talk later."

Dominick was looking out of the window when

83

she came back to the table, sitting down once more.

"I was just thinking, Dominick. Since your meeting with Archie, then his call to send you to a bar, has he been in touch since?"

"Yes, he called the next morning, after I'd met you both at the bar. He wanted to know if all had gone well with Sherry. I was at a loss as to what to say, regarding finding out that Amber was in reality Karen Harris. So I told him that Sherry had found Amber, but had not seen her for quite some time."

"So you didn't tell him you were meeting me?"

"No, in fact, when he called, we'd not arranged anything anyway. Not that it would have been anything to do with him, so I wouldn't have told him anyhow."

Karen glanced at her watch. "It's been good meeting you again, Dominick, but I'm working and have a few appointments this afternoon." She handed him a card, already in her other hand. "That's my mobile, call me and we'll go out, but I'm not in the country for the next few days, so it would need to be closer to next weekend."

He kissed her directly on the lips, Karen didn't pull away. "I'm not sure what to say, Karen, only thank you for meeting me and giving me the chance to tell you how much I want to be with you again."

She smiled. "It's not one-sided, Dominick, I didn't come here just to listen, I wanted to come. But we'll not spoil it by rushing in, let's just take it slowly, get to know each other again," she replied, before walking away.

He stood watching her leave, surprised to see a large Range Rover draw up outside. Karen climbed in and it left.

Karen leaned back before she pulled out her mobile telephone, calling Stanley. "After my talk with Dominick, I think it's important that we keep surveillance on him for the time being?"

"I'm with you on that. The recording of your conversation. I presume in view of the contents, it's not for placing on general file?"

"No, it shouldn't be. Not because of him wanting us to get together, I'm entitled to a private life and wouldn't be bothered if the conversation was just that. But it also contains references to an operation that was not run by the unit, it must be on restricted access and only with your or my permission."

"Again I agree and will place it in your personal files. Are you going back to the flat, or returning to France?"

"I'm coming back to France, I've logged a flight plan to leave at seven tonight. We'll talk in the morning."

Chapter 11

Harold Maclean from the UK, pulled his car into an overnight lay-by outside Roubaix in France, close to the Belgian border. A number of lorries were already parked, some with the curtains around the inside of the cab closed while the driver slept. Climbing out of his car, carrying a small bag, he walked over to a lorry, where the driver was leaning against one of the wheels of the cab smoking.

"Jance, it's good to see you again," he said, once he was close to the driver.

"And you. I was expecting you an hour back."

"Sorry, the crossing to Calais was very late, with the ferries arriving from Calais delayed by customs searching every vehicle."

"Yes, I've heard it's bad. Anyway, if you climb into the passenger side of my cab, we'll talk."

Once inside, Jance handed Harold a beer from a tiny fridge, taking one himself.

"To business," Jance began. "The ten women who answered the advert will be arriving in London from Germany to take-up the jobs they have been offered over the next two weeks, the first arrives tomorrow. We've found it best to spread the delivery, in case there are problems entering the UK. Although, with a forged passport and coming from an EU country, it is much easier. Each will have with them an underground ticket, with a small map directing them to the house from the underground station."

"You've vetted them?"

"Yes. They range from twenty-five to thirty-one,

are all single and have little money. They are reliant on the jobs to pay their way and agreed to have the cost of their travel deducted from their wages. It is another screw to force them into what you have in mind, when they already owe three grand. You have the payment with you?"

Harold opened the bag he'd brought from the car, so Jance could see inside. "There's fifty thousand there, as agreed."

Jance removed bundles and flipped through them. "That's fine. We have a deal."

"When can I expect the next batch?"

"One month, we've already placed ads and have a number of enquiries."

"That is good, keep me updated, will you?"

"I will. Are you interested in children? We have two girls aged twelve and fourteen to place."

"Can you get them into the UK?"

"We can, but via Ireland. They would be fifty thousand each, delivered to the UK."

"They are white?"

"Yes, both can speak fluent German and English." He handed Harold another envelope. "See for yourself, they are very good-looking girls."

Harold looked at the pictures. Each was in casual wear, there were also some nude shots. "They look bonny, where have they come from?"

"They're sisters. Their parents were working in a small bakery in Eastern Germany. The family got a job offer in Berlin, with accommodation included. They jumped at the chance and said goodbye to everyone they knew and set off. The parents have been disposed of, the girls kept for over two months. Not a word has come out from where they used to live, that the family are missing. I think the family's been forgotten after they moved away."

"Let me make a few calls when I'm back in the UK. I think, no, I know I can place them. But I'll confirm, then we can fix a delivery date."

"I'll look forward to your call."

***

Harold was back in the UK. Along with another man, he was sitting in the lounge of a house, waiting for the first woman he'd agreed to take off Jance to arrive.

At that moment the doorbell rang. Harold walked through to the hall, opening the door.

"Mr Maclean, I'm Josie Hunt. I'm from the International Agency."

"Yes, I was expecting you, would you come in?" he told her.

Already he had looked at the young woman, she was attractive, around five foot six and slim.

Coming into the lounge, he asked her to sit down. "You speak good English, I understand you lived in Libya?"

"I did, but everyone in my school was taught English. They told us it was essential in this world to have a good understanding of the language."

"They were right. Except I've bad news. The job you have come for has been withdrawn. But all's not lost, the agency has found a similar job, but it's in Teesside. You will stay here overnight and a car will take you to the new job tomorrow."

Josie looked a little put out. "I really wanted to

stay in London, I've a couple of friends I would have liked to look up. Can the agency not locate me here?"

"It's a bit difficult, Josie, not all jobs come with accommodation and to live in London can be very expensive without it being included. But I'll tell you what I'll do. Stay in Teesside for a month or two and by then, I'll have found a suitable job with accommodation for you in London. They are always coming up, so there should be no problem."

"Thank you, that's very good of you. Will the pay in Teesside be similar to what I've been offered in London?"

"Yes, exactly the same. Most jobs, helping parents in their homes to look after their children, pay the legal minimum, but of course it's worth far more to you, with no deductions for your food and accommodation."

"Then I'm happy to accept your offer."

***

The following morning, Josie had breakfast and was soon on the road, heading for Teesside. The man driving was in his early twenties and already had music blaring out of the CD player.

"Is it a long way?" she shouted at him above the noise of the music.

"About four hours, maybe a little more if the traffic's bad," he shouted back at her.

She leaned forward and turned the music down. "In that case, I'm not listening to your music at that level. I don't mind you having it on, so long as it's not deafening."

He glanced at her, smiled to himself, saying nothing.

They travelled on, with little passing between them, apart from odd comments. Eventually, after over four hours of travel, he turned off the main road down a side road, stopping at the entrance to a house, with closed gates. Winding his window down, he reached out and pressed a button.

"Yes, can I help you?" came a metallic voice.

"It's Benny, I've got the woman."

The gates opened and he drove through.

Josie never made a comment on the way he'd spoken. She was glad they had arrived and she'd not see him again.

By the time they came to a halt outside the large, but old country house, a woman was standing at the entrance.

Josie climbed out. "Hi, my name's Josie," she greeted her with a friendly voice.

"Yes, we were expecting you, if you collect your case, I'll show you your room."

A few minutes later Josie was standing in a large bedroom. It was dominated by a huge bed, a small table and two chairs by the window and a wardrobe. She was surprised, compared with the house's decorations downstairs and ornate furniture, this room was very sparse. But it was clean and the lady showed her an en-suite bathroom.

"We've already had dinner, but yours was put by. You won't be expected to work until tomorrow, after you've met the house manager."

"Will I meet the children then?" she asked.

The woman looked at her strangely. "I'm not sure

what you're talking about, perhaps it's best you speak to the manager in the morning. Once you've unpacked, come down to the kitchen, I'll heat your dinner up. The kitchens at the bottom of the stairs, turn sharp left and it's the door at the end of the passage."

***

"I'm expected to do what?" Josie screamed at the house manager after she'd been taken to the office the following morning.

"Did the agency not tell you, we're a brothel? Of course in this country its illegal, so we're very discreet, besides the fact you may go to prison for soliciting."

"I've come to look after children in a private house, not prostitute."

"But that job's no longer available. You agreed to come to Teesside and we've paid your fees in advance."

"Then ask for your money back, I'm leaving."

"So that's your last word, you've no intention of fulfilling your commitment, or paying back the cost of your travel?"

"If I have to prostitute, no," Josie retorted.

"Very well, I want three thousand pounds now for your travel, plus our fee of two thousand. I'll have one of the workers drop you off at the nearest railway station."

Her face changed. "I don't have that sort of money, I'll have to owe it and pay back when I find a job."

The house manager shook her head slowly. "No, Josie, if you can't pay now, then you work it off before you leave this house." She reached down and pressed a small bell push under her desk. Immediately two men entered the room.

"This woman owes us money and won't or can't pay. She needs a little persuasion, I think. Take her downstairs and make her ready," she barked at them.

Josie was grabbed by her arms and dragged out of the office, all the time screaming abuse at the house manager.

Five minutes later the house manager entered a room in the cellar. Josie had already been stripped and laid out on an old bed, her arms above her head, her wrists secured to the rails of the steel bedhead.

"One last chance: work or we'll make you work?"

"Do what you want with me, I'll not work for you," she retorted bravely.

"Oh, you will, believe me," she answered, at the same time pulling a ready loaded syringe from her pocket.

Josie stared at the syringe in horror. "What's in that?" she gasped.

"Just a little relaxant, Josie, nothing to worry about," she told her quietly, at the same time pushing the needle into her leg. "There, that was easy don't you think? I'll come to see you in a few hours, for your next tiny injection. You'll can be sure with regular injections, you'll have lost all your inhibitions before our busiest night. Sleep well."

"You bastard, I'll never work," she shouted after her as she left the room.

Once outside the room, the house manager looked at one of the men. "Remember, a bucket full of water poured over her every half hour, we don't want her sleeping it off too easily do we? Let the heroin do its work."

Chapter 12

Dominick had arrived home from work. He'd collected a takeaway, picked up his mail from the postbox at the entrance to the flats and running up the three flights of stairs to his flat. Going inside and shutting the door, he settled down at the table to eat his dinner.

Almost immediately, there was a knock at the door. Dominick looked towards the door, visitors would normally use the bell, prevented from entering the building by a locked entrance that could only be released by a tenant. Presuming it must be one of the tenants, he opened the door.

The man standing there he'd never seen before. The man spoke before he could say anything.

"Are you Dominick?"

"Yes, and you are?"

"Bile, I was a friend of Archie, we need to talk."

Dominick was a little taken aback. "You mean Archie Pelar, the reporter?"

"Yes, may I come in and I'll explain?"

"I suppose, I'm just finishing my dinner. I'll carry on if you don't mind. Curry is not nice cold," he answered, returning to the table, leaving the door open for Bile to come in.

"I agree, you finish it," he said, following him in and closing the door.

"So what do you want to talk about?"

"I was working with Archie, until he met with a fatal accident, yesterday."

Dominick looked up at him, obviously shocked.

"You mean he's dead? How?"

Bile shrugged. "Knocked down by a car, he was pronounced dead at the hospital. So I've taken over his arrangement with you."

"What arrangement? I had no arrangement with Archie, he was just a reporter wanting more information for an article he was writing on Sophie Marshall, the woman who'd been trafficked and I found."

"Yes, I know, but his article also includes Sherry Malloy and the woman who was with her? Archie managed to arrange a casual meeting with Sherry, I believe?"

"He did."

"Why did he do that?"

Dominick frowned. "He'd showed me two photos, one was of Sherry, the other photo of Sophie's sister Karen. He wanted to know if I recognise either. I did recognise Sherry, I also asked him if he knew where Sherry was, she had come to Switzerland to find her friend Amber. I'd been with Amber for a short time and wanted to meet her again."

"This all tallies with Archie's notes, but I understand he managed to have you meet Sherry, in a somewhat casual way. With her was a girl called Karen Harris? A girl you met a couple of days later in Regent's Park and had coffee with? How did that happen?"

"That's private, between me and Karen."

"Of course it is, but the photo Archie took of you outside the coffee house showed you and Karen to be more emotionally attached than just having a casual meeting in the park. So have you forgotten Amber and asked Karen out instead and she agreed?" he asked, at the same time laying a photograph on the table, showing him kissing Karen on the lips.

"Like I said before, that's between me and Karen."

"Give me a little slack here, Dominick, after all it was Archie who led you to Karen. As it is, Karen's very important to us both. In your case, I presume, you would like her to become your girlfriend. Am I correct?"

"Yes," he replied shyly.

"Of course you would, who wouldn't? She's an extremely attractive and, might I say, sexy young woman."

"She is, but what do you want of her?"

"Archie and I are investigative journalists, or in his case was, I've now taken over his work. Unfortunately for Karen, she's a public figure and has a massive following. If I let you read even a little of her life story, I can assure you, you'd be fascinated. Archie had worked for three years collecting the information on her and her sister Sophie. I want to complete his work, show the world just what sort of girl Karen really is. Not only in her stand against people traffickers, but her charity work. You have yourself a girl who has worked tirelessly to get where she is today, don't you think she deserves recognition?"

"Putting it that way, I do. But I know very little about Karen and won't be able to help you. All I know is she works abroad a great deal and has a flat in London, which is probably general knowledge. Although I'd be interested in reading more about her myself."

Bile couldn't believe the naivety of this man, how could he know so little about Karen and yet after only a short meeting, arrange to meet her again, besides kiss her as if they were lovers, or a long term girlfriend? But he kept these thoughts to himself and gave a weak smile. "Of course you would and so does the world. This is my deal. I need to ask Karen a few questions, away from the media. In order to complete Archie's work, I want to confirm a number of facts with her. I don't want to embarrass the girl in public and with Archie not being with us, I have to be sure what he's written is the truth and not fantasy."

"So you want me to arrange a meeting, if I can?"

"No, nothing like that. The last thing I want is for Karen to believe you're part of the arrangement. It wouldn't bear well for your relationship if she believes you're with her just to help the press and not for herself."

"Yes, I suppose that could happen. What do you have in mind?"

Bile removed a business card from his pocket and handed it to Dominick. "Karen often eats out and appreciates a good restaurant. The restaurant on the card is one of the best of its kind in London. When you have a date with Karen, call them and make a reservation. Just mention that it was Bile who recommended the restaurant to you. The meal will be on me and you will receive the best of attention, making it a perfect night for you both. Towards the end of your meal, I'll come in with my girlfriend for dinner. I'll recognise Karen, tell her what I'm doing and ask if she would like to look at my work before I go to print. If she agrees, that's fine, if she refuses, that's also fine, I at least gave her the opportunity. You will not be implicated, or even recognised. Will you do it for Archie's memory?"

"Why not, I do owe him. Then, as you say, you're only asking her if she'll look at your work. It won't affect our night."

Bile stood. "Then I'll look forward to hearing that you have made a reservation. Thank you, Dominick. As I said, I, like you, want the best for Karen. She deserves that at least."

Once he left, Dominick pulled out his smart phone and keyed in the name of the restaurant, looking at the write-up and the many reviews. Like Bile said, this was a very good restaurant, Karen would be impressed, he was sure.

***

When Bile left Dominick's, he made his way down the fire escape and through into the backyard where all the rubbish and recycle bins were stored. Climbing the low wall separating the block from the next building, he went to the back door. It was as he'd left it, ever so slightly open because of a small wedge he'd placed earlier. Once inside, he went down to the underground car park and climbed into his car. It was fortunate he'd been cautious, as he had seen a car parked close to the entrance of the flats Dominick lived in. It had arrived when Dominick did, and was still there, with two men inside. He suspected Karen didn't quite trust this man and was watching him. All he could hope now was their relationship would continue long enough for Dominick to book a reservation at the restaurant.

Chapter 13

Gabriel Duwain, after travelling by train from the Ukraine, to Berlin, followed the other passengers off a scheduled flight from Germany. As she left the airport a taxi belonging to Unit T drew up. She climbed inside and it sped away.

"Did you have a good flight, with no problems, Gabriel?" Karen asked.

"I did, thank you. What will happen to me now? After all, I've a forged passport."

"You'll remain with my charity, while we arrange for a legal one for you. It'll take a few weeks, but then you'll be able to travel all over the world without threats from the people who arranged your travel. With me going as you, if it turns out to be for the purpose of forcing you into prostitution, I'll also try to gain you compensation, so you can begin a new life."

"I don't know how to thank you for all this, Karen. You will be careful taking my place?"

"I will, besides Unit T will be close by. We'll soon have them all locked up."

After a short distance a car came up behind the taxi and flashed. The taxi pulled in and Gabriel transferred to the other car. Karen remained in the taxi.

The collection of Gabriel was the result of information given by a contact Karen knew in the Ukraine. A trafficker had set Gabriel up with a forged passport. The passport showing she was a German citizen had enabled her to come into the UK. The trafficker had arranged work for her, so she could pay back the debt. She'd understood by the arrangement that she would be looking after the two children of a wealthy couple in London. However, Gabriel was not going to meet the men who'd set all this up, Karen had taken her place. Karen had set up this elaborate operation following the discovery of a Ukrainian woman, who had been found wandering the streets of Leeds distressed and obviously confused as to where she was. The woman claimed she had come to the UK to work as a live-in housekeeper, besides look after two children. When she arrived in the UK via Germany, the trafficker had given her an address, along with an underground ticket and a little money. She was to go directly there, then his associates would take her to the house where she had the job and introduce her to the employer. It had been a hoax. There had been no job as a housekeeper, the house she was taken too was a brothel, there she'd been locked up, besides beaten a number of times until she agreed to work as a prostitute.

The women's dilemma wasn't unusual, trafficking was already out of control after the poorer countries such as Romania, Slovakia, Slovenia and Hungary joined the EU. Attracting some of the worst criminal groups, linked to drugs and prostitution, who were now directed at the more moderate EU countries, looking for easy pickings. What interested Karen, after the police directed the woman to Karen's charity office in Manchester, was the woman's statement. She talked about a number of other women in the same house, all of them arriving in the UK in response to similar offers of a live-in housekeeper or nanny job. The woman claimed most, if not all were being held in the house, some controlled by heroin. The woman had escaped after hiding in a delivery van calling at the house. As a child she'd stowed away in lorries and vans a number of times, in order to get a free ride into the local town from home, so when the opportunity arose, she'd taken it. The only problem Karen had was that the woman had been unable to tell her where she'd been held, but she was very useful in giving Karen information on how and which agency she'd applied to, besides a description of a trafficker she knew as Jance, who had arranged all her paperwork and financed the flight. This man's name, for Karen, had been linked to a Harold Maclean, whose name had come up a number of times in other investigations surrounding trafficking, but until now her intelligence unit had not been able to link him directly. Today, however, she was to meet him. Karen had also changed her looks. She'd black, curly hair, like Gabriel, with contact lenses that changed her eyes to brown. A fake tan gave her a more rugged complexion, her clothes were low-cost and worn.

"This is the street, Colonel, what number did you say?" the Unit T driver asked Karen, bringing her out of her thoughts.

"Twenty-two," she told him after glancing at the travel itinerary sent by Jance to Gabriel.

Climbing out of the taxi, Karen pressed the button of her watch once, to confirm to her surveillance team that she had arrived. They were already watching the house after being given the itinerary Karen had been sent by Gabriel, when they'd met off the plane. Karen's watch was her means of indicating the situation to her surveillance team. The one push told them she was okay and to just keep on with surveillance. If she pressed her watch button three times, she'd be in trouble and they were to come in fast. Two presses would mean she was leaving the house, but not on her own. They were to follow. They were able to follow her without always being in sight of the vehicle she was travelling in, by two trackers she had on her, both hidden in the lining of her clothing.

It was Harold Maclean, who opened the front door, after Karen pressed the doorbell.

Karen spoke to him in German.

"I can't understand you, don't you speak English?" Maclean asked.

"Sorry, I can speak English, I just didn't think. I'm Gabriel Duwain, are you, Mr Maclean?" Karen asked.

"I am, we expected you earlier, follow me?" he told her curtly.

They came into a room, where another man was sitting.

"You have your letter?" Maclean asked, not introducing the other man.

Karen pulled a letter out of her handbag, handing it to him. She was considering if she should sit down, but decided against it and remained standing.

"How is it you speak such good English?"

"My parents were English, inside the house, my parents always insisted I speak English. I can also speak French and German. I thought you'd be the same as Jance, that is why I spoke in German."

"Where are your parents now?"

"Both dead. They were killed, some time back. I've been living on my own since, until Jance told me he could get me a passport and a job in the UK. I jumped at the offer."

"We arranged for you to work in the Kirk household. There's been a problem. They have changed their minds about having an illegal in the house."

Karen expected this, suspecting that the job Gabriel had originally come for had never existed, meaning she could well be diverted to the illegal brothel where the woman who was picked up in Leeds had been. "You mean there's no longer a job?" Karen gasped, trying to look concerned.

"Got it in one. What do you think, Tex, could she be all right for the job on Teesside?" he asked, looking directly at the man sitting down, giving Karen the impression that she was being considered.

"Take your coat off," Tex demanded of Karen.

She took her coat off.

Tex shrugged. "Are these the best clothes you have with you?"

"Yes, it's my only dress, I do have a trouser suit, why do you ask?"

"You will need to be interviewed, the last thing we want is for you to look like a tramp. Get yourself into the trouser suit, then let's see how you look."

"Where do I change?"

"There's a bathroom at the top of the stairs."

Karen grabbed her bag and ran upstairs. Soon she was back, wearing the trouser suit.

"That looks better, do a complete turn," Tex told her.

Once she was standing facing him again, he

looked across at Maclean. "I'll give them a ring, Harold, then if they agree to see her, I can run her up tomorrow." He looked back at Karen. "You'll stay here overnight. If they agree, we'll leave at seven in the morning."

"Where is this Teesside, is it close to London?"

"No, it's four hours away, why?"

"Is it the same pay?"

"Yes."

"Then its okay I suppose."

"Well, that's all there is, that offers accommodation," Maclean cut in. "So until we sort it out, make yourself useful and get yourself into the kitchen. Tidy the place up and make dinner, with what's in the fridge, for the three of us."

After Karen left the room, Tex closed the door. "She's not a bad looker and will fetch good money," he commented, sitting back down and turning the television on.

"I agree with you there. You need to be back tomorrow night, we've another for the London house coming in then."

"I'll be back, have no doubts."

***

The following morning, Karen, with Tex were on their way just after seven. Karen had already sent the signal, via pressing the buttons on her watch, to tell her surveillance team she was on the move. Her only problem was, before she called Unit T in, she had to be certain this was the location where the woman who had come to her charity had been taken. That could well mean she'd need to spend two or three days there - something, after hearing what the woman had gone through, she didn't relish.

Two hours into the journey, they stopped off for breakfast. Tex wasn't very talkative, so during the time they travelled, it was mostly in silence. She had the feeling that he actually looked down on her, as if she was nothing. Karen smiled to herself, if, where she suspected she was being taken was the same place as the woman in Leeds, it wouldn't be too long before she was back to arrest him for trafficking.

On the final leg, he'd become more alert. Even talkative.

"So you've been to the UK before, maybe for a holiday?"

"No, I prefer the Med, its warmer. But the original job offer was for twelve months, with a possibility of travelling the world with the family and maybe even a permanent position. Will I have the same opportunity in this job?"

"I've no idea, you'll have to ask. But it's unlikely."

Karen frowned. "I thought it was a family, the same as the other job I was offered?"

"I didn't say that. I just said there was a job going. They will explain everything when you get there."

Karen still acted concerned. "Just what do they do?"

Tex shrugged. "I've no idea, but they have agreed to take over your debt, deducting a regular amount from your wages, until it's paid off, besides understanding your passport is a forgery and you don't have a work permit for the UK. On that basis, there's not many clients who would take you on, so count yourself lucky." He went silent when the satellite navigation burst into life to tell them to turn left. "I always miss that turning without the Sat Nav and I've been here a few times over the last months," he commented. "Five miles or so and we're there."

Karen wanted to persist in her questioning as long as she could, already he'd happily admitted he'd been here a number of times. This would be part of the prosecution's case against him. He'd no idea everything he said was being recorded. "If you've been there a few times, you must know what they do?"

"They're in the entertainment business, that's as much as I know. You could be in the kitchens, cleaning the rooms, whatever. Apparently there's a number of options."

"Excuse me, I've not come to the UK to clean, thank you. You should have made that clear before we left London."

"Yes, well, you're in debt to us for three grand already, then with placement fees it adds up to five grand. Have you got that sort of money?"

"You know I haven't, and then, why should I have to pay more than the three?"

"Listen, it cost us the three just to get you into the country. We then ask a fee from the client. That's our profit and you get yourself a job in the UK. Which is what you want, with wages far more than you'd earn at home. Five grand's only a hundred a week to pay off, with no living expenses you'll easily pay that."

"I suppose, but I still should have been told."

"Why? You've a job, what more do you want? Anyway, this is it, so no more talk. Sort it out with the client."

Karen looked at the large country house, as they turned off the country road, to approach it on what looked like a private road, through open gates. Most of what must have been a spectacular entrance had now been given over to car parking. The large ornate double entrance doors had been painted blue, with part of the stone steps up to the door taken out to make a disabled access route. The entrance looked cold and uninviting. As they came to a halt, the front door opened and a woman came out, running down the steps.

Tex climbed out of the car, the same as Karen. "This is Gabriel, Viv, can you look after her now, I can't stay?"

"Very well, I'll see you soon, Tex. Can you collect your bag and follow me, Gabriel?"

Karen looked across at Tex. "What if I'm not wanted or I don't want the job? How do I get back to London?" she asked.

"That's your problem, they have paid your fee, so if you don't like what they are offering, I can do nothing. Like I said, sort it out with them." With that, he climbed back into his car and drove away.

"If you'd follow me, we'll get you settled and then you can see the house manager," Viv told Karen.

***

Ah, Gabriel, you had a good journey?" the house manager asked when Karen was brought into her office.

"Yes, thank you."

She looked down at the papers left by Tex. "I see you're from the Ukraine. You speak very good English, what about other languages?"

"Thank you, Tex said the same thing to me. My parents were English. I also speak French and German."

"You're quite accomplished and yet you've entered the UK illegally. You understand if we don't look after you, there is a chance you will be deported?"

"I understand that, but it's the way of the world. Sometimes what you want is insurmountable without engaging in a little subterfuge."

The house manager sighed. "Well, I've not heard that before. As it is, you owe us five thousand pounds. That will need to be worked off, including your accommodation. We pay two hundred a week, for at least forty hours. Out of that you pay back one hundred to us for your loan and fifty for accommodation and food. That will leave you fifty pounds."

Karen frowned. "That's not a lot and well below what I expected."

"Yes, well, that's the going rate for an illegal. Of course, it is not as bad as you seem to think. Our clients coming to the club will give you tips, they can amount to over a hundred a week, sometimes, if you work hard for them, two hundred."

"That seems a lot, why would they pay me tips?"

Outwardly, the house manager looked confused, although in reality she wasn't. She knew Tex hadn't told Gabriel that this was a brothel. It was time to tell her. "I'm a little confused, Gabriel, I understood Tex told you what we do here? After all, we've paid him five thousand for you."

"No, he failed to be explicit about my actual duties. Told me you'd lay those out. So what are they?"

"You are here to service our members' sexual desires, nothing more. It is eight hours a day, with one day off a week."

Karen tried to look shocked. "I don't think so. I've not come thousands of miles to become a prostitute. I could have done that at home and for a lot more than five pounds an hour, with a possibility of tips."

"Very well, if you give me seven thousand, you may leave. I'd think about that for a moment. You will not get your forged passport back, you won't be able to work without a national insurance number and you'll most likely be deported back home. You've no grounds for asylum."

"You know I've not got that sort of money. I'd have to get a job to pay you back. Then, how is it my debt keeps rising?"

She gave a slight grin. "For a start, we're not a charity. We paid five thousand, you can hardly expect us to be happy with just getting our money back? Besides, by the sound of it, we wouldn't get a penny of it, unless you worked. How are you going to do that in this country? Then, if you left this country, you and I know you'd not be wanting to pay us. That leaves you with a dilemma, the same as us." She hesitated. "Well, not such a dilemma as far as I'm concerned. If you've no money, you will work for us, until you've paid all the money back. Then, if you still want to leave, you can."

Karen never said anything. Already she could see how easy it was for them to force a woman to prostitute, however, the house manager's next words were far more disturbing.

"I presume with you keeping quiet you're uncertain of what to say? But you see, Gabriel, there are only two ways you can go now. One, you accept your debt and work it off. Two, you flatly refuse to work - then we will need to give you a tiny push in the right direction, to make sure you do."

"When you say push, in what way? You can forget beating me. I've had beatings all my life, beginning with my father, who liked nothing better than knocking five bells out of me. It never worked, you harden and just take it."

The house manager pressed a small button located just under her desk, but out of sight of anyone sitting down on the other side, like Karen was. Immediately two men entered the room, closing the door behind them, but said nothing.

"We don't mess about with beatings, Gabriel, it often injures a woman to the point of them being useless for some days. Then, like you're claiming, it wouldn't affect you, we'd need to resort to snipping a few of your toes, or fingers off, delaying you beginning working for that much longer. So we have a far more practical approach. One nod to these men, and they will take you down into the cellar. You'll be stripped and left in a stone room, with only a pot to piss and shit in and nothing else, not even a chair. Believe me, Gabriel, you will soon understand why. That's after you're injected with your first dose of heroin. Just enough to make you feel a little strange, although it will give you the need for a little more and then a little more. Each hour will get that much harder, your body will be shaking, your head spinning, hallucinations will leave you screaming in terror. By the end of the week, with smaller regular doses, you will be addicted, except from then, anymore comes at a price. I'll stand there as you tell me, no, beg me, how you'll do anything I want of you, for the relief that tiny needle offers."

She fell silent, allowing what she said to sink in. On Karen's part, she was scared. The experience of drugs being forced down her in the past had left her in a coma once, with a fifty-fifty chance of survival. Then, drugs given to her by Nigerian traffickers very nearly destroyed her mind. Even today, she still had nightmares, besides having very real blanks in her memory. She had a choice, like the woman said. Bring the covert operation to an end by pressing her watch button, leaving them with very little to prosecute the illegal brothel and its owners with, or do as she was being asked for a day or so, until she could find out just what was going on.

"I need a decision?" the house manager suddenly told her. "Agree, or let's see if we can change your mind."

"I've no intention of becoming dependent on heroin. You must look at it from my side. It's come as quite a shock what I've got myself into?" she hesitated for a second, as if it was taking a great deal of effort to say what she was going to say. "I will work as you ask, although, I need time to get used to the idea. While it would be for less than a week, I have a proposition that you might find acceptable?"

"What sort of proposition?"

"I would be prepared to offer a lap dance. It is something I did when I was eighteen in local clubs and I used to enjoy it."

The house manager sat there, saying nothing for a short time. Gabriel was an attractive woman and if she could get her to accept her life, without resorting to drugs, which she already had a number of women on, good money could be made. "You know, Gabriel, most who come here require us to convince them to work. You're different in that you accept your position. I think many of our clients would take-up your offer to lap dance for them, it would keep clients who are waiting for a woman to come free interested, earning us a little extra beyond the overpriced drinks. You'll find me a fair person to work for, you can have the rest of the week to show us what you can do, after that we talk again, but I will be expecting you by then to also offer additional services, even if a lap dance remains part of what's on offer to a client."

Karen inwardly sighed with relief. "Then I agree, do you have clothes I could use?"

Chapter 14

Karen was taken around the house, and shown the main lounge where clients would gather. It was large, and had two poles in the centre on small platforms, which at times she'd be expected to show herself off on. She could already see this was a very established brothel, and was beginning to suspect it could only remain here if it was supported by backhanders to local officials, be it money, or even complimentary sessions with women. She would enjoy bringing this place down, when the time came. So to negotiate lap dancing sessions for the next few days, on the pretext of allowing her to settle in and accept her position, she was happy. It was something she didn't mind doing, knowing full well the place would be raided long before she had to move to the next stage and offer services beyond a lap dance.

The house manager found her suitable clothes and she was given a room on the first floor. This would be her permanent room, where eventually clients would come. However, her lap dances would be downstairs in a small room off the hall.

***

Karen looked at her watch, it was coming up to eight, the time she was to begin work. Already showered, she began to dress. First she put on the bra that pushed her breasts up high, with matching skimpy knickers, followed by a suspender belt, holding up sheer nylons. Karen buttoned her waistcoat top and clipped the short, flared skirt around her waist, positioning the waistcoat and skirt to leave her tummy button in view, before pushing her feet into the high heeled shoes. Karen always had nine items to remove, each one would go at a time to match the music, allowing her to be naked for less than twenty seconds; most of that time she would be facing away from the client wriggling her bottom, the last seven seconds facing him astride his knees. She was told not to wear any jewellery, even her watch; the house manager had offered to lock it away, but Karen told her it was of little value and she'd like to keep the watch with her. The woman agreed, so long as she left it all in her room.

Karen left the bedroom, going downstairs, joining the other girls in the main lounge.

The house manager came up to her. "You're a very attractive woman, Gabriel, you will do well here. Already I've made it known that lap dancing is available tonight. When a client agrees you dance for him, take a token from him as payment. Also, try to have him buy you a drink. Now it's time for you to mingle and find your first client."

Karen nodded slightly. "I understand."

When Karen walked away, the house manager was joined by Radley Hendal, the owner of the brothel. He was tall, spectacled, wearing casual clothes, but well dressed.

"Is that the new woman who you agreed could offer lap dances first, to get into the work?"

"Yes, it was her idea, when she realised she had to repay her debt to us after being given two options - agree, or be turned into a junkie. It was then she told me she'd done lap dancing when she was younger, although she didn't seem phased at moving onto offering all services by the end of the week."

Radley looked a little concerned. "I don't like it. It sounds too easy for her just to agree. Then, we never found the women who escaped, or had the police knocking at our door. Could this woman be a plant to find out what's going on?"

The woman shrugged. "You could say that about any woman brought here. According to our supplier, she checked out, without any possible problems. She was obviously very scared by the prospect of being given heroin. I suspect she has had heroin in the past and knows just what it can do. Particularly to one who's already been down that path."

"You're right. Perhaps I'm getting cynical and expect everyone to need a little persuasion. Although, keep an eye on her all the same."

"We always do, you never take a woman's word as gospel, particularly if she's mouthing what you want to hear and not offering an argument as to why she won't do as she's told."

Radley walked away, welcoming a number of regular clients as he moved around the large lounge. He also discreetly listened in to what the working women were talking about with clients, even listening to Karen's conversation for a time.

Finally, he left the room, stopping a client who had just handed his coat to the doorman and was heading for the lounge. "Derran, it's good to see you. Why not join me in my private room for a drink?" Radley asked.

"Sounds good, Radley. I'm always up for a drink, especially when it's free," he mocked.

Derran was one of the brothel's best clients. He'd

be there at least three nights a week, spending a great deal of money each time.

Radley knew the cost of a drink was nothing for this man, he ran a large plant hire company, employing close to three hundred people. "Only the best malt as well, Derran."

Once inside Radley's private room, they sat down, both holding a large glass of whisky.

"Had a busy day then?" Radley asked.

"I have, in fact, I should be celebrating with the wife, but she's got a headache as usual."

"So what's the celebration for?"

"I landed a contract with the Ukraine government to supply a large consignment of plant machinery, with a servicing package that will see good returns through the next three years. It's worth millions."

Radley smiled. "Then you must celebrate. In fact, I will give you a bonus, on the house. Although in this case I do have an ulterior motive, which I think you will enjoy," he came back at him.

"Sounds interesting, lead on."

***

Karen was carefully studying the girls. Already she could see, among the nine that were in the lounge, the typical glazed expression caused by drug taking. Karen's problem was, although they suspected women were being held here under duress and being forced to prostitute, if they didn't have concrete evidence, the owners might wriggle out, claiming the women were habitual drug takers and prostituting to finance their habit. Now she was here herself, with recordings of the manager offering her an alternative of a drug route if she refused to work, Karen had them. All she needed to do tonight was to see the general condition of the women offering services in exchange for payment, which strengthened her case. Karen intended to hit them hard and close them down, she also wanted their assets to compensate the victims, besides put them behind bars for ten years, or if the current legislation went through, maybe for life. Then there was Maclean and Jance. Those two were already implicated, with Gabriel being pushed through the system, before she'd been replaced by Karen.

A man approached her. He was small, clean-shaven, with glasses. He was also holding out his token, offering it to Karen. "I was told you dance," he said shyly.

She smiled. "I do, and your token will pay for that. But are you not going to offer me a drink first, maybe even have a short talk so you know a little about me?" she asked.

He just nodded and walked over to the small bar in a corner. Soon he came back with a drink, handing it to her.

Karen had watched him. She intended to follow the house manager's instructions, in chatting to each man and accepting a drink; she knew she'd be given coloured water, while the client would pay for a double whisky at an inflated price, but it would reduce the amount of times she'd have to dance,.

The man received no change from a ten pound note. Karen took the drink from him and smiled. "Thank you, shall we sit down for a few minutes?"

The man's eyes lit up. "I'd like that, what is your name?"

" Gabriel… and you are?"

"Patrick."

"You come here a lot do you, Patrick?"

"No, I've never been before. A man at work was talking about this place to another. I listened in and decided I'd come and see for myself. I live with my aged parents, spending most of my time on my computer, so I don't get out much."

"I see you are holding a session token, have you picked a woman to be with you later?"

"Yes, I want you. I noticed you the moment I came in and have looked at no one else. Do you want my token now?"

She shook her head. "I'm not available for sessions this week, next week perhaps. So I can only accept your dance token. Maybe we should go now, if you follow me?"

The small room they had set aside for Karen had just one kitchen chair and a stool. In the corner on a shelf was a CD player. Karen had selected a CD track that matched her time of four minutes for the entire dance sequence. The only other item in the room was a silk dressing gown, hanging on a hook on the back of the door.

Once inside, Karen slipped the bolt. It was a low-cost one, that if necessary the minder who patrolled the entire house could burst open with little difficulty.

"What do I do?" Patrick asked.

"You've never had a lap dance either?"

"No, never."

"In that case, sit on the chair, with your hands under your bottom. Take them out, try to touch me and the dance ends, you leave and don't see me finish. You won't get a refund. Do you understand?"

"Yes," he told her, at the same time sitting down, trapping his hands as she'd explained.

"That's good, just relax and enjoy my strip for you, before I sit facing you astride your knees, naked."

Karen touched a button on the CD player and the music began. Standing in front of him, she began swaying to the music, her eyes closed as if in a trance. Slowly she unfastened each of the four buttons on her waistcoat, before slipping it off, dropping it to the floor in a corner of the small room.

Coming closer to him she pouted her lips as if offering him a kiss, at the same time releasing the single button, holding her short skirt up. Pulling it away, she dropped it on her waistcoat.

Patrick was transfixed as she placed one foot on the stool, released the first nylon stocking from the suspender, rolling it carefully down her leg, removing her high heeled shoe, before slipping the nylon off over her foot and replacing her shoe. Doing the same with her other nylon, she stood in front of him, reaching around her back, releasing the catch of her suspender belt.

Karen turned her back on him, allowing him to watch her reach behind and release the bra, allowing it to fall off her arms, throwing it into the corner with her other clothes, before turning back to him, her breasts covered with her hands. She began massaging them gently, throwing her head back slightly, her eyes closing as if she was enjoying the massage, titillating him as her hands would allow a nipple to be exposed for a moment, before she withdrew her hands completely.

Karen was listening all the time to the music, knowing where she should be at each stage of the music score. Again she turned away, grasping the top of her knickers, wiggling her bottom slightly as she pushed the knickers clear of her hips, allowing them to fall to her feet, then stepping out of them.

She turned to face him once more. She could see he was staring down, trying to catch glimpses of her most intimate area as she walked towards him, pushing her breasts close to his face as she sat astride his knees.

Now she was jerking her buttocks, her legs well apart, but so close to him, he couldn't look down very easily to get an unrestricted view of her.

At that moment the music stopped and she stood, turning away quickly, grasping the robe hung on a hook, slipping it on.

"You enjoyed my dance?" she asked, fastening the robe.

"Yes," he gasped.

"Then I'm here till very late, if you want another dance you need to buy another token. You must leave me now, so I can dress."

After he left, Karen dressed slowly. She enjoyed lap dancing, this was why she hadn't brought the unit in, when in reality she only had to look around the lounge to know something was not right. Then, with her recordings, there was no defence. Even so, she decided to delay the order until the clients had left, leaving just the owners and workers inside the brothel.

Now ready, Karen left the room, returning to the lounge. Within minutes a number of clients had approached her, offering their special lap dancing tokens for a dance.

**

It was coming up to twelve, Karen had been told the next man was to be her last for the night. Since coming onto the floor, she'd danced for eleven men, which suited her, although she suspected such numbers would not earn what she could earn servicing clients and already she expected to be told tomorrow the deal was off and she'd have to work like the other women. This didn't worry her, she had enough on them to bring the unit in, so she would not need to prostitute.

However, once everyone was asleep, she wanted to check out the building in areas she hadn't been taken round. While this wasn't absolutely necessary, secretly Karen enjoyed the excitement of pitting her wits against the target, and often went beyond what was absolutely necessary, risking her life at times for no real reason.

Approaching a man sitting at the small bar, Karen smiled.

"Hi, I'm Gabriel, may I join you?"

"You can. I've not seen you before, are you new?"

"Yes."

"In that case we should be getting acquainted. Where's your room?" he asked, offering her a token.

Karen smiled. "I'm only offering a lap dance tonight. I assure you, you will enjoy it."

He seemed put out. "Why? You've got yourself a nice figure and seem fit enough to me?" Derran asked.

"It's my first night, so I'm just getting used to the place. I'll be available for all services later in the week," she answered.

"Interesting start to working here, I've not heard of that one before. Anyway, time's motoring, I've a shag booked for later, so let's get on with the dance shall we?"

"Don't you want to buy me a drink first?" she said, trying to boost her return for the brothel.

"That's for the punters. I'm a regular, Gabriel, and don't buy coloured water. Where's this room you're going to strip in for me?"

Karen sighed, a few years back men would be queuing up to buy her a drink, even if it was just coloured water, just to spend more time with her. "If you'd like to follow me."

Once inside the room, he sat down. "I like to see a woman's fanny, I'm not bothered watching you bouncing your little tits around, or pushing them into my face. So skirt, suspenders and knickers first, then sit astride my knees facing me, while you take the waistcoat and bra off," he told her.

While clients could tell her how they wanted her to undress, she'd learnt during her time working in Paris as a lap dancer, on a covert operation, not to do that, just follow her routine. Here, she would need to make an exception, she didn't want to attract attention to herself, maybe even receive a thrashing, for not keeping a client happy. Then, with it being a one-to-one and not in full view in the main lounge, she wasn't that bothered, although she would have preferred to expose her most intimate area for far less time. But she shrugged, trying not to show she had objections to his request. "If that's what you like, I can do that for you."

"Not what I like, what I want, now get on with it," he came back at her.

Karen followed her routine timings, but had already lost the suspenders and nylons, followed by the knickers, before she was on his knees unfastening the buttons of the waistcoat.

"Come on woman, you're supposed to be feigning intercourse, get the buttocks working, and start thrusting, before you arch yourself back while you lose the bra," he shouted at her.

Doing as he asked, finally she was naked; she thrust for a few more seconds, then stood, turning away, walking over and collecting her robe.

"It's time for you to leave, the dance is finished," Karen said, "thank you for allowing me to dance for you, I hope you enjoyed it?"

Derran stood and come up behind her. "Vy buly duzhe dobre, shcho chastyna Ukr vy pryyshly?" (*You were very good, what part of the Ukraine do you come from*?) he asked her.

Karen couldn't understand and said nothing, pulling her robe on. Already she was nervous, she knew he was speaking Ukrainian, but her knowledge of the language was very sparse.

" Dyvno, shcho vy Kanot zrozumity svoyu vlasnu movu." (*Strange that you cannot understand your own language.*)

Again she didn't reply.

He suddenly grabbed her hair, yanking her head back, looking at her. "Are you just ignorant, or can't you speak the fucking language, yet alone understand it? My wife is Ukrainian, I've been there many times."

She just looked back at him, very scared.

He grinned, keeping a grip of her hair as he dragged her over to the chair, before sitting down and bending her face down over his knees, holding her firmly. "Radley, the owner, who you've not had the pleasure of meeting yet, had a little chat with me earlier. It seems he doesn't like being told by one of his bought women what she should and shouldn't do. He's of the opinion you should be offering far more. He also told me I should demonstrate to you how that sort of attitude is controlled around here." Without another word, holding her head down with one hand, he yanked the robe clear of her bottom, then laid into her with the other hand. His punishment was hard, relentless and without any compassion. Karen was grimacing with the pain, tightening her buttocks, tears streaming down her face.

Finally, he stopped, pushing her harshly off his knees. She fell to the floor, still shaking.

"You want me to call Radley and tell him you are not Ukrainian?" he shouted at her.

"No, please don't, I know I shouldn't have deceived him, but I'll work hard, he'll have no complaints."

"Then it's time to see if you are not just saying that," Derran came back at her aggressively, at the same time standing up and grabbing one of her arms, pulling Karen to her feet, the robe falling off to the floor. "Come on, like I said earlier, I have a shag booked. But I'll save it for another day and try you, so let's find a bed to use shall we?" Already he was dragging her out of the room, not even giving her an opportunity to pick the robe up to cover herself.

She stumbled after him. Other clients were laughing as Derran dragged her naked past them. One who had seen her dance shouted after him: "If I'd known her final client of the night could shag her, I'd have hung about, Derran. Fuck her hard, she must be really frustrated and hyped up after all that stripping," he urged.

"Oh, you can believe that, I'll soon have her broken into our ways," Derran shouted back at him, as he and Karen carried on up the stairs, before going into the first room where a door was open, slamming it after him, pocketing the key.

"Get yourself into the bathroom and slap plenty of lubrication on, even up your arse. It's time you learned just what to expect here," he demanded.

Karen went through to the bathroom, she could have kicked herself, already she'd enough evidence, after being on the floor for only a couple of hours, to have called for the unit to raid the place. Now her delay in doing that, had left her in this position. All because of her arrogance; believing she was in control, preferring to show off with her dancing, enjoying seeing the clients' faces as she removed her clothes, rather than remaining focused on the job. Again, like so many times before, she had underestimated these people, always looking at a woman as a cash cow, expecting and getting obedience from them at all times, even if she needed a good thrashing to remind her. As far as they were concerned, she was bought and paid for, meaning they could do what they wanted with her, she had no say. However, her watch was in her room, not this one. Without it, she couldn't instigate a raid, until she was allowed back to her own room. She could see no way out but to let him do what he wanted of her.

"There you are," Derran said, when she came out of the bathroom. Already he was lying on the bed naked. "Get yourself on top and let's begin by seeing that arse of yours work the way it was intended, rather than wriggling it in your pathetic dance," he mocked.

For the next half hour, Derran's rape of Karen was unrelenting. For her this was the way she'd always been taken by men so she just accepted everything Derran had her do. He finally lay back, obviously satisfied.

"I'd a feeling you'd perform, given a little encouragement. In fact, I think you've already prostituted on a regular basis, am I correct?" he asked, climbing off the bed looking down at her.

"No, I was a lap dancer, but had boyfriends like any woman," she answered indignantly, never ever considering she had been a prostitute by choice in all her previous covert operations.

"Well, they must have known what they were doing with you, showing you ways to please a man, so expect me to take you on a regular basis."

"I suppose I won't have much option."

"No you won't, besides, a few of the regulars here will also want you. I'll need to warn them to start you off with a good hiding, before they take you," he mocked. "I think that really turned you on and made you subservient."

Karen didn't rise to his assertion that she needed violence in her lovemaking, although she knew that men acting that way with her, did make her eager to please, to avoid more punishment. Not that she liked it. "You must live locally if you come here regularly?" she asked.

"I do and also have the largest plant hire company in the North of England," he boasted. "Besides a wife and daughter."

"Then, if you have a wife, why do you need to come here?"

Looking at his watch, Derran looked back at Karen. "That's none of your business, you're here to shag and that's all. As it is, I've still got a quarter of an hour left, I must be slipping. They usually knock on the door, because the woman has her next client waiting and I'm running late. Get yourself up, face the bed and bend over, legs apart," he demanded.

Karen didn't move, in fact, she was shocked that he wanted more.

"I said, up and bend over, or this time, rather than my hand on your bottom, I'll lay into you with my belt," he told her aggressively, already picking his trousers up to pull the belt out from the loops.

Realising he meant what he said about hitting her again, Karen sighed, then stood, bending down as he'd told her. Her hands on the mattress, her legs slightly apart.

Derran came up behind her, slapping her buttocks. "Lower," he demanded, moving one hand around her, slipping it in-between the top of her legs, and gripping her tightly.

"Please, you're hurting me, I'm letting you do what you want with me, without objection," she begged.

"Stop complaining and get used to it," he told her. "Then I'll show you why my wife let's me come here. She doesn't like it up the arse." At the same time, he guided his penis with his free hand between her buttocks, forcing himself up her back passage.

Karen was grimacing with the pain, not able to move while he gripped her tightly.

Suddenly her resistance to his intrusion gave in, and he moved both hands to grip her hips. "That's a good girl, are you sure you've not done this before?" he mocked, working himself deep inside, before he began to thrust himself hard, relishing her objections that he was hurting her and not letting her tighten her buttocks to prevent him going deep. Finally, he was satisfied, pulling out, before pushing her face down onto the bed.

"I'll be back in a couple of days, Gabriel. I'll keep your little secret, but I want to see you really work hard, now you're broken into my ways."

"Thank you, I'll look forward to our sessions and I promise to give you a good-time."

He gave a slight smile, and nodded, before leaving the room.

Karen lay there, her thoughts going back to the time she'd spent in an Algerian brothel. However much she tried to reject the reality, it would seem her time working there, non-stop all day, had changed the way she reacted. There was no love, no affection in being with a man any more, just a knowledge that by giving the man what he demanded there would be no punishment. These thoughts made her feel very down, to think that she'd stooped so low as to go into an operation with her eyes open, prepared to do what she'd done with Derran, as if it was her normal way of life.

Sliding off the bed, she left the room, going directly

to her own and through into the bathroom, determined to wash his sweat off her body. Finally out the shower and dry, dressed in jeans and top, Karen pressed the watch button three times, to instigate the raid, which she should have done hours before.

Sitting down on the only easy chair in the room, all she could do was wait. Karen, unlike the rest of the house, would not be here, when Sir Peter sent in the police to takeover the investigation. She would have left with Unit T. The recordings of conversations with the house manager and the women obviously controlled by drugs ensured a conviction. However, she intended to remain within her covert identity, for the next part of the operation.

Chapter 15

To maintain her covert identity, Karen had been let out the back door by the Unit. She walked for some time and was picked up well away from the house, by a Unit T vehicle. Inside the car were two soldiers and a driver.

"Have we surveillance on MacLean's house still?" Karen asked.

"We have, Colonel. There has been no reports of them getting ready to leave, the car is still parked outside and has been since the man took you to the brothel. It's pointing that they don't know about the raid yet," Lieutenant Foster, sitting in the back told her.

"The team knows to go in if they look as if they're bailing?"

"Yes, they have those orders."

Karen called Stanley.

"Stanley, Karen."

"It's good to hear from you Karen, are you alright?"

"Yes, I'm fine. I'm going to get some sleep while we head back to London. I want to arrive at the house where I met Maclean around twelve. I'll tell him I've thumbed lifts, so that the time will hold up. Hopefully he'll fall for what I'm going to say to him and he could attempt to move me on. I'll keep the recorder running all the time, the same as I did with the house manager at the brothel."

"I understand, take care, Karen."

"I will and the surveillance will be very close."

"That goes without saying," Stanley replied.

Arriving in London, Karen was dropped off a short distance from the house where she'd met Maclean. Soon she was knocking on the door.

He pulled it open, staring at her in disbelief. "What the fuck are you doing here?"

"The place was raided by the police. I'd just finished work, got changed and went down for supper, then managed to escape out the back door in all the confusion. You and I need to talk," she said calmly.

"You'd better come in."

Karen followed him in. "So where's Tex?"

"He'll be back soon. When you say the place was raided, has the owner been arrested?"

She shrugged. "I've no idea, there were people everywhere, including police. The point is, you sent me to a place where they expected me to prostitute. I couldn't do that so they agreed for me to offer a lap dance, that's something I'd done in the past, but no more. Even then, that wasn't why I came to the UK. So I want my money back."

He smiled. "As far as I'm concerned, you came to the country looking for work and I found you a position that offered accommodation. No one told me it was a brothel, or what they wanted you for."

"Maybe they didn't, but I'm broke and can't even afford to get home. The house manager said you'd been paid five thousand, so I'd no option but to stay there to pay it off. How could I pay that much? Anyway, I want at least half, what you got for me. It's only fair."

At that moment Tex opened the front door with a

key and came directly into the lounge carrying two plastic bags. He stared at Karen. "Why the fuck's she back?" he said believing it was Maclean, who had brought her.

"Radley's place was raided last night. She's a bit upset it was a brothel and she was expected to work as a prostitute. It seems they agreed for her just to lap dance. Now it's been raided, she can't even do that. So she wants half what we got for her, so she can go home," Maclean said soberly.

Tex looked at Karen. "You don't get it, do you? We don't pay you, you get sold and people pay us."

"I didn't agree to be sold, or prostitute. I could have done that back home. I just want my money, then I'll go."

"Did you remember to collect your passport, then?" Tex asked.

"How the bloody hell could I?" Karen asked indignantly. "If I'd hung around, I'd be in prison now, or waiting deportation."

Tex grinned. "Then you're fucked, a new passport will cost close to a grand, maybe more. Have you that sort of money?"

"I will have when you pay me."

"Perhaps you would, Gabriel. Except I think we'll hold onto your money. In fact, as the job's fallen through, we have the opportunity to place you again. A similar place, just as pleasant and a little more discreet. There will be no raid there I can assure you."

"Excuse me, I want to go home, not to another brothel."

"And you will, I assure you. I'll even give you

your money. Until then, you need to be away from here, while I arrange for a new passport, which you'll pay for. If this place will let you lap dance, which you accepted at Radley's, will you go?"

Karen frowned. "How long for?"

"One month, then I'll come for you."

"And I'll just lap dance, not have to prostitute?"

"Yes."

She sat quietly, as if thinking. "I don't seem to have an option, with no passport and you not letting me stay here. Alright, but no more than a month and I want to be paid. I'm not working for free, I've got to find money for another passport."

"The work there will more than cover it, Gabriel, believe me," Tex told her. "Now get yourself into the kitchen and see what you can rustle up from the bags I've just brought in, while I make a few calls."

After Karen left the room and they could hear her working in the kitchen, Tex shook his head slowly. "I can't believe that women's naivety, Harold. If she has the idea we're going to get her a passport, she's off her head. Mind you, this time she'll be working out of a well secured room, servicing a queue of clients. She'll never be allowed to leave, till she's burnt out."

"Yes, and we'll make another five grand to boot," Harold added.

Karen returned to the room, carrying the plates of food she'd prepared.

Tex, who'd been talking on the telephone, replaced the handset onto its cradle. "It's all arranged, Gabriel. They have a need for lap dancers and will let you work there for a month, including accommodation. They said you won't be paid, but expect around six to seven hundred pounds a week from tips. That's alright for you, isn't it?"

"Yes, thank you. When do I go?"

"As soon as you've eaten, I'll take you. It's the other side of London, where you wanted to be anyway. I understand they have a lot of wealthy clients, so I think the tips are underestimated."

Chapter 16

Karen was sitting in the passenger seat alongside Tex, who was driving. She was concerned, when rather than leaving from the front entrance of the house, they left from the back, climbing into a car parked, along with a number of others, on a back street. However, she had pressed the button of her watch twice, to indicate she was on the move, relying on surveillance to keep track of her, using the signal from the two trackers, one hidden in the seam of her knickers, the other the seam of her jeans.

In less than an hour, the car pulled into an industrial estate. The buildings were old and dilapidated, badly in need of restoration, or even demolishing.

"Where are we?" Karen asked.

"I need to collect a few carpet tiles from a mate, then I'll drop you off," Tex told her, at the same stopping behind a large unit, with a side door alongside a large roller shutter door.

A man of African descent came out of the side door when he heard the car draw up. He was around five feet six, of muscular build, with short, cropped hair, dressed in jeans and a t-shirt. Pulling open the passenger door of the car, he looked inside. "Alright, Tex, I've got the tiles you called about, do you both fancy a drink, before you load up?"

"That sounds good, Ekua. Out you get, Gabriel, then you can give us a hand loading the tiles into the boot," he urged.

As Karen climbed out, Ekua stood back a little, now he moved quickly forward, pushed a cloth, he'd been holding, in her face, thumping her stomach hard, forcing her to gasp, inhaling whatever was on the cloth. Almost immediately Karen slumped down unconscious.

Tex walked around the car, from the driver's side and looked down at her. "This was the one wanting her money back," Tex commented, lighting a cigarette. "I should give her a good whipping for her arrogance. You do it for us, Ekua, tell her it's a going away present off me and Harold."

"She'll get plenty of those, if she's not prepared to do what's expected of her, have no doubt. Give me a hand to get her inside, will you?" Ekua came back at him.

With Tex grabbing hold of her hands and Ekua at her feet, they soon had her inside the unit, laid down on a large rug.

"Have you the money, I need to get away?" Tex asked.

Ekua was already kneeling down at Karen's side. He'd removed her shoes and socks, and was now unfastening her jeans. Looking up, he nodded towards a bag. "It's in there, five grand you said?" he asked, before carrying on undressing Karen, pulling both her jeans and knickers down her legs, then off the feet.

Tex picked up the bag and opened it. The money was in bundles of a hundred pounds and he began counting it out. By the time he'd counted it all, Ekua had Karen naked, he'd even removed what jewellery she was wearing, including the watch.

Tex looked towards them. "Why are you stripping her?"

Ekua shrugged. "It's far easier to be sure she

carries nothing she could self-harm with, or use to try to have a go at me, and besides in the past, I've had a few users hiding wraps in their mouth or taped to the inside of their legs. One fucker died when I gave her a calming drug and she gave herself a heroin fix, I'd no idea what she had hidden on her body. Taking a woman naked like this means she hides nothing, besides, if she's a user, I can use her addiction to make her work harder for the next fix," he answered, at the same time running his hands through Karen's hair, inspecting inside her mouth by pushing his fingers between her teeth and cheeks and feeling around.

Karen by now was coming around, opening her eyes, not understanding at first where she was, just as he pulled his fingers from her mouth.

Ekua grinned. "You're awake, I didn't expect you to wake just yet. No matter, you'll just have to grin and bear your inspection," he told her, slapping a strip of duck tape over her mouth. Then turning her onto her face, pulling her wrists together, he secured them firmly with more duck tape. While she was on her tummy, he took the opportunity to check her arms for needle marks, part her buttocks to inspect her back entry, then forcing her legs well apart, he ran his hand around and just inside her vagina. Satisfied, she was hiding nothing, he stood. "She's clean. I'll take her."

They shook hands and Tex left with the bag of money.

Ekua had positioned Karen, when she was brought in, towards the edge of the rug. Now he began to roll the rug up, with Karen in the centre, before using more duck tape around the rug to prevent it coming unrolled.

"Time for you to leave, Gabriel. A little uncomfortable, I grant you, but necessary," he told her, lifting the carpet, with Karen in. Walking to the back of his van, he slid it inside, slamming the door shut. Collecting all her clothes, including her handbag and bits of jewellery, watch and even hair clips, he pushed the lot into a black bin bag, taking it over to a rubbish compactor. Throwing the bag in, he pressed the on button, watching with satisfaction as the bag was crushed into the compactor and out of sight, along with other rubbish already inside it.

Ekua opened the large roller shutter door, backed the van outside, shut the door and locked up. Soon he was on his way.

***

Another two hours had past, after Ekua had delivered a number of carpets to retail shops, before he brought the van up a narrow alley behind a row of terrace houses. Most of the houses had removed the back wall, allowing a car to be parked off the passageway. Ekua, for his house, had done the same. He reversed into the small backyard and stopped. Getting out of the van, he unlocked the door of the house, pushing it open, jamming it wide with a brick. Going to the back of the van, he dragged the carpet out with Karen still inside. Carrying it over his shoulders, he made his way into the building, upstairs and through into a room. This was once a large family bathroom, but the bath had been removed, replaced by a bed, leaving just a toilet and washbasin. The window, already frosted, because it was a bathroom, had been boarded up. A single light in the centre of the room was the only illumination. Overall the room was shabby, with plaster falling off the walls, exposing the brick behind it.

Leaving the carpet on the floor, he ran back downstairs, locked the van up, then came inside, bolting the back door. Grabbing a small bottle of lemonade off the kitchen table, he went upstairs and into the room where he'd brought Karen. After shutting and locking the door, with him inside, he removed the tape from the carpet, rolling it out with his foot.

Karen lay there looking up at him, unable to talk, with the tape still over her mouth. She was desperately worried. With him stripping her completely, both trackers hidden in the top seam of her clothing would remain where she'd been stripped. Then, with her watch missing as well, she couldn't summon help. All she could hope now was that surveillance had placed a tail on any vehicle leaving, even with her tracker indicating she was still in the building.

Ekua helped her stand, led her to the bed and sat her down on the side. Reaching under the bed, he pulled out an ankle iron, already attached to a chain, which was fixed to the floor. The chain was only just long enough to allow her to reach the toilet and washbasin. He secured her ankle, released the duck tape wrapped around her wrists, before ripping the tape off her mouth.

"You look dehydrated, drink this," he said with concern, handing her the small bottle of lemonade.

She drank it gratefully. "Where am I, why am I naked and chained up?" she asked, trying still to be Gabriel.

"Tex has sold you to me. From now on, I'm your new owner, this is where you work. You're lucky, you'll

138

never be on the streets, in the cold and rain. I'll bring you the clients, you service them. We should get through at least ten, going up to thirty a day over the Friday and weekend."

She looked at him in horror. "I'm not being raped by a hundred men a week. You can beat me up, do anything you want, but the only way that would happen is if you tied me down so I couldn't move."

He shrugged. "What's all this griping? The last woman I had in here could do the ten in the evening and still have time to watch telly?"

"Then you'd better get her back, I'm not."

"She's dead, you've replaced her. So believe me, you will be working at that level very soon."

Leaving the room, he was soon back, with a t-shirt. "You wear this from now on. Anything else is pointless. In the small cupboard above the sink, there's a toothbrush, soap, a sponge and towel. There's also lubrication in a tube, if you want to use it. Keep everything in the cupboard, tell me when you run out of anything."

"What about a bath or a shower, don't I get to wash beyond a sponge?"

"There isn't one, this was the bathroom." With that, he left the room, locking the door behind him.

Karen pulled the t-shirt on over her head, it was oversized for her, but at least it gave her a little dignity. She looked around. This place was no better, or worse, than she'd experienced in the past, so she didn't dwell on it. Her thoughts were on how to overcome Ekua, which she intended to do sooner rather than later, after he'd told her what she should expect.

"Come on, wake-up, here's your dinner," Ekua shouted, at the same time shaking her like a rag doll.

Karen opened her eyes. She'd been tired, lying down on the bed, she remembered nothing else. Even now she felt light-headed, Ekua's voice booming in her head.

Sitting on the side of the bed, with no other means of sitting down, she began to eat the obvious takeaway meal, using a small plastic fork. After the food, she was given more lemonade.

"Right I'm off out. You get some sleep, tomorrow you begin work. I've eight already arranged for the afternoon, but that should double when it gets around that you're available."

She glared at him. "I told you, I'm not going to work, so forget it."

He never replied, just left the room, carrying the empty takeaway box with the empty bottle of lemonade.

Chapter 17

The following day, already Ekua had woken Karen, given her a bowl of cereal and a large bread roll filled with cheese. The only drink, again, was a small bottle of lemonade. When she'd finished the breakfast, he'd left her, but now, two hours later, he was back.

Karen was lying on the bed, gazing up at the ceiling. After last night's food, she'd not felt well, in fact, she was convinced he was adding drugs to the food, or drink. She suspected it was in the lemonade; after all, even when she'd arrived and he'd given her the first drink, she'd begun to feel strange. Because of this, immediately he left after breakfast, Karen forced herself to be sick, throwing everything up from her stomach; even cupping her hands and drinking plenty of water from the sinks tap to wash her stomach out, forcing herself to be sick once more. She was hoping by the time he returned, she'd feel a lot better.

Ekua had come close, looking at her carefully, even lifting one of her arms and watching it drop back on the bed when he let go. He seemed satisfied. "Right, your first client is due in twenty minutes, get yourself prepared, with plenty of lubricant. If you're not ready, he'll take you anyway and the day will get harder as more clients come."

"I don't feel well, my head's spinning and I can hardly see, besides, I've never done this before, I don't know what to do," Karen lied to him.

"So... what do you want me to do, give you the day off?" he mocked. "As for opening your legs and letting a client stick his cock up your fanny, that's not difficult to understand. But I'll show you how to prepare your body, so you can get through the day - only this once though, I'm not your fucking nanny," he told her, at the same time pulling her off the bed, and standing her up, before drawing the t-shirt up over her head. "Don't move from there," he demanded.

Karen stood there, while he walked over to the cupboard above the washbasin taking out the tube of lubrication. He came back, she was expecting him to give her the tube. But he didn't. Opening the tube, he squirted a little onto his finger. "You use this much," he told her, showing her his finger, then immediately, to her disgust, he dropped the hand immediately rubbing the gel around and inside her vagina. "Do this each time, otherwise you'll be as sore as fuck by the end of the day. Now, turn yourself around and bend over the bed, while I squirt some up your bottom. A lot of my clients like to finish off that way."

Karen began to raise verbal objections to see what he intended to do about that, at the same time pushing him away. "If you believe for one moment a man's going to stick his thing up my backside, you've got another thing coming. I told Tex I wasn't a prostitute, I lap dance, so it's not going to happen," she came back at him aggressively.

He sighed. "It seems you don't want to accept what has happened to you. No matter, let's see if a good thrashing will make you more amenable."

Leaving the room, he quickly returned with a whip, cracking it in the air. The handle stubby, the whip was long and menacing. He stood there looking at her. "One last chance, you've been dosed with tamazepam in your drink, I'm told it's used to keep people sedated and under control. You can't fight it, believe me. So are you prepared to work?"

Karen never moved. Knowing she'd have to take it, no matter what. Although she believed he'd need be to very careful with such a whip, not to injure her badly, then he'd get no work out of her.

"Arrogant bastard, aren't you? But I think you need reminding who owns you. Get yourself bent down over the side of the bed," he demanded aggressively, again cracking the whip.

Karen still didn't move.

Dropping the whip in frustration, he came up to Karen, grabbing her hair and dragging her up, determined to force her to turn around and bend over the side of the bed, all the time intending only to use his trainer on her backside. He'd hoped the whip would frighten her enough to bend over the side of the bed, well aware it could only be just a threat. To use the whip with her sitting as she was, risked cutting her face open, or losing an eye. Even bent over, to have any real effect in making her do as he wanted, he'd need to hit her hard, again risking cutting her skin, leaving her unable to work for some time.

Ekua was only as tall as Karen in her bare feet, except he was muscular, he had never considered that she posed any sort of threat to him. Feeling confident, with her already partially drugged, he'd the idea she might struggle, but that she would get nowhere.

That was his mistake. Karen may have been naked, vulnerable and perhaps easily injured, except she had the advantage of surprise and wasn't, as he suspected, drugged. As he dragged her up to a standing position, she kicked his legs from under him, at the same time pushing him towards the wall. Completely off balance, not expecting her to retaliate in any way, he crashed to the floor, hitting his head on the wall, leaving him immediately disorientated. Karen had already satisfied herself on just how far she could get around the room with the chain attached to her ankle and as such, she had weighed up the distance to where he'd dropped the whip, making it retrievable. To take him on further, naked as she was, left her far too vulnerable without some sort of protection, which only the whip offered. Ignoring him sprawled on the floor, she went to the whip, grabbed it and spun around to face him. "You throw the key to me, for this bloody ankle iron, or so help me, I'll whip you till you're fucking dead," she screamed at him.

Ekua suspected Gabriel would do as she threatened, the woman was desperate. "I've not got it, it's on the same ring as the door key. If you've not noticed, the keys are still in the keyhole."

Karen glanced at the door, Ekua was correct, the key was in the lock, attached to the key ring, another smaller key was hanging down.

He gave a hint of a smile. "Seems like you're fucked. You can't reach them, only I can." He hesitated for a moment, then grinned. "In fact, whip me all you want, but still secured by the chain like you are, I'll get to that door, have little doubt. All I have to do then is fetch my mate, he uses an electric cattle probe to keep his women in line. Believe me, Gabriel, you won't have a chance just holding that whip, we will take you down with his probe. The electricity it produces will, after we throw a bucket of water on you, make a whipping seem pathetic. So it would seem your attempt to escape, was ill-conceived, with no chance of success."

Karen had been well aware she wasn't in total control, but had never considered he wouldn't carry the key. The last time he'd come into the room, he'd locked the door and pocketed the key. With him just going out to fetch the whip, he'd not bothered to remove it from the lock, more interested in punishing her. Now, as he pointed out, if he brought in a cattle probe, which she'd had used on her a number of times in the past, she would have little chance of holding him off. The electricity it produced when touching a body, even more so if her body was wet, would have her rolling around in agony on the floor, begging him not to use it again and prepared to do anything he wanted. So his assessment of her attempt to escape was correct, she'd failed, besides leaving herself open for a severe punishment.

"I see you don't have an answer. You've one last chance. I've paid a lot for you, it would be foolish of me to punish you, as you deserve, to the point you couldn't work. Except, try to escape again, I'll cripple you, by burning the soles of your feet with a red-hot poker. Maybe snap a few fingers to stop you grabbing me, like you just did. Both will not prevent you working, even if at first you just lie on the bed with your legs open." He hesitated. "As it is, now you know escape is impossible. The attempt failed and just maybe, it will convince you not to try again. So I'll give you an alternative to being maimed for life. You agree to work, without any more objections. You will be punished for attacking me. A woman must learn, when she's owned as you are, who's in control."

Karen sighed inwardly, what option did she have, but to accept? She would also need to try again, if the unit didn't find her. To do that she had to be mobile, not crippled and unable to walk. However, Karen also wanted something out of this, to make her captivity a little more bearable. There would always be another chance. Maybe not at first, but he would slip-up and injured, she'd be in no condition to take him on. "You're right, it was stupid, but you can't blame me for trying."

"Why shouldn't I, when a minute ago you were intending to kill me? As it is, I want an answer, work or I'll force you to work?" he answered.

"Then I'll work with no further objections. But I have conditions for working as you want me to do. They will cost nothing, just make my time here more bearable."

He looked at her, seeing the determination in her face. With her standing there, it was the first time he'd been really able to study her. She had a nice figure, her breasts were obviously firm, she had a flat stomach and long shapely legs. All assets that would have the clients returning often. "You're not here to make conditions," he hesitated. "Even so, after this episode, which has proved to you there is no escape, we still need to work together, so what is it you want? Not that I'll agree, if they aren't reasonable."

"No more drugs in my drink and you don't punish me for trying to escape. Then, until I get used to prostituting for a living, no more than ten men a day. Rather than a t-shirt that covers nothing below my hips, I want a dress to at least give me some dignity. When I'm not working, I want a chair to sit on, with something to read."

"They sound reasonable, but you'll not avoid punishment for attacking me. Then ten a day's too low for Fridays and Saturdays. You'll do at least ten in the day, without the evening clients. Those days you may have up to twenty, maybe more."

She shrugged, she knew it would be the best deal she could make. "I agree."

"Very well, hand me the whip, bend over the side of the bed, the palm of your hands flat on the mattress."

When she was in position, he didn't hesitate. Pulling his trainer off, he hit her six times across the bottom and the top of her legs. Karen was shaking, the pain intense, but she took it.

"You have spunk, taking your punishment as you did. Don't try that again, or this small reminder will be nothing to what I can put you through. Now, get yourself cleaned up. Your first client will be here shortly. From now on, I'll bring a client to your door and you take it from there. They have around a quarter of an hour with you, I'll knock on the door, returning five minutes later, allowing him to dress and get ready to leave. The client will be given two condoms, make sure he uses them. If he wants to finish up your backside, he uses a new condom and it's the last thing he does with you." Then his mood changed. "Piss me about, think you've got one up on me and our agreement is out the window. You'll be servicing constantly from midday till the early hours. I'll take away your dress, the chair and even your book. Because, believe me, you won't have time to put it on, or open the first page of the book to read it, before the next client is waiting to use you. Do you understand?"

"Yes, I know when I've lost," she answered, turning to face him, wiping her running eyes with her arm.

"Very sensible, Gabriel, just keep reminding yourself why you're here." He said nothing more and left the room.

Chapter 18

As Ekua had told Karen, it wasn't long before the door of her room opened. A man came inside and the door was shut. Ekua never came in.

Karen stood, removing the t-shirt. "If you get undressed, I'll put your condom on if you want me to?" she said quietly.

The man passed them both to her. "You do that, then I want you on top to start," he replied, kicking his shoes off and releasing the belt from his jeans.

***

Although annoyed the attempted escape had failed, Karen worked as she agreed, with very little time between clients. By early evening, she'd already been with ten clients, the last just leaving. Her time with them had been relatively easy, compared to when she'd been sold into an Algerian brothel, when then, as now, a covert operation had gone wrong. That brothel was the pits, but had given her a great deal of experience, not only in learning how to keep herself clean and hopefully infection free, but more importantly, how to handle man after man demanding sex from her. Without that experience, she'd have been in trouble today. As it was, the techniques she'd learned gave the man what he wanted, with her doing very little, often finishing in minutes, making the rape each time - and Karen always considered it rape - that much more bearable.

Ekua came into the room, carrying a food tray. "You did well, everyone's happy with your performance. Most have booked you again for later in the week."

"Yes, well, I can't cope with one after another. I

need time between each one. You forget I've never had more than one man in a night," she lied. "To be faced with ten, all wanting full sex, one after another, I just about coped. I need better breaks between, to get myself ready."

"I can only promise quarter of an hour between some at times. Often it will be half an hour, maybe an hour. So you learn on the job and just put up with it. Anyway, while you're enjoying your food, the one you missed this morning because of your little tantrum has turned up. He already paid this morning, so after him, that's it. You start again at twelve tomorrow, with three already booked in over the lunch hour."

Karen's face fell. "We agreed ten and I've done ten."

"We did, but that starts tomorrow. You're lucky, I had fifteen already for you today, but managed to put four off till tomorrow. In the morning you'll get your dress and chair, besides a book to read."

She never responded, carrying on with her food. The drink wasn't lemonade, but water. Karen knew by the taste that there was nothing in it. Why should he doctor it, he had her doing what she'd been sold to do.

When Karen finished the food, Ekua took the takeaway box off her, including the bottle that contained the water. "He'll be here in an hour, make sure you're ready." At that moment his mobile rang. Ekua walked to the other side of the room and talked for a short time, then replaced it in his pocket. "Looks like you will be busy Friday, there's twenty-six booked already by my partner, with the same Saturday. So you'd better learn quickly how to cope, we'll certainly hit thirty at this rate." Then he left the room, carrying the empty food containers.

Karen sat on the chair he'd provided, messing with the chain. It was substantial, however the links were not welded together, just bent with a slight gap on each link of the chain. Even so, the chain was thick and it was impossible, without having something to jam into a link, to actually bend it out of shape and increase the gap and separate the chain.

She had dozed off when the door opened and a man came in. He was small, wore heavy rimmed glasses and looked nervous.

Karen stood, giving a weak smile. "Have you got your condoms?" she asked.

He handed both of them to her. "Ekua told me you'd put it on for me."

"If you want," she replied. "Get yourself undressed, how do you want me? On top or underneath?"

"What do you like?"

Karen frowned. "Have you been with a prostitute before?" she asked, surprised at calling herself a prostitute. But that was what she'd become and she had to get used to it.

"No."

"Okay, just get undressed, lay down on the bed, I'll put your condom on."

As he dropped his trousers, all the change in his pocket fell out. He began collecting it, with Karen helping. Among the coins she found one and a two pence coin. Slipping one of each between the mattress of the bed and its base, she gave him all the rest.

By the time he left, Karen was thankful her time

with this man had been so easy. She was convinced he'd never been with a woman before, he'd virtually come while she slipped his condom on, then after that, he couldn't even get himself hard again. They spent most of the time lying on the bed together, doing nothing, although she allowed him to play with her breasts, after he'd asked if he could. It was the least she could do, after all, the man could have been so much worse.

It was two hours later, after Karen was convinced Ekua wouldn't be back for the night, she crawled under the bed to the ring in the floor that the chain was attached to. In her hand were the coins she'd hidden when the last client dropped his money. Already she had looked at the ring and found it had been secured to the wooden floor with screws that had a single slot and not the star type. Seeing the coins earlier, she'd had an idea and now wanted to see if it would work. Trying the coins in the slot of a screw, they both fitted, the two pence being the best, but the curve of the coin meant it wouldn't sit flat in the screw's slot. Coming out from under the bed, and looking around, going to a corner of the room, she could actually get close to where the brick was showing. Immediately Karen began to rub the edge of the coin backwards and forwards over the brick face.

An hour later, with her fingers hurting - although by now she'd wrapped the coin with the hem of her t-shirt to hold it - the round edge of one side of the coin had worn down on the rough brick and it was flat. Returning to the ring, she tested the coin; it sat flat in the screw head as she wanted. Even so, she wasn't finished. She was very aware that she'd have no chance of unscrewing the screws just by holding the coin, it was too small to get a proper grip on and produce the force needed to turn the screws. Karen needed a lever of some sort. She began checking the links of the chain securing her, to see if she could get the coin into the gap on one of the links. If she could, the link would become her lever. She couldn't, the coin was just too thick. Undaunted, she started to rub the side of the coin on the brick. This was even slower and more difficult, as she struggled to hold the coin flat, besides move it backwards and forwards.

By the morning, with her fingers sore and aching after holding the coin for so long, she'd succeeded. The coin fitted nicely into the gap of a link. Karen had herself a screwdriver of sorts. Climbing onto the bed, she lay down and fell asleep. The night had been long; with no knowledge of the time, Ekua could be here at any moment, with her breakfast.

***

"Come on, Gabriel, wake up. You certainly sleep well, you were the same yesterday," Ekua shouted, shaking her.

Karen opened her eyes and got out of bed, sitting down on the chair he'd brought in the day before. He placed the tray on her lap and sat on the side of the bed.

"After breakfast, you've got around three hours before you start work. Most are on lunch so you've six between twelve and two. You need to reduce the time you're with a client, or you'll not get a break, the next one will be waiting. So don't hang around, shag hard and try to make them come quickly. Get them out dead on the quarter hour, then you'll have a few minutes to clean yourself up."

"I'm not a bloody machine you know. I need time to at least wash, and tidy myself up. Yesterday I worked my arse off trying to make some of them come," she said, indignant at what he expected of her.

"Stop moaning, women like sex just as much as men. Get on top of them, have them grip your buttocks and work you. With your body arched back, hands behind your head, pushing those tits of yours out, pretending to have an orgasm, he'll be turned on and really come quick."

She sighed. What planet was he on? "I'll do what I can, if he's not finished, it's his fault, you just make sure you don't let the quarter hour overrun."

He stood, taking the empty tray off her. "That's my girl. You know, Gabriel, I'm jealous. Most men would enjoy just shagging all day, like you get to do, and doing nothing else. Get some rest, I'll be back just before you're to begin work." Then he left the room, slamming the door.

As soon as he left, Karen did not dwell on what he wanted her to do, she was under the bed. Using her home-made screwdriver, she slotted it in, praying it would work. At first she believed the screws were too tight for her screwdriver, with the two pence beginning to bend out of shape before the screw began to turn. At last, the screw began turning. She tried each one and as with the first, the initial resistance took its toll of her two pence. However, after she'd got them all to finally begin to turn, the flat she'd created on the two pence was so distorted, it wouldn't even stay in the ones she'd already loosened. Karen sighed. It would seem she'd have to make a new flat on the other end of the two pence, before she could finally remove the screws. Even so, with her success, she was confident that with a repair to her screwdriver, she'd have the screws out sometime today, which gave her a boost. This was important. Tomorrow was Friday and the promise of thirty men made her stomach turn. Now resigned to servicing another ten men, she still had to plan her next step very carefully.

***

Ekua hadn't been wrong about the lunchtime clients. By the time the last one left, she'd had enough. In fact the last one had given her a good smacking for not responding like he wanted. Karen just took it, she'd been punished many times under the same circumstances, she just accepted with some clients this would happen.

***

By early evening Karen was sitting in the chair, eating her dinner. Ekua was at the far side of the room on his mobile telephone. She would have liked to finish it here, by taking him on. She'd had time in the afternoon, after the last client left, to make the coin flat on its other side, but that was all. Then, if Ekua kept to the pattern as yesterday and this lunchtime, immediately after she'd finished with the last client, he'd be in with her food, giving her no time to remove the screws, even if they came out easily. On that basis, it would be Friday morning at the earliest before she could make her break. Plenty of time, she decided, to plan it meticulously.

"Finished?" he asked, bringing her out of her thoughts.

"Yes, thank you. When's the next client due?"

He smiled. "You're getting keen then, enjoying being fucked are you? You've around an hour before they begin to come in."

Karen didn't rise to his comments, wanting to ask another question. "I'm already beginning to stink from the body odour of the men, can't I have a shower or bath sometimes? One sponge and a bit of soap is not exactly the way to wash myself down. And then, the towel is just a hand towel."

"I'll think about it. As it is, I've got to see if I can trust you. I'm not putting myself in a position like last time. Maybe when my partner comes on Sunday, we'll both take you to shower in the bathroom off the main bedroom. In the meantime, I'll fetch a larger towel." He glanced at his watch. "I'll leave you now, make sure you're ready for your first client of the night," he said, collecting her empty tray and leaving the room, locking it after him.

Karen was reading when he came back less than ten minutes later, giving her a towel and leaving again. She was glad of it. Taking the dress off, she washed down at the sink, before drying herself. She intended to look after her hygiene, even down to inspecting herself for lice or other mites that could attach themselves to her from a client. If there had been no immediate possibility of escape, she would have asked for a douche to wash herself out and even shave herself, to keep infection down.

Karen was with her eighth client of the day. He was a big man, obviously worse the wear for drink and he had already taken her on her back, now she was on top, doing her best to finish it quickly, so he'd go. But he was having none of it, gripping her buttocks, slowing her down, knowing what she was trying to do. Suddenly he pushed her off. "You call that fucking, you're shit, more interested in getting it over with. My wife's better than you."

"Maybe," she came back at him, "but she's not been fucked seven times already today. So what do you want of me now?" Karen asked with resignation, just wanting him to go.

"Get yourself standing at the side of the bed, and bent down. Maybe I'll get better satisfaction taking you up the arse?"

She did as he told her. Most clients in the past, telling her to do this, would smack her bottom a few times, more to strengthen their dominance over the woman with this added aggression, he didn't. Just pushed himself up inside her back passage, gripping her hips and beginning again. Suddenly there was a knock at the door. Karen, relieved this man's time was up, pulled forward, so the man came out of her, and moved away. "That's it, you've had your time. You should dress and leave."

"I've not fucking come yet, you finish me off woman, or I'll give you a good thrashing," he shouted at her.

She shrugged, grabbing her dress to put on. "I can't help it if you haven't come by now, at this rate, we'll still be at it for another fifteen minutes. Get rid of the condom and wash your cock, I'll try with a handjob. Otherwise, take it up with Ekua, he'll already have my next client waiting; or finish yourself off with your wife."

"Fucking arrogant bitch," he retorted, hitting her directly in the face, sending her backwards and falling to the floor. Already her eyes were stinging, with blood

157

coming from her nose and mouth. But he hadn't finished, kicking her time after time in the ribs.

As she lay there obviously in pain, her head spinning, he quickly dressed, before bending down, grabbing her by the hair, dragging her up. "You want me to fuck my wife, because you can't be bothered to fuck like you should?" he shouted at her. "No fucking prostitute talks to me like that," he added, hitting her hard in the stomach. She bent double, only to be hit again in the face, knocking her out. He looked down at her, kicked her a number of times, but this time with his outdoor shoes on. "Maybe, by giving you a good thrashing, it's knocked the arrogance out of you? Either way, I'll be back next week. If by then you've still not learned to keep that mouth of yours shut and work like I expect a woman who I pay for to work, I'll lay into you again and again until you learn."

Karen didn't hear his comments, after his brutal attack, she'd slipped into unconscious.

Ekua unlocked the door, coming into the room. "Time's up, Sid," he said, then stopped dead, staring down at Karen, before going to her and kneeling at her side. "What the fucking hell have you done to her, she's got another ten tonight."

"She's fucking useless, needed a good hiding to remind her, she's been paid for and should work to satisfy the client, not herself."

"There's reminding her and fucking trying to kill her. What about my losses tonight, she can't work like this? You should pay for my losses. As it is, give me a hand to get her on the bed, so I can see how bad she is."

"In your dreams. I'm not getting blood all over

me, besides, she's even wet herself. Do it yourself. As for paying for your losses, you're better without her, she'd not have lasted the night, before some other client got frustrated and gave her a good beating," he retorted, then walked out of the room.

Ekua sighed, he'd sort Sid out later, but Gabriel needed replacing, fast.

Pushing a few buttons on his mobile, he waited till it was answered. "Tanny, Ekua. Sid's done his usual thing and beaten the fucking woman up. She's in a bad way, I need a replacement fast and her taken away."

"When's the next client?" Tanny asked.

"Half an hour, I could delay him another fifteen minutes."

"I'll have Mandy brought over. Tell them to put the woman you have in their van and dump her."

"She cost five grand and I've only had a grand back up to now. Can't Mildred look after her, maybe when she's better put her on the hotel run?"

"I'll look at her when they come back. If it's just superficial I'll do that, but we're not a hospital, so if she's got broken bones, she's fucked for weeks, it's better to get rid."

"Yes, okay, tell them to hurry, I'll clean up."

Coming off the phone, Ekua unfastened the iron around Karen's ankle and dragged her to the far corner of the room. By the time the men arrived with Mandy, he'd pulled the bloody sheet off the bed, bagged it in a plastic bin bag along with Karen's t-shirt and mopped the blood from the floor, including where she had urinated.

While Mandy readied herself for the clients,

Karen was wrapped in a large polythene sheet and carried downstairs and through the front door into a waiting van. Minutes later it sped away.

Chapter 19

The morning after Karen had been removed from the house, following her beating, Stanley was on a video link to the meeting room at the charity offices in London. In the charity office was Lieutenant Foster, second in command to Karen. He had called for the meeting.

"Perhaps, Lieutenant, you can give me a rundown on just how far the operation has progressed and why you want this meeting? It's been two days since we've heard from Karen. I need an update for my report and to satisfy me that Karen is not in any danger," Stanley began.

"This is why I've asked for the meeting, Stanley, there have been developments. As you're aware, we tracked Karen from Maclean's house to a warehouse that supplies wholesale carpets to shops. We knew she was on the move, with her signal from the watch. Fortunately, surveillance was locked onto a tracker hidden on her person and we were able to follow them to the warehouse. The man who was with Maclean, didn't use the car at the front, but one parked on a back road. Then it gets messy. Her tracker was definitely indicating she was inside the warehouse, although we didn't see her taken inside. We couldn't get a team in to observe that quickly enough. When the car left again, the tracker remained transmitting from the warehouse."

"What happened then?" Stanley asked, making notes as the lieutenant spoke.

"A van left a short time later and began delivering carpets to different retail shops. Finally, it parked behind a row of terrace houses. Stayed there all night, before leaving in the morning and returning to the warehouse. Again, after a short time it was out delivering."

"And Karen's tracker was still indicating she was inside the warehouse?"

"Yes, it was, she'd also not sent a distress signal from her watch. We could only assume she had things under control and didn't want us to intervene. You know Karen, when it comes to us not reading the situation correctly and going in too soon, wrecking her operation."

"I do, and I understand your position, but two days is a long time without moving from the warehouse. Had you considered there was a problem, maybe with the watch?"

"Of course. Particularly when the tracker, with thirty hours of operating time, was becoming weak, it was decided that we couldn't hold out any longer without satisfying ourselves she was not in any danger. Last night, after the delivery van had left the warehouse and the surveillance team was telling us it was parked behind the house again, it was decided to send in soldiers to search and locate her, so she could verbally confirm all was well, besides furnish her with a replacement fully charged tracker."

"What was the outcome of the operation?"

"We found the commander's tracker, along with her watch and the clothes she was wearing. We have to assume she'd been made to undress, perhaps to put other clothes on. The ones she'd been wearing had been placed in a rubbish compactor, where they were found by the team going in. How they made her undress, without her pressing the watch for assistance, which she would have done, knowing the risk of having no tracker, or means to call us in, we can only surmise. But she's not in the warehouse, that's certain. The tracker still carried on working, protected from being crushed by the clothes around it, which is how we found it."

"Perhaps it would have been better if it had failed, then we would have had to go in," Stanley commented. "I presume you've now implemented a search of all the locations the van has delivered to since?"

"We have, that's going on as we speak. The final location where the van parked overnight, we intend to go in and look around after the van leaves for the warehouse. The driver of the van usually leaves for work at around ten."

"Can you keep in direct contact with me on that part of the operation, Lieutenant? I've a feeling that house holds the key to Karen's abduction."

"I agree and I will do that, of course."

***

Lieutenant Foster entered the house with two other soldiers, all dressed in jeans and jumpers, giving no indication as to who they were. Entry had been easy, the lock on the back door had been a three lever mortice and posed no problem for them.

As usual the search was careful and thorough, finally they were all in the room where Karen had been kept, after satisfying themselves the house was empty. A woman was sleeping on the bed. A soldier came up to her, shaking her hard. She opened her eyes, looking a little stunned.

"What the fuck do you want, I don't start till

twelve, so piss off. Then… where's Ekua, he tells me how many and what time they're coming?"

"We're looking for a woman, around thirty, black hair and five eight."

"There's only me here, I came last night, the one in this room before me, had pissed off a client and been badly beaten up for it."

Lieutenant Foster was looking around the room, finding the chain under the bed.

"What's this for?" he asked.

She shrugged, indifferently. "It's used to restrain difficult women. Most that Ekua uses don't believe they should be here, so it stops them leaving. For me it's a job, I can come and go as I please and will be here until the last woman's replaced."

The men looked at each other. Could the woman she was talking about have been Karen? "This Ekua, he's a pimp?"

"Course he is, didn't you know?"

"No, so he's your pimp?"

"Mine," she retorted, obviously indignant at his suggestion. "I don't work for him. I work the hotels for Tanny. I have a house to live in and a room of my own, when I'm not working. As for Ekua, you get this room, you work, live and sleep in it. Besides, he doesn't even have a shower, you have to sponge yourself clean by that sink."

"So you came here last night, who took the woman who was here before you?"

"How do I know?"

"What about this Tanny you are with, would he

have taken her?"

By now she was well awake and suspected, with not knowing who these men were, Ekua owed them, in some way, and they had come to collect. She'd already decided she could be in some sort of trouble from the way they were talking. It was time to be cautious and direct her and Tanny away from Ekua's business. "No, why should he? She belonged to Ekua." Then she lowered her voice. "Mind you, keep it quiet, but by what I heard last night, she was in a pretty bad shape. Ekua will have dumped her somewhere, you can be certain. But don't tell him I told you."

Lieutenant Foster was worried. "When you say dumped her, you mean killed her and dumped the body?"

She shrugged indifferently. "How should I know that? I'm only telling you, Tanny hasn't got her."

"How do I get in touch with this Tanny, to check this story of yours out?"

She looked scared. "Listen, I've told you all I know, maybe more than I should, but if this gets back to Tanny, I'm as good as dead. I'll not answer any more questions. Just go, will you?"

Lieutenant Foster shook his head. "It's not as simple as that. What you're suggesting indicates not only abduction, but possible murder. Withholding information, seems to me you could well be party to what has been going on here." He showed her his warrant card. "I am Lieutenant Foster of Unit T. You will be arrested for trafficking and face at least ten years in prison. If it's murder, then life. If you want to take that risk, keep stum, otherwise you talk and keep talking until I'm satisfied I know everything you know."

Her mouth dropped open. "You're from Unit T?" she gasped. Every woman on the game knew of Unit T. Most of their pimps were terrified of being targeted by them. "I've told you all I know."

Lieutenant Foster left the room, leaving the soldiers to guard her. He called Stanley, telling him what he'd found out.

Stanley went cold, he hoped they had not killed Karen, because they had held off going in. "Have your soldiers pick up this man calling himself Ekua. Then put the screws on him. We could be in a race against time to find Karen, Lieutenant. Let's pray we're not too late."

"I hope not as well, Stanley. We'll also get Tanny's address out of her, if we have to take her apart, just in case he took her. Until we're certain what happened, this could be a crime scene, maybe for murder. The police must be informed."

"I'll talk to Sir Peter, let him handle the local police. Whatever happens, you must have Tanny's address before the police take control."

Coming back into the room, Lieutenant Foster came directly up to the woman. "One more chance, where's does you pimp Tanny live?" he shouted at her aggressively.

"I don't know where, he just turns up at the house I live in. I've got his mobile number," she said, pulling her mobile from under the pillow and handing it to him. "It's under Tanny."

He snatched it off her. "Right, I want a full description of him, leave nothing out."

While she gave it to one of the soldiers, Lieutenant Foster called Stanley. "We have his number Stanley, can you scan it and see if we're looking at a smartphone, then get your guru Jamie there, to access it and activate its GPS?"

"Hold on, Lieutenant. He's attempting access as we speak."

Minutes went by, with Lieutenant Foster holding.

"We have it, Lieutenant. We're lucky, it is a smartphone and Jamie locked onto it as soon as he answered, sending him a bogus message from his provider to upgrade. Stupidly he's accepted the upgrade. We'll keep your vehicles GPS updated as you drive."

"I'll leave immediately, Stanley. Are we mobilising?"

There was silence for a few moments. "Yes, I'll mobilise, if you concur, at o-nine-thirty hours."

"I concur. This operation is to find our commander. We don't want interference."

"Then Unit T is in lockdown. All personnel in the UK will be directed to join you. Find Karen, Lieutenant, for all our sakes."

"We'll find her Stanley, believe it," he answered soberly, hoping beyond hope they were not too late to save her life.

Chapter 20

Karen had been collected by the two men who worked for Tanny, with her replacement left with Ekua. Now the men had returned to the drinking club Tanny was in. They parked at the rear and went to find him.

Climbing into the van, Tanny closed the door, leaving the men standing around outside, smoking. Inside, Tanny switched on the small light set in the roof, before reaching into his pocket, taking out a small, powerful torch and disposable gloves, the kind supplied by fuel stations for customers to protect their hands when they filled up with fuel. After putting the gloves on, he pulled back the polyethylene sheet that covered Karen in order to inspect her. Her eye was now very puffy, her face covered in dried blood, one side of her face very swollen. There was still a trickle of blood coming out of the side of her mouth. She was unconscious.

He came closer to her face, shining his torch into her eyes, then frowned. Carefully, he opened her eyelids and removed the contact lenses, looking at them for a moment. These were not lens to see with but colour changing contacts. The woman's eyes were blue. Pulling open her mouth, he checked her teeth were still intact. They were, but the inside of her mouth was badly cut as well as her tongue. Turning his attention to her body, he used his torch to check down her arms for signs of drug abuse. Finding nothing, he ran his hands over her ribcage, particularly where the bruising was, before finishing over her breasts. Moving down her body, he pulled each leg up, bending it at the joints, checking for possible fractures or breaks, then carefully feeling her feet he noticed her manicured nails. This was a woman who looked after her body. Parting her legs, before using the torch for close inspection of her vagina. Turning Karen over, he looked over the rest of her body, before parting her buttocks and checking the back passage. Satisfied, he turned her onto her face, again covering her with the polythene before making a telephone call.

"Issac, I've got the woman I called you about earlier. She's been beaten up, but it's only a few cuts and bruising. It was a one-off beating and there's no old scarring on the body."

"What about the current injuries? Will she be permanently scarred?" he asked.

"No, apart from bruising, most of the injuries are internal. They'll quickly heal and the bruising will soon go. In a couple of weeks she'll be fine, believe me. She's a nice figure, firm breasts, no implants or marks from needle use on her arms. Bit difficult to say if she's snorting drugs up the nose, because of her injuries.

"She sounds suitable for my use. You said earlier, she's not a prostitute, you're certain of this?"

"She's not, believe me. Ekua told me she came from Maclean and had only just entered the UK. Ekua claimed he'd only used her for one day, before a client who was worse for drink took a dislike to her. He wants rid, can't look after her so he'll take a hit on what he paid. I've been around prostitutes for years, after checking her over, I believe him. There was one point, she wore contact lenses to change her eye colour. Hers are a deep blue, why she'd hide such nice eyes, I'm not sure."

"You can never tell with women, they see imperfections men don't. Providing what you tell me is confirmed by my people, I'll agree to the ten grand fee and send the contact lenses with her, so I can look at them."

"Do you want me to deliver? She's already in my van."

"No, we'll collect within the hour. Our outlets and the way we move people around is our affair and not even you should have those details."

"No problems. My van's parked up behind Loceeds drinking club in the West End."

"We'll be with you in around forty minutes. Remember, I'm still in the market for girls around twenty. If you find suitable ones give me a call."

"I'll do that, but they're rare, most I see are off the streets and already shagging for all their worth just to keep their habit financed, or a bed for the night."

"I understand. Keep in touch."

***

Karen was awake, at first confused as to where she was; feeling around in the dark, she soon decided it must be a vehicle of some sort. She felt sick, her head and chest hurt. In her mouth, she could taste blood, often spitting it out to prevent her choking. Already she was aware she couldn't escape in the condition she was in. Even so, she was alive and once the pain had gone and she was taken back to work, she still had her screwdriver to remove the screws so she could make her escape.

Soon she began to hear male voices coming from outside the vehicle, then suddenly a door was opened. A man looked inside, shining a torch in her face. She

170

scrunched her eyes up, blinded for a moment after the dark.

"She's awake," the man who was shining the torch commented.

"Let me get in and inspect her," another male told him.

Karen was subjected to a similar inspection to the one Tanny had done while she'd been unconscious. However, awake this time, the pain as the man moved her was intense, making her gasp and even scream once, before her mouth was covered.

"Give me the syringe," the man inspecting her asked. Immediately the needle was pushed into her arm. Moments later she was asleep. Then he carried on with his inspection.

"Well, is she what you want?" Tanny asked. After the man finally climbed out from the back of the van.

"She'll do, we'll take her. You can check the money, while we get her into our van."

Chapter 21

Tanny was snatched, when he came out of his house, later the next day. He was bundled into a vehicle, his head covered with a bag, his wrists bound together, and driven out into the country. Soon he was in an old barn, used for the storage of furniture. The bag over his head was removed and he was forced to sit down on a kitchen chair, already placed in an open area.

"Where the fuck am I, and who are you two?" he demanded.

Both men were Unit T soldiers, but they had no intention of admitting that. "Who we are doesn't matter," one began. "You're here to answer a few questions. Believe you're not going to answer them and walk away, you'd be wrong. You'll crawl away, before a bullet's put in your head. Think very carefully before you open your mouth?"

"What do you want to know?"

With no idea if it was Tanny, who had moved Karen, they decided to take a line of questioning as if he had. "The woman you collected from Ekua, where is she?"

"Which woman?"

"Bad answer," the man said, thumping him hard in the stomach. "Shall we begin again? Where's the woman you collected from Ekua?"

Tanny was gasping from the blow, spitting onto the floor, before looking up at him. "If you're talking about the prostitute that got beaten up by a client, she's gone." Again a blow came to his stomach. "I asked where she is, not the potted version that she's gone."

"Fucking stop that," Tanny gasped. "I'm answering the questions. As to where she is, I've no idea. She was picked up, money exchanged and that's it, she's taken and you'll never see her again."

"Who picked her up?"

"I did, and passed her on to a man I know only as Issac. There's a number of movers of people like him, not that it will be his real name. You get to hear around the place what they're in the market for. If you have such a person, you call a mobile. Gabriel, the prostitute I'm talking about, was owned by the pimp Ekua. He had to sell her on after a client beat her up. She's been replaced for him, he lost money, but at least he's earning again. I looked her over, the injuries, although quite bad, were in my opinion superficial. So I took a flyer, called Issac, told him all about her and he agreed to look after her while she was injured, before selling her on."

"Where did you take her?"

"I didn't. They met me behind a drinking club called Loceeds, checked her over and paid. They took her."

"What's this Issac's number?"

"On my mobile under Issac."

The man looked at Tanny's phone, finding the calls he'd made; one of the more recent ones was to Issac. He looked back at Tanny. "This Issac, he's still in the market for women?"

"Yes, but no more of Gabriel's age. He wants them around twenty, not using or on the game. They also have to be attractive. I'm not sure where he places them, but he always demands the best and will pay. I told him those

173

sort are not easy to come by, but that I'd keep my eyes open and call him."

The man sighed. "Then you have a choice. Take the rap for selling Gabriel, or pass the responsibility on to this Issac."

"What are you talking about? I helped the woman, found someone to look after her. She was already with Ekua, servicing up to twenty clients a day. After she recovers, Issac will pass her on to a similar set-up, so what's your beef? You should be thanking me."

"You'd be right, if that was the case with Gabriel. As it is, she was trafficked, forced into prostitution and is still in that position. Her brothers are on the way from the Ukraine to sort it out. We're just helping, finding them the route she's taken. You either help us move on to this guy Issac, or we tell them it was you who took and sold her. They will take you apart, limb by limb, have no doubts. If I were in your shoes, I wouldn't let the buck stay with you - need I say more?"

Tanny stared at him in shock and obvious fear. He just ran a number of girls already on the game, finding them clients. It was easy and wasn't really dangerous, as it didn't involve stepping on the feet of the bigger gangs. To pass a woman on for a few grand had been good business, but it seemed she wasn't what he believed she was. "What can I do? I've only the phone number, which you've got now? Can't you tell them that?"

The man shook his head slowly. "Why? This way they get their pound of flesh and will go home believing she's lost. Although, thinking about it, if this Issac wants more girls, just maybe we could get you off the hook.

How much did you get for Gabriel?"

"Ten grand and I had to pay four to Ekua. Why?"

"Pay us two grand, we'll fit you up with a girl to suit Issac's needs. You call him, have her taken and you'll never hear from us again. We'll follow the vehicle and move on to Issac himself, with Gabriel's brothers of course. He'll wish he never met them, believe me."

"Oh yes, I'm going to do that. The next thing I'd know, Issac's men would be knocking on my door, blaming me for setting him up. I may look stupid to you, but I'm not. I survive in a pretty rough business."

The man sighed, glancing at his partner. "When do they arrive?"

"Tomorrow morning, why?"

"Tell them we have the man who took their Gabriel and give them this location," he said. Then he turned to Tanny. "You're right, we could have told Issac it was you, but we wouldn't have. Why should we, the brothers want their sister back, whoever is holding her will be butchered. I'll let them take it out on you, try to call this Issac and make our own deal, then move on. If he bites, well and good, if he runs, whatever, you will satisfy her brothers' anger." He began to walk towards the entrance.

"Wait," Tanny shouted after him. "Gabriel will be out of action for two weeks at least. So she will be going nowhere. He'll want her virtually perfect before selling her on, to get top money. So what's a couple of weeks that can net him close to twenty grand of profit? I'll help you out, if you keep her brothers away from me. I'll call Issac in about a week, or ten days' time. Tell him I've found another woman. If he accepts her, will that be it for me?

But you supply the woman, I've not got one to suit him. Then you leave me alone."

The man stood for a short time, looking at Tanny. "I agree, but you and I stick together like glue, you work, sleep and shit by my side. Try to double-cross me and I will put a bullet in your head. Understand?"

"I do."

Chapter 22

Karen was looking around the room. She knew she was in a hospital; it was sparse, but with practical items around her, like a narrow cupboard by the side of the bed and a television fixed on the wall, in such as position that whoever was in bed could watch it. The type of bed, was typical of the hospitable type, the pillows clinically clean, the sheets and bedspread white and bland.

Around her face was a bandage. Around her chest was another. Both her face and chest ached, her throat was dry, the inside of her head banging. As she lay there she tried to think back to what happened. The men coming into the room, one after another, the drunk who did nothing but insult and abuse her, before he hit her, then nothing. That was apart from believing she'd woken in a van, with someone pushing and prodding her giving her pain; and again, nothing. Now this.

How long she lay there staring up at the ceiling, she'd no idea, before a woman wearing a white coat, followed by a man similarly dressed, came into the room.

"I see you are awake," the man said, at the same time bringing his head closer to her face, looking at her injuries. "I'm Doctor Johnson, you're very lucky. At first we believed you had a dislocated jaw and broken ribs, but x-rays have shown that not to be the case. You're badly bruised, particularly your side, where the man must have kicked you. Your jaw is fine, again bruised, with a little damage to the inside of your mouth, where the skin was cut by your teeth. Given a week or so, you'll be back to your old self. Anyway, after a brief check over, perhaps you'd like a little soup? Anything else for the moment would be difficult, as you won't be able to chew with the cuts in your mouth still raw."

"Where am I?" she mumbled, constrained by the bandage.

"You're in a private hospital. Brought in by your father Issac. He's waiting outside to see you. Anyway, everything seems fine and the swelling is going down nicely. I'll leave you, the nurse will bring the soup very shortly."

Both left the room, then moments later a man came in. He was small, overweight and heavy rimmed, glasses. With his lack of hair, his head was shining under the room lights.

"We haven't met, Gabriel. I'm Issac and as far as the hospital doctor looking after you is concerned, I'm your father. I don't want you to give the impression to him that is not the case, do we have an understanding?"

"Why should I do that?" Karen mumbled.

"It's really very simple. Your debt to Ekua has been taken over by me. I own you and soon you will be moving on to a new owner. Already your debt has amounted to fifteen thousand pounds and it is climbing every day you're here. I've a very large stake in this hospital, any attempt to try to convince the doctor you're here against your will, or have been abducted, will be looked upon as the ramblings of a woman confused after a good beating. That will be met with sedation, preventing any more outbursts. The nurses looking after you are in my employ and will always be present when the doctor's here. So you lie quietly and let the doctors work their magic. The day after tomorrow you'll leave, to be taken somewhere to fully recover. Now do you understand?"

"Yes."

"Very well, we'll meet again very soon. You have a good future, no more being forced to prostitute, just one man, Gabriel. For a woman like you, that's a good thing, yes?"

"Given those as the two choices, you're right, it is a good thing," Karen answered.

***

Karen had been brought to a house set in its own grounds, the driveway, she estimated as being a quarter of a mile long. It was a large, rambling sort of a house, which had obviously been extended many times in its life, but not sympathetically. It was as if the owners had no real interest in architecture, and just wanted more space inside. Helped out of the car by the driver, she was immediately taken inside, upstairs and into a bedroom. The room included a settee, coffee table and a television.

A woman followed them in and the driver left.

"I'm Hillgar and run the house," she began. "You're a guest, however you have restrictions. While you recuperate, you will be confined mostly, to this room. At meal times you'll be collected and brought to the kitchen. You have any questions?"

"What about clothes, do I get anything better than this housecoat I've come from the hospital in?"

"You will, just as soon as the bandages around your body are removed. In the meantime, I will ensure you have a nightdress to wear in bed. Do you have any more concerns?"

179

"Only about what will happen to me eventually."

She smiled. "I cannot tell you that. However, Issac will talk to you in the next few days, then you will be told what is expected."

Without another word, she turned and left the room, closing the door. Karen heard the lock of the door click.

Wandering around, she looked in the bathroom. Toothbrush, soap and a towel had been provided. The bath looked really inviting and Karen couldn't wait for the bandages to come off so she could have a long soak. Going back into the bedroom, she sat down on the settee. In some ways she was glad about what had happened to her. It had opened a completely new type of operation that was going on. Of course, she was aware of the traffickers that took women to order, for the most discerning of clients. Even she'd been originally sold this way. But for this to be happening in England, it interested her. Convinced that whoever she was sold to would not be able to hold her, she would escape with knowledge that would certainly prove very valuable in breaking a more lucrative area of trafficking.

Chapter 23

Karen, wearing a dress that finished slightly above her knees, which complemented her figure, besides high heels and stockings, entered the main lounge of the house just before lunchtime. This was a room, she'd never been in. It was large, with a number of lounge chairs and a huge fireplace. The far wall had doors that led to what she believed was a conservatory.

It had been nearly two weeks since she'd arrived. All her bandages had been removed, the swelling of her eye and face had gone down, the bruises on her side had all but disappeared. Now, with a little make-up and eyeshadow that Hillgar had given her, she felt better in herself and more than ready to take these people on.

Issac was sitting with another man, and they stood when she was brought in. "Gabriel, you look a great deal better than when we first met, please come and join us."

Karen smiled and sat down opposite them both, saying nothing.

"You would like a drink? We have all the spirits and mixers?"

"Vodka and tonic would be nice, thank you," she replied, again with a smile.

Issac made a drink and handed it to her.

"Perhaps I should explain your position first?" Issac began. "You've entered the UK illegally, on a forged passport. There was a cost for that and your travel, yes?"

"Yes, three thousand Euros."

"It may have started at that, Gabriel, but you were stupid, getting mixed up with traffickers. They buy and sell naive people like you, who can't go to the police without admitting they are here illegally, risking prison and deportation. Since then, every time you're sold between such people, they make profits, and you're the one who finally pays. But you have no work permit, so you earn in the black economy, often a pittance taking years to pay off the debt."

"I suppose. Now you have taken me, I owe even more," she answered with obvious resignation.

"You do, but it is also your lucky day. I don't place women into prostitution, servicing twenty, maybe thirty clients a day. You are passed on to one man. You agree a time to clear your debt with him, after that it is your choice if you stay or move on."

"Can I ask you who the person is that I'm likely to be passed on to?"

"I have a number of clients wanting women such as you. For me it is important to show you off at your best. Remember, a man who pays a lot for you, will look after you. So providing you reciprocate, you will have an easy life, far better than what you've just left."

"How can I do that, show myself off that is?"

"This gentleman with me is Breccan, he's a photographer. Now you're well again, Breccan will be creating a small portfolio for potential clients. For this, you will be photographed with what you have on, in your underclothes and naked. Please do everything he asks of you."

"But I still have signs of bruising on my body."

"For Breccan, that's not a problem, his computer programme will get rid of such blemishes. We cannot wait longer until you are completely clear of the bruising. Clients will be aware of your background. Maybe before you leave here, they will have gone anyway."

Karen didn't want, or like to be photographed naked, with the results bandied around, but she couldn't see any way of avoiding it. She suspected that while the conversation remained relaxed, in the way he was talking to her, this would only last while he believed she was co-operating. The moment she stopped, she'd see a different side to him. He was, after all, a trafficker and dealer in women. So to sell her, if he wanted photographs of her naked, he would have them. With this at the forefront of her mind, Karen had no intention of creating confrontational issues, resigning herself to being photographed in the nude. "Then I'm happy to be photographed. You've been very good to me and I appreciate the opportunity given to me, rather than others pushing me down the prostitution route."

"I'm glad you're realistic enough to see that."

Placing the drink on the table, she looked at him watching her. "When does the photographic session begin?"

"This afternoon, following dinner, which you will join us for." Then he changed his tone slightly. "Tell me, Gabriel, why were you wearing contacts, that weren't lenses, but ones that changed the colour of your eyes?"

Karen had realised her lenses had been removed and as such, it could be noticed that they only changed her eye colour. "My doctor at home recommended them. You see, my blue eyes, as you may have noticed, are a very deep blue, making them extremely sensitive to light, particularly in the sunshine. I didn't want glasses, vanity I suppose, so I saved up to buy those," she hesitated. "They cost me a lot of money, so when I was put with Ekua, rather than risk getting them lost or damaged, I kept them in and would only take them out when I slept. With me being beaten up by one of his clients, they were still in my eyes. I suppose the hospital took them out?"

"Yes, something like that. In view of what you've told me, I'll see you get them back, with the correct storage and cleaning fluid. I myself, at times, wear contacts for sports I participate in, so I know that they need to be kept sterile."

"Thank you, I appreciate it. In strong sunshine, I can be virtually blind."

Issac glanced at his watch. "I think it's almost time for lunch. Shall we all go?"

**

Breccan had set his photographic area up in a room with bookshelves all the way around it. He had a large white backdrop, held up with stands, curving across the floor. On the set was a white, painted, kitchen chair and that was it.

"Right, Gabriel," he said in a broad Irish accent. "To get relaxed, just move around, looking in different directions, then stay still when I tell you. Let's go."

For the next few minutes, she did as he asked. Sometimes with a smile, other times serious looking. This was followed by shots of her just in her bra and knickers, using the chair to raise a leg. Karen was enjoying the experience, Breccan always enthusiastic about how she posed.

They'd stopped while he checked the photos on his computer, before he looked up at her. "We will do the naked shots now? Similar poses to when you were in your underclothes, using the chair, but keep your high heels on, to show off your legs."

Karen had been enjoying the shoot, until now. She liked to show her body off. Sighing inwardly, she never said anything, just pushed her knickers to her feet before stepping out of them, then removing her bra.

Again he had her moving into different positions; the only time she wanted to refuse was when he had her bend down, touching her toes, while he photographed her from behind.

"That's good, just one or two more, Gabriel. This time off the stage, stand at the side of the window, one hand on the sill, looking out," he urged.

It wasn't one or two shots, but a number, until he finished. Karen dressed and looked at the photos. She had to admit he'd made her look good in all of them, not that she liked the nude shots. Then, her time standing naked by the window, with the sunlight streaming in lines down her body, with her in silhouette, were clearly taken in an attempt to show her as being a sexy and desirable woman to a client.

"You like them?" he asked.

"Yes, they are very good." What else could she say? They'd use them anyway.

"I'm glad you approve. I'll call someone to take you back to your room, then I'll go and see Issac. He should be more than happy with what we've managed to achieve."

Issac went through the photographs, selecting what he wanted to be printed.

"She's a natural, Issac, followed instructions perfectly, and it shows in the photos. You have a very attractive and sexy woman there. She should fetch good money."

"Yes, she will. In fact, I've already got two clients who've taken a great deal of interest in her. The photos by the side of the window will be the clincher for a bidding war between them. I've also had a call from Tanny. He's got us one around twenty. Here's a photo he sent, what do you think?" he asked, handing him his mobile telephone.

Breccan looked at it for a moment. "He's doing well for you, Gabriel is a good- looking woman, this girl is similar. She too will photograph well. When do you collect her?"

"Saturday night. Then she'll be shipped across in the early hours of Sunday. You come Monday morning and we'll have her photos out before the end of the day. Anyway, get Gabriel's package put together with all her other details and let's get her placed by this time tomorrow, shall we."

Chapter 24

Early Saturday morning, three days after the photo shoot. Karen was asleep when she was shaken gently by a man she'd not seen before.

"Up you get, wash, dress quickly in the jeans and top, you're wanted," he told her when she'd opened her eyes.

Doing as she was told and after a breakfast of cereal and juice, Karen was taken into the main lounge.

"Ah, Gabriel. Good news, you leave today, in fact, now. I'll miss you, you've been very cooperative and done everything we've asked of you."

"Where am I going?"

"Africa. You will be taken to Dublin. From there, by ship via France and Spain to your final destination which I believe is Nigeria. But he has a number of locations, so you could be anywhere," he answered, not knowing himself exactly where she'd end up. He handed her a small box which contained her contact lenses along with some cleaning fluid. "I think you may need these, I'm told the sun is strong where your new owner lives."

She took the box from him and smiled. "Thank you. This man I'm to be with, he's Nigerian?" she asked slowly.

"He is. I'm told he looks after himself, pumps a great deal of iron and is a big man, six feet five in fact, besides being very wealthy, you've fallen on your feet."

"So I'm in Southern Ireland now?"

"No, Northern Ireland at the moment. You came over by boat, did you not realise?"

"No, I thought I was in England and would be placed with an Englishman."

"You aren't racist, are you?"

"Not that I know of, except, would I prefer a European? Yes, I would. Which was why I came to England."

"Well, in your position, you can't have everything you want. He will feel no different when the lights are off."

Karen sighed to herself. Maybe not in his eyes, he didn't have to put up with him. Then to be told she was in a country she didn't know she was in and being shipped on to Africa, besides, forced to live with a Nigerian. This wasn't her idea of the future she had in mind. Raped and drugged by a Nigerian in the past, she was scared of them, knowing as a woman she'd received no respect, maybe even be handed around when he tired of her. Somehow her captivity had to come to a close, before she was put on the ship.

"What about a passport," she asked meekly, hoping he'd forgotten she had none."

"All taken care of. So I'll say goodbye, Gabriel, enjoy your new life."

***

They had been travelling for less than an hour and were approaching a road junction signposted M1, Dublin. Karen was sitting in the back of a two door car, two men were in the front. The driver she knew as Conn, the other man she's seen around, without knowing his name. Conn was a small, weed of a man, always had a cigarette in his mouth, and was the one who'd often take her to the kitchen to eat. He'd say very little, in fact, she felt he looked down on her, his words often given as orders. Although not restrained, with no back doors, she couldn't have made a break, even if she'd wanted to. Her plan, while in Issac's home, the way she had acted, doing everything they wanted without objection, had resulted in a more relaxed attitude towards her. Because of that, she didn't believe she'd been considered a risk, in fact the very opposite. Not that this relaxed attitude had, as yet, created an opportunity to make a break.

While they had travelled and thankful she'd not been blindfolded, Karen studied every road, every signpost. Already she'd noted that the house she'd been taken to was off a road that ended up at the A3. A signpost before the junction had indicated five miles to Armagh and twelve miles to Monaghan, going the other way. They turned towards Monaghan. Except before arriving there, after crossing the border they turned onto the N2, heading towards Clontibret, with the signpost showing Dublin to be eighty miles away.

"Stop at that cafe, before we get on the M1, I want cigarettes, the man sitting at Conn's side said.

Pulling into a car park, the man at Conn's side looked back at Karen. "You want coffee?"

"Yes, thank you, no sugar."

He climbed out, Conn remained, lighting a cigarette.

Karen released her safety belt, pulling the belt gently out the holder. This action was already giving her an idea after she realised that its length, fully pulled out, was considerable. She leaned forward, looking over the front seats. "So where are we?" Karen asked in a friendly way.

"We're less than an hour from Dublin. That's where you're going," Conn answered.

"I thought I was going on a ship?"

"You are, it's already in the dock. You'll board tonight."

'*I don't think so,*' Karen mumbled under her breath, at the same time, with her safety belt still fully pulled out, looping it over the headrest, grabbing Conn's hair with her other hand and turning his head, so she could force the belt down the side of his face ending up around his neck. Pulling both sides of the belt hard, she literally began to strangle Conn. Already he was struggling, his arms flailing, trying his best to get the belt off, which was blocking his windpipe, leaving him gasping for air. "I like you, Conn and don't want to kill you," Karen said quietly. "But I'm fighting for my freedom here, so unless you want me to strangle you, start the engine and drive away from this place. Don't believe for a moment I won't kill you, or can't. I was trained in the military. You will be dead in seconds. Now drive."

Conn at first did nothing, believing she was bluffing, still trying to get the seat belt off. But he'd no chance, the seat belt was strong, with nothing to grasp hold of. Even now, Karen's tightening of the belt was close to being unbearable for him. Deciding he'd had enough and she wasn't bluffing, already beginning to feel faint, he reached down to start the engine. Conn had a family at home, this job didn't pay that much and certainly not enough to cover risking his life for Issac. He was a man who wouldn't lift a finger to help his family, if he didn't return. Seconds later they sped out of the car park.

This was just in time, as the other man had come out carrying the coffees. He stood there not knowing what to do. Placing the drinks down on an outside picnic table, he called Issac.

"What do you mean, he's pissed off with Gabriel. Where were you?"

"I'd gone to a cafe for cigarettes and drinks. I was gone less than three minutes."

"She was restrained wasn't she?"

The man bit his lip, Conn had told him it wasn't worth it, when they couldn't find the key to the handcuffs. After all, he'd said *'It was only a two door car, so she couldn't get out without being seen, and all the time she was in the house, she'd followed every instruction, never objecting.'* He took a deep breath. "Course she was restrained, why even bother to ask?" he retorted.

"I've told you many times, never leave a woman with just one person when she's being moved. She's too fucking valuable. So it looks like Conn's trying to go into business on his own and has decided to sell her himself. He'll die for that. Have you called his number?"

"No, I called you."

"Then wait, while I try to get in touch with him."

Issac slammed the phone down, looked up Conn's number and dialled. The phone rang for a few seconds before it was answered.

"What the fuck have you done with Gabriel, Conn?" Issac screamed down the phone, not even waiting for Conn to speak.

"Issac, it's not Conn, I dropped him off a mile or two back. It's Gabriel. I decided I didn't want to spend my life being fucked by a Nigerian, who I know from experience often treats a woman like shit. You'd better pay him his money back, they don't take too kindly to being ripped off."

"What are you talking about? I own you and you fucking owe me. I looked after you when you were injured, fed and clothed you. This is how you repay me?"

"You did, didn't you? I should thank you. Thank you Issac. As it is, I decide what I do with my life, not you. Take care, maybe we'll bump into each other sometime?"

"Cut me off and I'll fucking kill you," he screamed down the phone.

But Karen had cut him off and was already dialling her unit. She listened for a moment, the regular bleeping immediately told her they were in mobilisation and lockdown. Without her satellite phone, and the code it emitted, she wouldn't be able to get in touch with them. It was a protocol she herself had set-up to prevent possible informers inside the camp from making contact. Now it had backfired on her.

Chapter 25

Tanny looked at Sherry when she approached, wearing hipster jeans and top, with the two men he'd done a deal with, not knowing they were part of Unit T. Sherry had even changed her name to Sam West, for the operation.

"She looks even more attractive in the flesh, get yourself in the back of the van," Tanny told Sherry."

Sherry looked at the two men she'd come with. They nodded their agreement and she climbed into the van. Tanny closed the door.

"When are his people coming to collect Sam?" one asked.

"As soon as I call to say I have her, they will come," Tanny replied, pulling his mobile telephone out from his pocket.

"Then we'll go, if this comes off, that's the last you'll see of us."

"They'll take her, believe me. She's perfect. Once she's gone I can do no more. You're on your own and need to keep close to her."

"That's our problem, not yours, now call him."

Tanny dialled Issac. "Issac, its Tanny," he said when Issac answered.

"Have you got that girl with you?"

"I have, when do you want her?"

"We're coming now, I need a girl fast."

"I'm parked behind the drinking club, Loceeds, as before. The usual price?"

"Yes, after they check her for me, I'll pay." The phone went dead.

Tanny climbed into the back of the van, closing the door and switching the light on. "They are on their way, hold your arm out."

"What's that?" Sherry asked, looking at the syringe. "No one told me I was going to be drugged."

"Well, you are; if I don't do it, they will. At least what I give you will wear off quickly, after that, just feign being asleep."

Sherry sighed and held her arm out, the next moment she slumped forward. Tanny slapped her face a few times, seeing no response. Then unfastening her shoes he pulled them and the socks off, before removing her jeans and knickers. Finally, he had her top and bra off, laying her down on a blanket. He had no option but to strip her before they came, to be certain a wire hadn't been attached to her body. If Issac's men found such an item, it would be him who'd take the heat, with Issac believing he'd been double-crossed. If that was the case, he'd be lucky to get out alive.

Tanny looked down at her and smiled. "I bet they also failed to mention you would be taken naked? If there had been more time, I might have fucked you myself," he commented, rubbing his hand over her breasts, before checking her arms for signs of drug abuse and that she'd no hair clips in her hair. He had to be sure she was as the men told him for this deception to work and Issac to take her. Although, if their following of her didn't work and they lost touch, Issac had an attractive and sellable girl, besides being very happy with him, with a real chance of more business between them.

Wrapping the blanket that Sherry was laid on

around her, Tanny climbed out of the van and stood smoking.

Shortly another van arrived, it was Issac's men.

After a few words, one of the men climbed into the back of Tanny's van, looking Sherry over very carefully. "She's good, we'll take her, give me a hand to get her into our van," he told his partner, after wrapping Sherry up in the blanket again. Tanny checked the money he was given.

When both Issac's men were inside Tanny's van, a Unit T soldier, slipped out from behind large rubbish bins, clamped two magnetic trackers under the van belonging to Issac's men, before moving back into the shadows.

This was a 'belt and braces' approach, as already they had the entire area under surveillance, ready to follow Sherry no matter where she was taken. Stanley had been deeply concerned, knowing Karen would not be happy using her. However, Sherry on her part had jumped at the chance to help Karen, no matter what the risk. She loved her like a sister and would go anywhere, do anything for her.

***

"We have a problem, Lieutenant," a surveillance soldier manning his computer suddenly said.

Lieutenant Foster looked at him. "In what way?"

"It was believed she'd be taken to a house, now it seems that's not the case. The van has turned down a narrow track towards a cove. Visual has reported seeing a naked girl, her mouth covered with tape and her hands tied behind her back, brought out the back of the van and walked down to the beach. They confirmed it to be Sherry.

She was placed in a small launch, a blanket covering her, and it's just left. Visual couldn't have got down to the cove in time to stop them. This wasn't envisaged and we don't have the facilities to follow, without using the helicopter, which is at least twenty minutes away."

Lieutenant Foster stood for a moment, looking at the monitors, his surveillance team was using to track Sherry. "Send the helicopter. There is no other way. Not that I hold out much hope. But now we know what the route will be, for the next girl we send in, we'll have this situation covered."

A soldier looked at him. "You mean you're abandoning Sherry?"

He shrugged. "What can we do, she's on her own, all of us know there's always a possibility. Her only chance, as with Karen, is for us to locate this Issac and where he works from. At the moment we keep a lid on what happened. I've already a backup girl. We wait a few days and get this Tanny to call Issac again. He'll be more than happy to deal, after all he's getting very saleable girls. That's what traffickers do. If Karen was here, she wouldn't panic, she'd do the same thing, believe me."

Chapter 26

Karen had left Conn at the side of the road, then headed for the airport. With the unit in mobilisation, there would be no way of contacting Unit T, unless she could get to her aircraft.

Without a passport or money she had no means to prove to the authorities who she was, Karen decided to call her manager at the London branch of the LBNF charity on their free phone number. Instructing the manger to go into her flat and collect her real passport out the safe, along with credit cards and money, beside a complete change of clothes, including underclothes and shoes, before catching the next flight to Dublin. The manager never questioned why Karen needed the items, that was not her place. So if Karen wanted her passport and money, she'd follow her instructions to the letter.

"You've saved me a real problem, was it a good flight?" Karen asked as they embraced in the airport foyer.

"It was, Lady Harris. I have everything you asked for. We should go through to departures, the return flight leaves in less than an hour. They're already calling for the final passengers."

"No problem, we'll make it. I'll just use the toilets to get changed," Karen answered, taking the small cabin bag and heading towards the toilets.

Arriving in London, Karen left her manager before making her way to the heliport and taking the shuttle to Gatwick. Once there, she went through to the private aircraft park and boarded her own plane. Opening a secure hatch in the rear bulkhead, where she kept her guns, and other items, Karen took out a satellite transceiver. She keyed in a special code which would enable her to bypass Unit T's block because of mobilisation and connect her directly to the intelligence unit.

"I need to talk to Stanley, its Karen," she told the operator, giving her access code number. Immediately she was put through.

"Karen, it's good to hear from you. Where have you been, I've been really worried this time?" Stanley asked.

"It'll keep, Stanley. Why are we in lockdown?"

"It's a long story, Karen."

"For the moment, give me the potted version as to what's happening?"

Stanley went on to tell Karen all that had happened and what he and Lieutenant Foster had decided to do.

"I agree with what you did, can you have them pull Sherry? They have no idea what she's going into, believe me."

"With you safe, we can abort anyway, I'll call him immediately. What are your plans now?"

"I intend to return to France, get everything down in a report, so we can issue arrest warrants. But I'll hold off logging a flight plan, till I'm happy Sherry is out."

"Do you want me to take us out of mobilisation?"

"Not yet, Stanley, let's have an update from Foster first, shall we?"

"I'm calling him as we speak, Karen, do you want to listen in?"

"Yes, but don't mention that and don't put me on two-way communication."

"Lieutenant Foster, Stanley. I've spoken to Karen. She wants Sherry pulled out immediately. She's told me that the girl's heading into a hornets' nest. She doesn't want Sherry anywhere near it."

"Excuse me, you say Karen's out?"

"Yes, she's in London. It seems she was ahead of us and has found her own way out."

"Then I need to talk to her. Sherry's lost, we're preparing to send in another girl, but not for a few days."

"Sherry's lost, explain, we in intelligence know nothing of this."

"We withheld that information pending a helicopter sweep. It returned only an hour ago. Sherry was transferred to a launch, we think from there she was put on a fishing boat. We don't know. By the time we could get a helicopter in the area, we'd lost the launch they took her away in."

"Can you hold, Lieutenant, I need to talk to Karen." Stanley switched back to Karen. "I can't believe what I've just heard, Karen. We sound like bloody amateurs, the way it's been handled."

Karen was surprised to hear the calm and unruffled Stanley swear, but she didn't comment. "I can't help but agree with you, Stanley. The repercussions can wait for the moment. Sherry's in serious trouble, believe me. But there's a slim chance they will take her to where I was held. I've not got an exact address, but I do have a general idea, watching the roads as I travelled to Dublin. Log a flight plan for me into Belfast International and book me a car. I'll update you with all the background details as I fly. This is a race against time, Stanley. Now I've escaped,

I've a feeling they will use her instead of me. She could end up in Nigeria, if we're too late."

"Do you not want a unit there to back you up?"

"No, take us out of mobilisation and leave a unit in London on standby. Once I have further information about her whereabouts, they should be ready to move."

"Well be careful, like you said, these are not nice people."

"They never are, Stanley. That's the name of the game for us."

Chapter 27

Issac had left his house and travelled to the docks. There he went aboard a small fishing vessel. In the hold, Sherry was secured firmly to the bulkhead, a blanket wrapped around her.

She'd boarded this vessel via another fishing boat working out of the UK. Transferred at sea, when the boats came together, the crew of both vessels had stood there making lurid remarks and laughing after she'd been brought from the hold naked and urged forward by a stick being struck across her backside. She was transferred over to the other boat via a short plank.

"Release her," Issac told the captain.

She was released.

"Drop the blanket and stand up," he shouted aggressively at Sherry.

Sherry stood. She was still naked, no clothes had been provided, apart from the blanket to keep her warm.

He came up to her. "Open your mouth," he demanded.

Sherry did as he asked.

"You have good teeth, close your mouth," he ordered, at the same time running his hands through her hair.

"Put your arms out in front, palm side up."

Once she did that he looked along each arm for signs of needle use. "You can put them down," he told her, at the same time stepping back from Sherry, looking over her body, before coming up close and reaching around grasping her buttocks. "Let me feel you clench that bottom of yours," he told her in a low voice, pulling her tight against his body.

Sherry clenched her buttocks, while he gripped her hard. "That's good, you can release now," he commented, after letting go of her. "Turn around."

Again, Sherry did as she was told.

Issac moved closer, reached around her grasping her breasts, feeling not only the firmness, but for any telltale signs of implants. "Firm buttocks and nice tits, so there will be no waiting about for you," he commented, pushing her away. "Turn around and face me."

Sherry, fed up with being fondled, turned to face him, hoping his inspection of her was over.

Issac pulled a hanky from his pocket and began wiping his hands, as if he'd touched something obnoxious. "I've a client who was expecting a woman to be supplied, but she's no longer available, you will take her place," he told her in a matter of fact way, wiping his hands.

Sherry said nothing, just stood there looking at him. She wanted to be able to recognise him again. Then, when Unit T caught him she wanted to be the one to wipe that smug look off his face.

Glancing at his watch, Issac replaced his hanky and pulled a sheet of paper from the same pocket, handing it to the captain. "We've missed the Dublin sailing, they had to leave on the tide. They supplied these coordinates and expect to be there in three hours. I want you there as well to transfer her."

The captain looked at the coordinates. "We can make it, but I'll need to refuel first. Are you coming?"

"No, I've things to do. Just make sure she gets on

that ship."

"Where am I going?" Sherry suddenly blurted out. She had believed she'd cross over to Ireland and Unit T would be there. Now she was scared no one would realise she was to be put aboard yet another boat.

Issac grinned, showing a row of gold teeth. "It's like this, Sam. That's your name, I believe. Not that it matters, your new owner will give you a more appropriate name. Anyway, I digress. I had a woman called Gabriel earmarked to take this trip. Due to circumstances, she's no longer able to go, so you're to take her place. Your new owner is a Nigerian, he's very wealthy and an important man. He likes white girls and if you keep him happy, perhaps you'll last six months, maybe more. After that, who knows, he never tells me where they end up, just requests a replacement. Anyway, it's meaningful work for a girl with a body like yours, if nothing else." Then he looked back at the captain. "Find her something to wear and secure her. Call me when she's been transferred," he said. With that, he left the hold.

Sherry stood unmoving, stunned. Where was Lieutenant Foster, he had promised to look after her? Then, if Karen was operating covertly and calling herself Gabriel, she must be out. Which meant the operation to find Karen had been a waste of time. Although Gabriel, or rather Karen, could be in more trouble than she was and that might be why this Issac was sending her in Karen's place.

"Well, you heard Issac, get her something to wear," the captain, who'd enjoyed watching Sherry being inspected, barked at a crew member. He left the hold quickly.

Clothes were found, a blanket was put over Sherry's shoulders, and she was forced to sit down again. Her hands were tied behind her back and secured to the bulkhead.

***

When Issac left the boat, he started driving back to Northern Ireland, but rather than go directly home, he was on his way to Belfast. Soon he was on the estate where Mace lived. He despised this area, the rubbish strewn around, the walls daubed with slogans and filth. Small gangs hung around watching, immediately aware of a stranger entering, texting others that a stranger was in the area. Even so, to operate in Ireland, Issac knew he had to deal with the Murphy's, and put up with the wall of fear that surrounded them. They were not only a useful outlet for him, but with their involvement in most criminal activities north and south of the border, if you didn't deal with them, you didn't operate.

Issac entered the small semi-detached house rented by Mace, holding a large A4 envelope. At the front door two men, who would have fitted in better standing outside a nightclub, quickly frisked him for weapons - that was after he'd handed them his gun. That was a small single shot weapon that he always kept close by him. It has been used on occasion to regain control of a situation.

"Issac, come and sit down. Forgive me for not standing, my arthritis, it's giving me a little jip today."

He went over to her, leaning down to kiss her on each side of the face. "No problem, Mace, you just stay sitting down," he told her, before taking a seat himself.

"Tea, coffee, or something stronger?" she asked.

"Tea's fine, I need to drive. Last time we met, I could hardly see the car's dash, let alone the road," he answered with a smile.

"Yes, that was a good night. But we did need to celebrate. After all, we had moved five women and made a hundred thousand into the bargain."

"We had. So what are you up to these days? Can I interest you in two good-looking girls from Scotland. Both are already working the streets and ready for a move?"

She shrugged. "Maybe, what is the cost? As it is, we're going upmarket these days. I have girls coming in that command over a thousand for a night and already most are fully booked. I tell you, Issac, the money is pouring into London, from wealthy foreigners frightened of losing their money back home, it is spawning a new demand for these high-class girls."

"Yes, so I understand. Except it seems you have tapped into a source that can place these girls. That is good, Mace. The street girls, although lucrative, are hard work, earning little in comparison."

"They have their place, but are costly to keep under control, opening up opportunities for the pimps to pocket part of the earnings."

He frowned. "But you only use family?"

She smiled. "Sometimes they can be the worst, Issac, believing they are immune and can do as they like. They soon learn, after I give them a gentle reminder when they step out of line."

Issac knew of her reminders. He'd met a few of her relatives, some limped, another had three fingers missing.

This small woman ruled with a rod of iron. But he liked her for that. If she made a decision, no one questioned it. So dealing with her directly, he never had a problem.

"I need you to do me a small favour, Mace."

"It has a value?" she asked, always looking for and expecting payment.

"Of course, in fact, five thousand."

She raised an eyebrow, this was a great deal of money for a favour. "What is this favour?"

"I've lost a woman. She'd been sold for forty thousand. I want her back."

"Understandable, but a little remiss of you, Issac, I thought you had better control of your workers. Anyway, why do you believe I can find this woman?"

"She escaped from a car heading towards Dublin. The car has been found abandoned in a supermarket car park."

"It sounds like she not only escaped from the car, but took it as well? What was the driver doing to allow that?"

"There were two of them, one left the car for cigarettes, the woman overcame the driver and had him drive away. He was thrown out of the car and she carried on towards Dublin."

Mace shook her head slowly. "If I was in your shoes, I'd have both of them severely punished. Even your workers must learn. Was the woman not secured?"

"According to the one that got out for the cigarettes, she was. Except it's come out since, they had mislaid the key for the handcuffs, decided she was no threat and took her without restraint of any kind."

"Then it's essential to teach them both a lesson. Do you know where she is, so we can collect her for you?"

"No, but she's an illegal, has no passport, no money and no friends. She has to surface somewhere. It won't be at the police station, you can be certain of that."

"That envelope you're holding, are they photos of the woman?" Mace asked.

He nodded, handing the envelope to her. Mace pulled out the photos. One was Karen in a dress, the other her in underclothes. She looked at the photos for some time, passing them to Bile, who'd been leaning on a wall listening to the conversation. As she passed them over, she gave a very slight shake of her head. Mace wanted no comment from him.

"Tell me, how did this woman end up with you?"

Issac told her how Karen had originally gone to Teesside, returned and been sold on, finally passing to him after she'd been beaten up.

"Very well, we'll take the contract and collect her. That is, if she's still in the country. She seems a resourceful woman to dupe you all like that. Moving on to other business, I believe Heaney is meeting you tonight?"

"He is. We're discussing the collection of asylum seekers from Dublin and taking them across to the UK."

"That's correct. We've already done a dry run to test the route from France and with help from my associates at the docks, we're able to pass them onto Heaney. The point is, Issac, they are of no value to us after that. They've paid their travel, so we're not interested in what happens later."

He frowned. "So when we collect them from

Heaney and they are on the fishing boat, you're saying I shouldn't transfer them to the UK fishing boat? What do we do with them?"

"Precisely, why waste fuel and time? As to what to do with them, they did reach Europe, so just throw them overboard a few miles out. Give them the chance to swim the rest of the way."

"That's cold-blooded murder."

"Yes, you have a problem in that?"

"Will there be women and children?"

"At times, of course. In fact, some may be useful in your own business. I've heard the children can fetch good money."

"I'm not sure, Mace. These people have been through hell to get to Europe and we're going to kill them."

Mace sighed. "Issac, if you want to transfer them onto your UK fishing boat and take them to the mainland, do it. I'm not bothered either way. We'll pay a hundred a person, under ten years go free. All the risks are with you landing them, not us."

"I'll think about that. It's time I wasn't here. Find Gabriel for me, Mace. That woman owes me big time."

"We shall see."

After Issac had gone, Mace looked at Bile. "Get me the pictures of Karen we took off the wall in that reporter's bedroom."

Sorting through them, Mace dropped a few on the floor in front of her, alongside the three Issac had left.

"Would you fucking believe it, Bile? The stupid fool had Karen Harris and let her escape."

Bile looked down at the photos. "I think you're

right there Mace."

"I know I'm right. Men only see one sexy lady, women see different, beyond the sexual attraction. That woman has some balls, with what she'll go through to take traffickers down. But we can forget looking for her, she'll be long gone. Get Heaney on the phone, Issac is compromised and could bring us all down if he blabs to Unit T. Believe me, from what I've heard of Harris's interrogation methods, he'll be singing like a bird after ten minutes in her company."

"Then why didn't she take him earlier, she was in the house for two weeks?" Bile asked, while he dialled Heaney's number.

"That's a good point. I think she couldn't. Issac always moves his women naked. That way he's not got to search them. Karen was injured, in fact, like Issac said, unconscious when she was collected. Whatever she carries on her person to keep in touch with her unit, she'd have lost when they stripped her. So once in Issac's care, she would need to bide her time, be cooperative in every way, play the meek woman giving them no cause for concern. That's why they never bothered about restraints in the car. She was a pussycat, or so they believed."

"I've got Heaney," Bile suddenly said, handing her the handset.

"Heaney, Mace. Issac's compromised, you know what to do."

"I do. Do you want chapter and verse on his routes into the UK?"

"Good idea, we may be able to take them over. Talk to you tomorrow."

Chapter 28

Karen landed in Belfast, immediately collecting the hire car that Stanley had arranged. She had the intention of visiting Issac and finding out where Sherry had been abducted to. However, there was a problem. If she walked in, he'd immediately recognise her as Gabriel. This was something she didn't want to happen, believing her look as Gabriel could still have a use. To overcome this problem, Karen intended to go in as a Unit T soldier, complete with helmet and visor. To this end she brought from her aircraft her combat bag, as well as an M4 carbine and a handgun from her secure cupboard.

Within twenty minutes she was on the road, heading for Armagh. Her satellite navigation unit was telling her she'd be there within the hour, she knew by following the A3 towards the border that she'd need to begin looking, after ten miles, for the road where Issac's house was located.

**

By twelve-o-clock that night. Leaving her car some distance away, Karen was soon in the grounds of Issac's house. She'd changed and was dressed in all-black combat clothes, bulletproof vest, steel capped shoes and a helmet, with a bulletproof visor that would help protect her eyes in a shoot-out. She also wore a leather strap that crossed her body and was attached to the belt around her waist. On this strap were spare clips for her M4 carbine. Around her waist, she had a holstered handgun, a torch and two pouches with extra ammunition for the handgun. Around her ankle, was her knife, fixed upside down in a sheath. On her arms and the helmet was Unit T's Dark Angel insignia, although she'd left off the label over her breast pocket giving her name and rank. To complete her preparation, she pushed a few tie wraps into her pocket, usually used to secure trees to a post; they were useful as a temporary replacement for handcuffs. This was Karen as she'd dressed many times, often working covertly, alone, although she was reduced in firepower by not taking grenades, they were a usual part of her attire when on a mission. Even so, to meet her with the visor down and gun in hand would instil fear in an adversary, giving her the edge. More importantly, she had lost her individuality, becoming just a soldier.

Moving towards the house, she could see three cars parked at the front. What concerned her was that in one car were two people. She suspected they were both male. The windows were closed and they were just sitting there talking. Bypassing them, keeping close to the shrubbery, she began to move around the house, looking at every window, every door, to decide where she could enter. Passing the conservatory, Karen could see through into the lounge. Issac was in there with a man she'd never seen before. They seemed to be arguing, Issac using hand gestures to reinforce what he was saying. Further round the house, she arrived at the kitchen where she had her meals. Hillgar was sitting at the kitchen table, a cup in front of her and an empty plate. Karen suspected this was her final drink before she retired. All Karen could do was wait. For her to get into the house, she needed Hillgar to go to her room.

Eventually the kitchen light went out. Shortly, in

a top room of the house, the light came on, before the curtains were closed. Karen knew, from conversations in the kitchen with Hillgar, that was her bedroom.

Going up to the back door, Karen raised her elbow, putting it through the window of the door, confident the sound wouldn't be heard. The kitchen was quite a distance from the main area, with the kitchen door, a corridor and another door leading into a short passage before you could get into the entrance hall of the house.

Opening the door, she slipped inside, at the same time lowering her visor. Moving cautiously, she entered the house. In less than a minute she was in the entrance hall. The door to the lounge was slightly open. Inside, she could hear the conversation between Issac and this other man; they were obviously having heated exchanges.

Leaving them for a short time, Karen searched the upstairs rooms of the house, checking each room, particularly the one she'd been locked inside. She had hoped that Sherry was there, but they were empty. Disappointed, Karen returned to the entrance hall, bolted the front door, and slid the small bolt on the door leading to the kitchen.

Switching her M4 carbine to maximum output, which would allow her to spray a room in seconds with the entire contents of her clip, Karen then kicked the door of the lounge open.

"Both of you, on the floor, face down, hands behind your heads. You're prisoners of Unit T and have five seconds to comply, before I begin shooting, with this M4 carbine, it's capable of cutting you in half at this range," Karen shouted.

They turned to look in shock at the fully armed soldier standing there, visor down, the insignia of Unit T clearly visible on her helmet.

Issac didn't hesitate, doing as she ordered.

The other man was initially slow to do as she requested, believing that this soldier could be on her own. If she'd been with a military unit, or an armed police incursion force, the type of entry would have been very different, with armed personnel everywhere, each protecting the other, causing confusion for the people inside. Her mode of entry was all wrong, unless she was alone. "I'm part of a paramilitary group, with others outside. You're obviously alone and have no business with me, because of that I will leave. Attempt to stop me and my men will come in, you will have a fight on your hands, which you cannot hope to win."

Karen looked at him for a moment, why was such a man here? Then she'd not seen anyone else outside, beyond the two in the car, not that it meant there weren't any more. The area was too large for her to do a complete search on her own. Either way, she was not about to back down, so she decided to bluff. "Then you will understand, as a soldier yourself, I would have already searched both the grounds and the house. I'm also fully aware of the two men in the car. Delay any longer and there will be one less of you. I also have no fear of gunmen, no matter who or what they claim to be."

He looked at the insignia of Unit T. If she was one of them, she'd be one of their Dark Angel soldiers, and would certainly have checked outside. Then, with her being alone, she might even be Karen Harris. For such a person, his words would fall on deaf ears. She was a professional killer and very capable of carrying out her threats. Even if he could reach his gun, her protection of vital organs, with the bulletproof jacket, would mean he could only wound her, not disabling her enough to stop her bringing her gun to bear on him. Doing as she asked, he was soon lying on the floor face down.

Karen took out a few tie wraps from her pocket and threw them towards Issac, considering the stranger as the higher risk. "Issac, use the tie wraps and secure your friend's wrists behind his back, then do the ankles. Delay and I won't need to secure anyone, you'll both be dead."

Issac wondered why she should know his name, but didn't ask, doing what she told him to do.

"That's good, now secure your own ankles and lie face down again, hands behind your back."

Once he'd done that, Karen came forward and secured Issac's wrists, also checking the stranger to ensure he was secure.

Placing her gun on the table, she dragged Issac along the floor, before turning him over, sitting him up and leaning him against a wall. Collecting her gun, she switched it to safety, slinging it over her back. Pulling her handgun from its holster, Karen screwed on a silencer, taken from a pouch on her belt.

"Right, ready to answer a few questions, Issac? I have one rule you should be aware of. Refuse to answer, or tell me a wrong answer, and I fire this gun. It's modified and has twenty rounds. Each round will hit something very painful. You won't die, I'm too good a shot for that, unless I decide you do, then it will be a bullet in the liver, so it will take hours of agony before you die. A small cost on your side, for what you've put so many women through, before you answer to your maker. Have we an understanding?"

"You'll get nothing out of me until I'm away from this place. Mace has double-crossed me, claimed I was harbouring a Karen Harris from Unit T. She's sent this man Heaney to kill me, after I tell him my routes to and from the UK."

"You weren't harbouring her, you had her secured, she was Gabriel. The one you intended to sell to Fasido," Heaney cut in.

"I don't think so," Karen said. "Gabriel is with us, she's on her way to France as we speak."

"I couldn't care less who she was, if you want information, I still want out of here, call your troops in," Issac demanded.

Heaney sniggered. "She's got no troops, have you?"

Karen ignored his question. "I'll get you out if you tell me where the girl is who went in place of Gabriel."

"You're talking about the girl Tanny sent?" Issac asked.

"Yes."

"She's aboard a ship on its way to Africa. Now I want out."

"What's the name of the ship, is it going directly there, or calling at ports on the way?"

"I don't have its fucking itinerary," Issac retorted. "Fasido bought her, he arranged transport. But if you want the name of the ship, that's with me, till we're a long way

215

from here."

"Then you're both fucked. The girl is lost, because neither of you will leave this house... alive, that is," Heaney cut in.

"You shut up. We go, Issac," Karen decided, reaching down and cutting the tie wraps around his ankles.

Pulling him up, she pushed him out of the lounge door and down the corridor towards the kitchen.

At that moment there was banging on the front door, followed by someone shouting through the letter box.

"Heaney, are you there? We need to go," a male voice shouted.

"Shoot the door open, Dara, I'm tied up, Issac's getting away," Heaney shouted back.

Seconds later, after a machine gun started up, Dara and the other man from the car burst through the front door, running into the lounge.

"What happened?" Dara asked, cutting Heaney's bonds.

"A fucking Unit T soldier turned up, holding an M4. I wasn't going to argue. She's on her own, she and Issac left out the back door. We'll get them both," he said, finally standing and pulling out his gun.

"Let's go," Dara said. "Shaun, you get ahead of them. Take the car, she must have parked on the road. Disable her car, then hide and cut them both down, if they get past us."

***

Karen and Issac had come around the house, well clear of the cars, and were running down the drive towards the road where Karen had left her car. They'd not been running long when the car, which had been parked with two men inside at the front of the house, was approaching fast. Both stumbled into the shrubs, keeping down as it passed. Then they were up and running once more. Already Issac was gasping, he wasn't a fit man and the drive was close to a quarter mile long.

"I've got to stop for a moment," he told her coming to a halt, breathing heavily.

Karen didn't object, she could see he was struggling, if they didn't stop, he'd not make it at all.

Pushing him to the side, out of sight, she went down on one knee, the M4 in her hands, concentrating her watch on the house; although, she was concerned about the car passing, unsure how many were inside, but suspecting they intended to cut her off. Karen pulled her mobile out, with the intention of calling for assistance. She pressed a preloaded number for the army barracks in Armagh. By giving them a coded number, they would respond to a Unit T request for assistance. She listened, then the mobile phone bleeped with the message, 'no signal'. She stared at the signal bar, even tried moving the phone around, but it showed nothing. "Don't mobiles work around here?" she asked.

"No, sometimes in certain places they do, but not very well, I use a landline."

Karen looked back at him. "Then we have to make a run for it. The car's not far. Can you move yet?"

He nodded. "Yes, I'm good to go."

"We'll also need to get off this road and into the shrubs, or we'll never make it to the road."

"There's a small track a little further on, it leads into the woods, it's used by trackers for rabbits, that sort of thing. It eventually curves back to the road," Issac said.

"Then head for it, you lead the way, I'll protect you."

With one last look around, they moved. But in less than fifty yards a gun started up from behind them. Heaney, who'd not left in the car was approaching from the house and had seen the flash of her gun, caught in the moonlight. Now he was onto her and moving forward close on her heels, raising his gun and firing.

Issac stumbled and fell. Karen dropped to the ground, spun around scanning the area with a night sight. She saw movement, aimed her gun and began firing.

After that, all hell broke loose. Gunfire was coming from two directions, pinning her down, her efforts to stop at least one of the men were proving fruitless.

"Give up soldier, come out with your hands up," Heaney shouted, when her gun silenced as she reloaded. "You've got nowhere to run and will soon be out of ammunition. We've no beef with you, you can walk away. I'll give you three minutes before we use grenades, you won't stand a chance."

Karen shook Issac."We need to talk, I can't hold them off," she whispered.

Issac never answered, or moved. She moved closer, putting her hand to his neck. There was no pulse, Issac was dead.

"Shit, that's all I need," Karen said to herself.

"One minute, then you die," Heaney called.

"Issac's dead. Your bullet found its mark. I'll

move away, so you can check yourself," she called back.

"No, you come out, with your hands up, or you don't come out at all and die there," he came back at her.

She knew that with one clip left and a handgun, she couldn't hope to fight on if he began to throw grenades. "I'm coming out," she called, throwing her M4 onto the drive, stepping out with her hands up.

"That's sensible. Remove the handgun, draw it out with two fingers and drop it to the ground," Heaney told her, his powerful flashlight blinding her. "When you've done that, move away from them, into the centre of the drive, lie down, face to the ground, hands above your head."

When she had done as he told her, Dara came out from another direction, walked past Karen and went to Issac. "He's dead, a bullet directly through his heart. Did he tell you anything?"

"No, there wasn't time," Heaney answered.

"What about the Unit T soldier?"

"I'll keep my word and not kill her, but we'll not let her walk away. We'll deliver her to Mace, she may have a value, for interrogation, or whatever."

Dara walked over to Karen. "Stand up, get rid of the helmet, remove the belt and your bulletproof jacket, then empty your pockets. You're coming with us."

After she had done as they asked, Dara checked her pockets before grasping her arm, urging her forward and down the drive towards the road.

"So what's your name?" he asked.

"Private Garter," she answered, followed by a military number.

He slapped her across the head with his hand. "Don't get fucking smart with me, or I'll put a bullet in your head. What's your full name?"

"Francis Garter."

Nothing more was said. Heaney had called Shaun with a small walkie-talkie, to tell him to bring the car back. As soon as it stopped, Karen was pushed into the back seat, Dara climbed in alongside her.

With Heaney driving they were soon leaving Issac's house behind.

Chapter 29

Karen was sitting quietly, trying to plan a means of escape. However, once inside the car, Dara had used one of the tie wraps from her pocket to secure her wrists. Now, after a thirty minute drive, they had turned onto the M1, heading towards Belfast.

Every minute was bringing her closer to Mace, a woman she feared. As soon as Mace found out her real name, her destination wouldn't be a brothel or a pimp, she would have her killed. Karen was very certain of that. Her only possible salvation was the fact that neither Dara nor Heaney had considered, beyond the obvious weapons they had taken off her, whether she carried anything more. They had missed her ankle knife. All she could hope for now was that with arriving in the middle of the night, she might possibly be dumped in a room until the morning and have a chance to use it.

Her other disappointment was Sherry. The slim chance of Issac telling her the name of the ship she was on, was now gone. All she had was a possible country and a name, which might be the Nigerians real name, or only the one they knew him by. Although Karen was at least satisfied that if she hadn't tried, Issac would have been dead by Heaney's hand anyway.

***

Further along the M1, a police patrol car was parked at an observation ramp, watching the cars. The motorway was quiet, with only a few vehicles heading towards the city.

"Looks like it's going to be a long night, Bill," one of the policemen commented, eating a sandwich made by his wife.

"I think you're right."

At that moment, the ANPR registration recognition pinged, showing that a car had just passed with no insurance.

"That's all we need to spoil my break, Jack, a bloody uninsured vehicle. Let's go and get him," Bill commented, putting the half-eaten sandwich back into his lunch box.

With their blue lights flashing, they set off after the uninsured vehicle.

"Fuck, the police are on our tail," Heaney commented, looking in the rear-view mirror. "I wonder what they want?"

"Well, we can't stop, not with the woman in the car and weapons in the boot. Go for it, lose the bastards in the city," Dara urged.

Heaney didn't need telling twice, putting his foot down to the floor. The car shot forward, quickly climbing to speeds in excess of a hundred miles an hour.

"Yahoo! This is the way to live," Dara shouted with obvious excitement.

Back in the police car, Bill sighed. "Looks like the driver's going to try to outrun us. Does he know what we're driving here?"

Jack laughed. "I don't think so somehow," he said, glancing at the speedometer as it approached the hundred mile an hour mark, with the car ahead still gaining. "Call ahead, Bill, we need to have them intercepted, before they kill themselves, or some other poor bugger."

Minutes passed by, Heaney was driving like a

madman, urged on by Shaun and Dara. Dara had forgotten Karen, more interested in looking out of the back window, giving the finger to the police car following. Karen bent forward, pretending she was trying to protect herself, in case they had an accident. However, she saw this as an opportunity to try to escape. Her intention was to cause chaos in the car, hoping it would be enough for them to lose control and damage the vehicle enough to bring it to a halt. It was a risk, she could be injured or even killed, but once with Mace, she would be in the same position. By now, her hands were down by her right ankle, gripping the knife between them, pulling it from the sheath, bringing the ultra sharp blade between her wrists, trying to slice through the plastic of the tie wrap.

Dara turned back, saw her leaning down and slapped her across the head. "What the fuck are you doing down there. Get sat up," he shouted, grabbing her hair and wrenching her head back.

Karen did come up, but holding the knife in her right hand, the plastic tie cut; although so too was her wrist, blood gushing from a deep gash. Not that it mattered, Karen swung the knife up, stabbing him in the chest.

Dara screamed with the pain. "The fucking bastard's got a knife, she's stabbed me," he shouted, at the same time trying to push her away, hitting her across the head with his flailing arms.

The fight between them was intense, both of them rolling about in the back. Heaney was shouting at Shaun to help Dara and knock Karen out. But that was more difficult to do than just leaning over and hitting her. He released his safety belt, turned around, his knees on the seat, trying to get a grip on her. Karen was not having it, she was pulling away from him, then lashed out with the knife, slicing him across the face. He screamed in agony, going ballistic. In the confines of a car, travelling at over a hundred miles an hour, the fight was sending the balance of the car completely haywire. Heaney was fighting to hold it on the road as it careered across the carriageway. He slammed on the brakes, to slow the vehicle and gain some control. That was before Shaun, in error, punched Heaney in the face, as the car lurched.

The police car behind could only watch as the car careered out of control, hitting the barrier more than once. Sparks came from underneath as a tyre burst, the rim scraping the road.

"The driver's going to kill himself if he doesn't slow down," Bill commented.

Neither of the police were in a panic, they had seen it so many times before, with hotheads losing control of their vehicle trying to outrun the police.

At that moment the car flipped, hitting the barrier and sliding along on its roof, coming to a halt further down the road.

The police car screeched to a halt, both of them outside in seconds, Bill collected a fire extinguisher from the boot.

Another police car drew up, they called the fire brigade and ambulances.

***

Sir Peter Parker was asleep when the telephone began to ring. He glanced at the clock, it was just after four in the morning. Lifting the receiver, he turned away from his wife who was still sleeping.

"Parker here," was all he said.

"Sir Peter, this is Detective Batton from Belfast, Northern Ireland. I'm sorry to call you at this hour, but you're the only person we think can help us."

"That's alright, Detective, what can I do for you?"

"There was a car chase on the M1 earlier, three men and a woman were in the car. All apart from the woman were wanted by the police. The woman has no identity, but is dressed in combat clothing, with Unit T insignia on each arm. There was also a helmet with the same insignia inside the car boot, along with weapons. We cannot call Unit T directly, apparently we need to go through your office."

"You were right to call. How is the soldier?"

"She's in theatre as we speak. One of the men is dead, the other two are badly injured. The one who's dead was killed by a knife wound."

"Then it's important to place armed guards with the woman. I'll contact Unit T and have them come to take charge of her safety. I'll catch the first flight to Belfast that I can. I'll call you with an ETA."

"I will do everything you ask, Sir Peter. Although the woman's already under armed guard, not knowing who she is."

***

Sir Peter was on a scheduled flight to Ireland the same morning. He'd called Stanley and they both suspected the woman in the car was Karen, so as a priority Stanley had dispatched the Dark Angel unit currently waiting in London.

225

By the time Sir Peter came out of arrivals, two soldiers were waiting for him, with a unit car outside the terminal. Once inside, he wanted to know the situation.

"It is the colonel, Sir Peter. I've had confirmation from our forward vehicles. They arrived at the hospital three hours back and have the wing she's in secured. I don't have any details of her condition," the driver told him.

Soon the vehicle drew up at the hospital. A man waiting at the entrance came over as soon as the car stopped and Sir Peter climbed out.

"Sir Peter Parker? I'm Detective Batton. Would you like to follow me?"

"How is Karen?" Sir Peter asked.

"That is her name, then?"

"Yes, Unit T has confirmed the woman to be Colonel Karen Harris, their commander."

"I see. Well, according to the medical team, she had a nasty crack to the head, which knocked her out. She's also lost a great deal of blood from a deep wound to her wrist and is currently having a blood transfusion. Beyond that, it was a modern car, they take some stick and although the car is completely written off, the passenger cage held so injuries are considered minor."

It was over an hour before Sir Peter was allowed in to see Karen. She was lying in bed, a drip in her arm. One arm was bandaged up, both eyes were black and swollen, her face red.

"Well, you've been in the wars, Karen. They tell me you will survive and you're complete, with nothing missing," Sir Peter said, leaning over her and kissing her on the forehead. "But I can't see you being on the beach for a while. Are you well enough to tell me what you've been up to?"

"I failed, Peter. Sherry is missing, caused by a botched surveillance operation. A man called Issac took her, so I went to see him. I didn't expect there to be a splinter paramilitary force there, so we had a little skirmish. I lost and they killed Issac."

"I wouldn't say you lost, Karen. You're still alive and the men are in custody. But Sherry worries me. I understood her times on covert operations were finished. Both you and Sherry told me that was the case?"

"It was and I wouldn't use her again. The problem was, I wasn't there. Sherry, being Sherry, volunteered to help find me. Surveillance underestimated how Issac shipped women around, so they didn't have any means of tracking her in place, once she'd been placed on a boat, in different clothes and without the trackers on her anymore. The problem as I see it now, is where she is and what boat's she on?"

"Could it have started its voyage from Ireland, the ship I mean?" he asked.

"Who knows? Sherry was taken in London, she was brought to a cove in Wales. After that she could have been taken anywhere." Then she hesitated. "Although, I was supposed to have been on a ship. I was also told the ship was in Dublin docks. There's just a chance, Peter, that Sherry is on the same ship. Can you check what has sailed over the last twenty-four hours and hopefully there will be a ship going towards Africa with Sherry still aboard and not transferred to yet another ship."

227

"I'll do that, of course, but you know searching a ship is very difficult and is a labour- intensive task. Unless you have a lot of searchers, she could be moved around the ship as you searched."

Karen sighed. "Then we've lost her. Without the definite name of the ship, like you say, it would be like looking for a needle in a haystack."

"Well, you don't worry, just concentrate on getting yourself well again. I'll work with Stanley and leave no stone unturned."

"Thank you, Peter. I appreciate it. I love Sherry a great deal, I can't imagine her not being around anymore."

Chapter 30

Mace placed the morning paper on the table after reading the headlines, reporting a high speed chase, besides the crash and arrest of Heaney. "I'm not liking it, Bile. Unit T is getting closer. Never before have they poked their noses into Ireland, north or south, like now. Then Heaney gets arrested, and Dara's dead. What the hell's happening?"

"It gets even worse, Mace. According to an orderly at the hospital, the reason Unit T are there and taken over security on the woman in the car with the lads, is because it was Karen Harris. I have been told the press heard she's there and everywhere's in chaos as they try to get close to her. They have no chance, even the orderly can't go on the floor she's on. Unit T brought in their own medical team. He thinks they are moving Karen. Local army vehicles have arrived and are closing the area off around the helicopter landing pad. I called our people at the airport and the C4 is being prepared to take off. It seems they intend to move her by helicopter to the airport, then she'll leave on the C4."

Mace gave a hint of a smile. "It figures, Unit T will not want Karen remaining at a hospital difficult to protect her in. It also begs the question, how badly is she injured? Could it be life-threatening and she's being taken on to a specialist hospital?"

Bile shook his head. "I can't find that out, no one knows."

"Well, let's hope it is. You must get to see Heaney in prison. Call Charles, tell him he's to represent Heaney, then go with him to see Heaney as his assistant. I need to know exactly what was happening, leading up to the road accident. On another issue, this man Dominick, hasn't he booked the restaurant for him and Karen yet?"

"I called him a couple of days back. He told me he's not seen or heard from Karen for a while. He did talk to Sherry. Sherry said Karen was away and couldn't be contacted. He's asked Sherry to tell her he called."

"Well, if it was Karen in the car, she's not going to be in any condition to go out with Dominick for a while, anyway, just keep in touch with him. Maybe get him to call the number Karen gave him and see if he can find out how she is. We'll bide our time there. If she likes the guy, she will get in touch and they will go out for dinner."

"I'll do that. He and I are getting on, now he doesn't see me as a threat or risk to Karen. More like a man who wants to do right by her."

"He's a stupid man. Anyway, don't forget, you're meeting Crustkin, to view the first batch of girls on Friday. Everything's in place, but he's saying it will still be a month before they are ready. Push him, will you, we need the girls fast, to start earning money."

"I'm onto that, have no worries. I'll go and call Charles, see if we can get to see Heaney and find out if what he's done could affect our operations."

"Yes, do. I'll rest more soundly once I understand just what happened."

Chapter 31

Karen was back at her home in France. The Unit had spirited her out of the Belfast hospital, using an army helicopter to take her to the airport. Karen wasn't on board the C4. With a pilot sent over by the Unit, she had opted to return to France in her own aircraft. So, Karen had been taken by stretcher to a remote part of the airport, where her aircraft had already been prepared for take-off. While the press watched the C4, Karen was long gone.

Ally ran into the house and through to the kitchen. "Hi Madge, what's for dinner?"

Madge looked up from the table, where she was preparing the meal. "Nothing for you young lady, until you've changed out of those dirty jeans. Then, while you go upstairs, can you take this tea to Lady Harris?"

Ally's eyes went big. "Karen's back, when did she come?"

"By ambulance earlier today. She's had a road accident, so don't jump on top of her like you often do."

Ally grabbed the tea, running upstairs and directly into Karen's bedroom. She stopped dead, staring at Karen. "My god, what happened, Karen? You look awful."

"Thanks Ally, that really makes me feel good. Is that my tea?"

"Oh, yes," she answered, placing it on the bedside table. "Do you want help holding the cup while you drink some?"

"No, I'm not that bad, thank you. But don't tell me you've been to school in those jeans?"

"I have, we were on a nature trail thing this

afternoon and told to wear something appropriate. I'll go and get changed; are you coming down for dinner, or having it up here?"

"I'd have a little trouble going down at the moment, besides, the camp doctor says I've got to stay in bed for the next couple of days."

"Then I'll have mine here with you. You can tell me everything you've been up to. Where's Sherry, is she with you?"

Karen looked at her for a moment. "I'll not lie to you, Ally. There's a good chance we've lost Sherry. A mission went wrong and she's missing."

"But you'll find her, won't you, Karen? Tell me you will find her?" she said, tears beginning to form in her eyes.

"You know I'll do my absolute best, Ally. But we live in a dangerous world, the risk is very high. Sherry knows that all too well."

Ally just nodded. "I'll go and get changed," she said soberly.

***

The following day, Stanley was with Karen. Earlier Karen had dictated to one of the secretaries all that had happened. The secretary had typed it up and passed it to Stanley before their meeting.

"After reading your report, Karen, I really can't see how you could have done anything any different. My only concern was you going into Issac's alone. Even so, it wouldn't have been much of a problem if Heaney and his men hadn't been there."

"I agree, have you issued arrest warrants for all

the traffickers concerned, as far back as Maclean?"

"We have, the police are at this moment making the arrests. What are your intentions about Sherry?"

"What can I do? Short of going to Nigeria, if that's where she is, and seeking out this man Fasido, I'm at a loss. All I needed was five more minutes and I'd have had the name of the ship. Now I've the difficult task of deciding if Lieutenant Foster was reckless, using her the way he did. He of all people knew she'd been taken off that type of work, the girl's not cut out for it. She works well with a team, follows orders to the letter, but falls flat on her face when alone. Personally, I think it was an ill-conceived operation that may have cost Sherry her life."

"I have to agree, although with you not there, he as her commanding officer had the final say. But you know what Sherry's like. As soon as she heard you could be in trouble she was there, begging to help no matter what. How's Ally taking it, she loves Sherry a great deal?"

Karen sighed. "She's bearing up, accepting that we often take risks, but not accepting this was one risk that little bit too far and Sherry may not be coming back."

"Well, while you're on sick leave, I will be looking into this man, Fasido, where he lives and what he does. Like you say, it may not be his real name, but at least we're not abandoning Sherry and doing nothing. As for you, you need a break away from everything. To have some time to get everything that has happened into perspective."

"What's this thing called sick leave? I'm going nowhere. I want Mace and you can be certain I'll get her for something."

"Karen, be realistic. You will take her down, you know that, I've no doubt. But Mace has been around a long time, another month will not make much difference. But for you, it will make all the difference. Go to the coast, take Ally and chill out."

"Chill out with Ally. Do you know what it's like living with her? Sometimes I dread coming back to my own home. She's a teenager, they're on another planet."

He smiled. "I told you when she first came that you wouldn't cope with her. But with your pig-headedness, you claimed you could. Alright, you didn't have the early years with her while she grew up to get used to her and her ways, you just dropped in on her life when she was fifteen. How do you think she feels? Her parents and her sister are dead. That girl's got some spunk to pick up her life and carry on. Most fall apart and need professional help. You knew it was going to be hard, but for all her faults, you couldn't have a more loyal and loving girl. Can you actually be contemplating going on holiday without her?"

"You're right. It's a lot to expect. Ally's not going to allow me to walk out of the house, live it up on sunny beaches and party at night without her. She'd kill me while I slept and pinch the bloody ticket."

He smiled. "Not quite kill, Karen, but she would pinch your ticket."

"Then I'll go at the end of next week, by that time I'll not look so much like a panda, hopefully."

***

Karen had been home for nearly two weeks. She felt better in herself. The swelling of her eyes had gone down, the injuries virtually healed, the stitches on her wrist had been removed. She was now sitting with Ally after dinner.

"I'm going away for a couple of weeks, Ally. Nothing special, just lazing about on a beach, maybe enjoying a little nightlife. I'd like you to come with me."

Ally shrugged. "I can't its still school term and besides, I've got my exams coming up."

Karen was taken aback somewhat, expecting her to jump at the chance. "It's all sorted at the school, the tutors will even coach you when we return, you'll not miss out, Ally."

She looked at Karen. "I don't know how you can just sit there and calmly tell me you're going on holiday. Two bloody weeks you've been back and you've not lifted a finger to find Sherry. Well, I for one am not going to forget this. The kids at school always said you were a cold-hearted bastard. I always defended you, saying they didn't understand the pressures you were under. Now I understand. It's you, you, you, all the bloody time. Even when you came back after the car crash, you just calmly told me Sherry was lost, then went on to more important matters, like telling me to get changed for dinner. So you go on your bloody holiday, but don't expect me to come with you and hold your hand, I won't." With that she made to leave the room.

"You come back here, Ally. No one, not even you, speaks to me like that and walks away," Karen shouted after her.

Ally spun around, there were tears in her eyes. "Then bloody learn, Karen, to take what you so easily hand out. I'm leaving this house, I'm sixteen and can go. Hazel's parents said I can move in with them. Don't

235

expect me back, or even talk to me again. I hate you and all that you stand for."

Karen watched her run up the stairs, heard her door slam. She didn't know what to say, or how to handle a child. Ally had not even given her the chance to explain what they were doing about Sherry. What did she expect her to do, don her combat gear and fly out to Nigeria on some wild goose chase?

Sighing to herself, Karen followed her upstairs. Going directly to Ally's room, she didn't even knock, just pushed the door open and went inside.

Ally spun round, shocked at Karen walking in without knocking, she always knocked. Ally was also scared of Karen, not that she would admit it.

"You're an ungrateful bitch," Karen began. "I gave you a home, a future and did my best for you. I know I could never replace your mother, neither do I know how to bring up, or discipline a child. Even so, I'm entitled to some respect. You can't give me that any more. I presume you've been whining to others, telling them how unhappy you are, making me out to be an uncaring and selfish person, to the point Hazel's mother has offered to take you in? You'd better take up the offer, Ally. This is my house, my home, and as far as I'm concerned, you're not welcome here anymore. As for Sherry, I've had the entire intelligence unit looking for her since she disappeared. If Sherry is still alive, they will locate her, then I will collect Sherry no matter where she is in the world. I may not be able to show my emotions, probably because since I was seventeen, I've lived a violent, besides degrading life, with very few people I could really trust. Sherry is a girl I could, we've stuck together through hell at times. She's my best friend, my only friend. She trusts that I will never give up on her, the same as she wouldn't give up on me." Karen hesitated. "I believed you were the same, a girl both of us loved and we'd do anything for. You had guts, a determination to carry on with your life, the same as Sherry, who had to sit and watch a man put a bullet in her mother's head." Karen hesitated again and took a deep breath. "Pack your bags, go to your so-called friend, see how long they put up with someone with your attitude. I'll call you a taxi, but you pay for it yourself, or walk. You'll get nothing from me ever again." Then Karen left the room.

Ally was shaking. She should have realised Karen wasn't being complacent about finding Sherry. Now her stupid words had driven a wedge between them and she didn't know what to do. Packing a few of her clothes and collecting a teddy she'd had all her life, Ally went down the stairs and out the front door. Sitting down on the step waiting for the taxi, already tears were streaming down her face, but Karen never came out to comfort her.

***

The following day, Karen left early, flew to Paris and parked up her aircraft. Two hours later she was on a plane heading for New Orleans. From there she'd booked a cabin on a large cruise ship, leaving the next day for the Caribbean. It was all she could find at short notice after Ally had refused to come with her.

A little later in the day, Ally walked into the intelligence unit. The security at the door prevented her going further than reception. "This is a restricted area,

Ally. Are you here on an appointment?" one asked, but not in an aggressive way. Already he could see she looked very down.

"I wondered if Stanley was free?" she answered meekly.

"I'll give him a call for you, Ally. Just take a seat."

Stanley came through, a little bemused. "Ally, why are you not with Karen? Her aircraft left this morning?"

Ally said nothing, just ran to him, flinging her arms around his neck, burying her face in his shoulder, sobbing her heart out.

He looked at the receptionist, who just shrugged. "I think you'd better come to my office, we should talk," he said gently, pushing her away and taking her hand.

Holding a glass of coke, Ally told him what had happened between her and Karen.

He sighed. "I won't tell you how stupid you've been, Ally. I think you know that? Unit T is not only Karen, but hundreds of other personnel. Yes, she's the commander, someone has to be, but we all work for her, support operations that are constantly going on, besides doing the thousand and one jobs that complete a successful prosecution. What did you really expect Karen to be doing about Sherry? Karen had just come out of the field, she was injured, so needed a little time to recuperate."

Ally shook her head slowly. "I don't know, but she didn't seem to me to be doing anything, it upset me. I believed she'd just written Sherry off and was carrying on with her life as if Sherry had never existed. Then the kids at school were telling me this is how she was, cold, uncaring and treating people like shit."

"And you listened? When did she treat you like shit, or any other person at this camp for that matter? Karen, at eighteen, was spending every penny she had to help others, using most of her salary trying to keep her charity going after the money from the papers, for her story, ran out. She was stumbling between operations, which would often leave her traumatised, but she kept going, knowing what the girls were going through with no one helping, or coming for them. You only touched your toes in Karen and Sherry's world, Ally. They've been beaten, starved, degraded and duped into brothels, I can't image what they were like, in an attempt to help others," he said, hesitating. "As it is, I've had to virtually order Karen to take time off to get herself together again, on the promise of calling her the minute we locate Sherry. Believe me, then she'll drop everything to go for her and bring her home. I'd hoped you'd have stuck by her, Ally, made her feel at least she had you. Karen will be devastated if Sherry is lost and there is a very real chance of that. Thousands are lost and never found again, even our resources may not locate Sherry."

Tears were beginning to trickle down Ally's face. "What can I do, Stanley? I cried myself to sleep last night. I'd decided to go back and apologise, ask her if she'd forgive the nasty things I'd said. Then I heard that she'd already left the camp."

"Personally, I've no idea, or how much this has hurt her. People do argue, particularly in families of different generations, so she may have calmed down by the time she gets back. Let's hope she has, or we find Sherry and she can help patch things up between you two."

Chapter 32

Standing in a small queue at reception on the ship, it was soon Karen's turn. She handed them a passport and the email conformation of the cabin along with a credit card to be logged so she could purchase the many extras around the ship without keep swiping her card.

The woman looked at them all, typed in the details on her computer and handed her back the passport and credit card, along with a key card. "Your cabin's on the second deck towards the rear of the ship, Miss Marshall. Use your key card for any purchases on board. Enjoy your cruise."

Karen nodded and headed off. As usual, when travelling alone, she would revert to her birth name, never using her title.

The cabin was an inside one, with no window. It had been all that was left at such short notice. She wasn't bothered, the way she felt, after recent weeks, she didn't want to be the centre of attention, walking around as a passenger with a suite of rooms and dining at the captain's table. Karen only ever wanted the family life she had when living at home. Then, she'd go to church, help out in the fundraising at the fetes. Hang around with her friends with a treat for her birthday to go out for dinner with her parents and sister. This was all she ever wanted, and to have a man who loved her and children of her own. Her abduction killed that, she'd come home a different girl, a girl that had killed indiscriminately and with a huge chip on her shoulder. She'd been terrified that if she admitted what she'd done, the authorities would put her in prison for the rest of her life, so she built an impenetrable wall around herself, but it had backfired, in that whenever she let it down even slightly to allow a man into her life, he'd get killed, or sell her down the river. She knew she was alone, her parents gone, her sister wanting nothing to do with her. All her dreams of a family life were now pointless, she'd moved on, her values, the way she lived, even her sex life - if she could call it that - was so far away from what she wanted, it hurt at times even thinking about it.

After unpacking and attending the lifeboat drill, Karen was leaning on the rail, gazing at the many buildings along the shoreline, not really seeing them. She didn't even know why she was here, living out of a suitcase, queuing for food and sitting down to dine at night with strangers probing her for who she was and where she came from. Not that they'd be interested, it was more to open up a conversation, to boast that this was their umpteenth cruise and nothing like the last, or how many places they had been to. Other times she'd be wandering around aimlessly, with people looking at her wondering why she was alone. Why she'd let Stanley push her into taking a holiday, Karen couldn't imagine. Even after her parents' death and the weeks that followed, when she was out of Unit T, trying to find her sister, at least her life had a purpose. Now she'd lost Sherry and Ally, besides being on a ship for ten days with no one to talk to or have a laugh with. As it was, everywhere she looked there were couples or families, obviously excited about the prospect of the fun time that lay ahead.

For Karen this was no longer her world. Her world

was prostitution, violence and a constant battle to remain one step ahead and stay alive. She'd even considered asking Dominick to join her on this break, but why? She didn't play happy families any more, he'd be here just for someone to spend the night with; except, although the bruising to her body had all but disappeared, she was still experiencing pain with certain movements. So the last thing she wanted was to be rolling around on a bed. Besides, most men that had meant something in her life were dead and as proved with Ally, she wasn't capable of bringing up a child, even after someone had already done the hard bit.

***

The following day, at half-past six in the morning, Karen was already in the pool, attempting to do her usual twenty lengths. The swim at first gave her pain, but she soon got used to it. Now most of the time her head would be below the water, with hardly a splash as each arm propelled her forward, determined to complete her swim. At twenty lengths, she came to a halt, before swimming to the steps. A man offered his hand as she began to climb out. She accepted his offer gratefully, she felt exhausted.

"Thank you. I think I'm a little rusty, that was hard," she said, walking to a sunbed close by and picking up her towel.

"For someone rusty, I must say you didn't look like you were struggling, powering through the lengths like you did. Do you usually swim for a team?" he asked.

Karen looked at the man. In his forties, tall and quite muscular, he was also wearing a swimming costume. She began rubbing herself down "No, I do it for exercise.

At this time the pools deserted, so you're not constantly checking if you're likely to crash into someone."

"Very wise, I do the same. You should sit down for a moment, get your breath back. Can I fetch you a coffee? They've just put out the cups."

"No thank you. I'm off for a shower, then breakfast."

"Go on, let me tempt you with a very small cup of coffee. I promise it won't spoil your breakfast and you really look as if you need to catch your breath."

She gave a weak smile. "You're right, I do, half a cup will be fine."

He was soon back. Karen had sat down at one of the small round tables, behind the sunloungers. She was combing her hair.

"Let me introduce myself. The name's Todd Scott, I'm from New York," he said, offering his hand, after placing two coffees on the table.

She shook it, he had a firm handshake. "Karen Marshall, I'm from the UK."

"You are?" he asked, raising his eyebrows slightly. "You have a slight French accent, I expected you to say France. Were you born in France?"

"No, the UK. I work in France and can speak French fluently, with a little German and a smattering of phrases in other languages."

"Then you have the best of both worlds - the English accent, with the hint of French, making your speech sound very sexy. But tell me, with you speaking many languages, do you travel in your job?"

Karen gave the hint of a smile. "I do, but it's not

much fun. It's a lot of packing and unpacking in hotels. Then for a woman, staying in areas where you're not too certain about and going out alone, you end up at the hotel bar, getting funny looks, or men trying to pick you up all the time. Anyway, I'm away from work and want to forget it."

"I like the attitude, too many people take their work home with them. I know we've just begun, but are you enjoying the cruise?"

"Yes, I like the ship, particularly not having the need to dress for dinner, I intend to use the Lido self-serve all the time."

"So you don't want to dine posh, I thought that was part of the cruising experience?"

Karen shrugged. "When your cabin's inside, windowless and very small. It doesn't get priority for anything. Last night I was given my place on a table of eight for the late sitting. It was right next to the door waiters were coming in and out of, carrying trays. I'd only been in there for fifteen minutes before I nearly had a complete tray spilt all over me, besides constantly pushing past each other and knocking me. Then the waiter forgot my order, after serving everyone else on the table, he stood there like some idiot asking me what I ordered. I got up and walked out. At least in the Lido, I get to put what I want on my plate, even sit by a window. I may do the gala dinner, that's if my seat's still vacant."

Todd wanted to make a comment, but instead changed the subject. "I must admit it doesn't sound a very good start for your holiday. Did you go to the opening show?"

"I did, not that I'm into Broadway shows, they're filled with the sort of songs my parents would listen to from musicals. Most twenty plus years old, trundled out every year by amateur theatrical groups in the UK. Did you?"

"No, living in New York, I've seen the real thing, with all the great names. It never sounds the same with amateurs. So I sat outside for a while, then ended up in the bar, listening to the late-night comedian. I was tempted to go to the nightclub, but it had been a long journey coming to the ship, I decided against it. How about you?"

She shook her head. "It's not a place I'd go to on my own. I'd end up standing at the bar, feeling conspicuous with people looking at me."

"Men are the same you know. But we are expected to go and talk to a female. That can be harder than standing there like you'd be doing."

Karen smiled. "Put that way, I suppose it might be." She finished off the coffee. "Thank you for the coffee, you were right, I needed it. I should go," she said, at the same time standing.

Todd also stood up. "It's been an interesting conversation for seven in the morning. But seriously, Karen. I'm with two other guys, this is our vacation. We can't have you sitting in your cabin and not going to the nightclub because you're on your own. We'll always end up there by eleven every night, come and join us, no ties, no catch, just be with us, so you don't feel you're alone. At least you'll have a good end to your day, a few drinks, maybe even get offers from the single men around, to go on the dance floor and let your hair down."

She looked at him for a moment. "I'll not promise, but thank you for asking and perhaps I'll see you all in there."

"Not, perhaps, just come, Karen, it's your holiday. When the kids have gone to bed, the night belongs to the adults," he urged.

She gave him a smile. "Maybe," she replied and sauntered off. He watched her walk away. This was a woman at ease with herself, which made you immediately relaxed in her company. Maybe it was because she came across as a weak and nervous female, needing a man to look after her, men would always want to do just that. He knew she wasn't. Neither would she bat an eye at walking alone into a nightclub. This was Karen Harris of Unit T, who held one of the highest awards in his country, the Congressional Medal of Honour, given her by the president - she was no fool, besides being a very capable covert operator.

After Karen left, Todd made his way back to his cabin. Picking the telephone handset up, he dialled another cabin. "Get yourself in here, Johnny," he said after someone answered.

Johnny came through. "What is it?"

"Would you believe I went for my usual swim and had just dried myself ready to leave, when Karen Harris appeared."

"Why was she around at that time?"

"The same as me, using the pool."

"Did you speak to her?"

"I did more than that, we sat down and had a coffee."

Johnny frowned. "You were careful what you said to her? She's not stupid."

"I do know how to handle such a situation. It was only the usual talk you'd say to anyone you met on holiday."

"Did she give you any inkling as to why she's in the US?"

"No, nothing like that. But when she came out of the water, even with a one-piece swimsuit on, it was pretty obvious Karen's been knocked about somewhat. There are a few bruises on her body, still not completely disappeared. She also looked tired, didn't reject my offer to help her out of the pool. And then, her swimming initially was erratic, as if she was in pain, before it settled down. The reports coming back from the UK that it was her in the car crash in Ireland could be true. I asked her to join us in the nightclub, she didn't flatly refuse, so I think she will."

"Possibly. Send a report through, anyway. The bureau wants us to stick to her like glue, it seems they don't trust her motives, coming to the US and remaining downmarket. This woman's a multi-millionaire, and books a cabin you can't swing a cat in. Apparently she's done it before, taking a low-cost motel room. But that time she had a meeting with a trafficker, followed by rescuing a number of American girls abducted to be used in Europe, besides making one hell of a drug bust."

"Yes, I read the report. But that was on dry land, it's a bit different out at sea. You know, she's not even using the dining room, intending to go to the buffet in the Lido every night. That's bizarre for a woman used to being served, eating out in the best restaurants. I'd have thought she'd have booked the specialist restaurants, rather than serve herself."

"Well, whatever. As it is, we need to find out why she's here."

"Precisely, I'll give Joe a knock, then we'll go for breakfast and plan our surveillance rota. I'm beginning to like being part of surveillance on Karen, if we get to go on cruises. Even if the short notice meant we're accommodated in crew cabins. At least we get to eat in the main restaurant."

Chapter 33

The third man Sherry had been with that day, pushed her off him after he finally finished. She'd been on the ship for ten days, locked in a cabin, her meals brought to her, besides being taken to the washroom twice a day. The first morning, she'd been visited by the ship's captain and told in no uncertain terms that she'd be expected to service the crew while she was on the ship. For Sherry there had been no option when, after her objections that she wasn't a prostitute, he'd just laughed and agreed with her. After all, he told her, with a snigger, she wasn't in a position to charge anyway. Then his mood had changed, telling her to agree, or he'd have her whipped, then tied down. It was her choice.

"You leave later tonight, I'm the last man. He pulled out a small bundle of notes. The crew had a collection, you earned twenty-five dollars while you've been aboard," he told her with a grin. "That's less than fifty cents for a shag, you'd not make a living at it, love," he mocked.

Sherry didn't rise to his comment. Karen had told her in the past, do what they want of you, never risk being injured for your pride. That way, when the time came to make your escape, you'd be in a condition to do just that.

***

It was nearly five hours later when she heard the chain of the anchor winding down. Twenty minutes after that, a crew member came into her cabin with a dress and sandals.

"Get yourself dressed, it's time to go," he told her.

"Where am I going?"

"How the fuck do I know, there's a rowing boat arrived to take you."

"What country are we in?"

"We're not, the ships off the coast of Ghana. After you're taken off, we carry on to Cape Town."

Nothing more was said, the man grabbed her arm and was pushing her ahead of him, along the corridor and outside.

The captain came up to her. He grabbed her hair and yanked her head back, his face inches from hers. "You were well looked after, had a cabin of your own. Tell anyone any different and your new owner will leave you with his men. Understand?"

"Yes."

"That's sensible, have a good life girl, shag well for him and keep him happy, he'll look after you. Otherwise, after his men have used you, he'll feed you to his dogs. Now get down the rope ladder."

Soon Sherry was sitting in a rowing boat; four men were rowing hard towards the coastline. She was very despondent. Her only means of escape now was to get a message out to tell Karen where she was. How she could manage that, or even know where she was actually being held, Sherry had no idea. This time, she had the belief there would be no escape, or rescue. Her only glimmer of light was that in the past Karen had been in the same situation and she'd got out. Sherry hoped she was strong enough to follow in Karen's footsteps.

***

After leaving the rowing boat she was put in the back of a

Land Rover. It took the rest of the day before they turned into a compound. There were men with guns everywhere, open backed lorries filled with sacks and a number of parked cars. The vehicle went around the back of the main house and she was taken inside by a man who'd come out of a door to meet them.

Sherry and the man went up some back stairs, through a door onto a corridor. This seemed to run the length of the house, with doors off it all along. Urged down the corridor, he pushed her into a room.

"This is your room, the bathrooms through that door. Food will be brought, then settle down for the night. I don't want reports of you wandering around the house. Understand?"

"Yes, I'll not move out of here."

"That's good. Tomorrow, select a dress from the wardrobe and put it on. Sometime in the afternoon I'll come and fetch you to see Fasido." He hesitated. "If he likes you, this will be your room."

"If he doesn't, what then?" she asked meekly.

"Then you're fucked, so you'd better make sure he does, or you will end up in the low building you can see from your window. It's where the workers live. You'll be servicing twenty to thirty a day, till you're burnt out. Then, don't bother to ask what happens next, it offers no future." With those chilling words he left her alone.

Although, she noticed he hadn't bothered to lock the door. 'Why should he,' she thought. 'Where could I go?'

***

The following day, in the late afternoon, Sherry selected

a figure-hugging dress that ended a few inches above the knee, with high heels, hoping he'd find her attractive dressed that way. The man she'd met the day before took her downstairs into a large lounge. Sitting around were a number of men. A dark-skinned man, over six feet and well built, wearing a t-shirt and trousers, came up to her. He looked at Sherry, then a photograph he held in his hand. Sherry was nervous, seeing the way he initially looked at her; now, the longer she stood there, the more nervous she became. It was obvious from his mannerisms that he didn't want her.

"What is this Baba, I have paid thirty thousand for a child? She is not the woman Issac told me was coming," he demanded with obvious annoyance.

Sherry had caught a glimpse of the photo he held, she immediately recognised it as Karen. Now she was really scared, Fasido was close to rejecting her.

"I was told the woman you were to receive escaped the car she travelled in. Issac assured me this woman was younger, more attractive and would have cost far more."

Fasido looked annoyed. "Issac does not tell me what I will like, he supplies what I agree to buy. Has payment been made?"

"It has, that was the agreement once she boarded the ship."

"Then you call him, tell him I want the money returned. Take this woman away."

"I can't."

"You can't what?"

"Have Issac return our money, he's dead. Bile from the Murphy gang in Ireland called. He dealt a lot with Issac in the past. He told me they know the woman you paid for. Bile also said they have a plan to take her once more, but they'd want forty thousand for her."

"You are telling me I need to pay eighty thousand for the woman? Shit, you tell Bile from me, he'll get ten and like it, or we do no more business with them. Now leave me and take this girl with you."

Sherry was literally shaking, terrified of being handed over to his men, after what Baba had told her would happen. "Can I buy my freedom, if you don't want me?" she blurted out.

He looked at her, with interest. "You have money?"

"I have. It was my inheritance after my mother died. I never knew my dad."

"How much is this inheritance of yours?"

"Twenty-five thousand pounds. If you have a Barclays bank in this country, I could get it transferred."

"You think she tells the truth, Baba?"

He shrugged. "If she doesn't pay, then I'll slit her throat. We've nothing to lose."

Fasido turned to a man sitting on a settee, playing on a laptop computer. "Stop fucking about with games and tell me, is there such a bank called Barclays in Ghana?"

The man pressed a few keys and looked up. "There's one in Kumasi."

He stood for a few minutes. "How will you get your money?" he asked Sherry.

"I don't have my bank card, it's at home, but I share a flat with a girl. She could take my card, if I give her my pin number she can have the money transferred to the Barclays here."

Fasido again looked towards the man with the computer. "That is possible?"

"If the girl had the card and pin, maybe with a few personal details, such as age, date of birth. Possibly even the last couple of transactions on her current account. Then yes, it could be done very easily."

"Take her to her room," Fasido shouted at another man. "You girl, I will have a telephone brought, you call this flatmate of yours. Have her transfer the money. Once it is there, Baba will take you to Kumasi. You give him the money and you can walk away. Remember, we have many friends in Kumasi, I will ensure a few are in that bank, so try to be clever and tell the people in the bank what is happening, my friends will hear and drag you out of that branch if necessary. You will be sold. Have no doubt, many will pay good money for a white woman. They like to demean them, have them crawl at their feet. You do not want that, do you?"

Sherry shook her head.

"Of course you don't. Pay the money girl, arrange for your own transport home after Baba leaves you. I wouldn't hang about in Kumasi once your protection with Baba is gone, it is not the place for a white girl."

"Thank you, I will get you every penny. I just want to go home."

He nodded. "Take her away."

Once Sherry had left the room, Fasido sat down with obvious satisfaction. "Seems to be our lucky day, Baba. We get most of our money back, and you, once she's handed over the money, take her to Dillo's sale room and have him put her up for auction. She should fetch at

254

least twenty thou, maybe even more."

"I'll do that, you want me to still call Bile?"

"I do, tell him ten thou and get me my woman."

Chapter 34

The telephone in Karen's cabin began to ring. She turned over and looked at her watch, it was just after five in the morning.

"Hello," she said, picking up the telephone.

"We're sorry to be calling you at this time Miss Marshall. There is an international call for you. The caller gave his name as Stanley and said you'd know who he was. He also said it was urgent."

Karen smiled, she knew it was too much to believe they'd leave her alone. "Please put him through."

"Karen, you don't know how difficult it's been to contact you."

"No, I don't, unless you tell me. But remember, it was you who told me to go on holiday, this was all I could find. So what do you want me for, Stanley?"

"You know we're holding the mobile you use for informers to contact you?"

"I do, I left it with you, so that one of the females in your intelligence unit could answer, pretending to be me. Have you had a call?"

"We have. It was Sherry, but calling herself Sam. I think she realised it wasn't you who answered, but still called the woman Karen. She wanted you to take her bank card to the bank, with her pin number which she gave over the phone, and have all her inheritance, twenty-five thousand pounds, transferred to Barclays international branch office in Kumasi, Ghana, so she can get access to it. My intelligence woman wanted to know why and all the usual things you'd ask your friend, but Sherry told her she'd an investment too good to pass over and she must promise to do it. She finally agreed, telling Sherry to call back the next day so she could give her information on how to draw it out. We now know where she is, Karen. I've already begun to dispatch a total of ten Unit T soldiers, in civilian clothes, to Kumasi. They land at the international airport tomorrow and the following day. I believe, although she can't tell us, she's done a deal to buy her freedom. They can't be trusted out there, but they will do nothing until they have the money. We'll make sure she can't get at it, without her going to the bank with them. Our soldiers will be there, have no doubt, Karen."

"Sherry did well to get in touch with us, Stanley. It also gives us a country and maybe a location if she doesn't turn up, or something unforeseen happens. I've a mind to involve the local police, but as we don't know who we're dealing with, or what the real situation is that she's in, we'll hold off until we have more information. Ghana is similar to Nigeria, full of scam merchants, using the internet to extract money from gullible people. I agree she's probably trying to buy her freedom, saying she got twenty-five thousand saved. They'd accept that, the amount is low enough to believe her, but still an attractive sum. Either way, they'll take her money and not let her leave."

"I agree. But she'll suspect that herself, so will be relying on us to pull her out. I was thinking that a bank draft, with photographic identity of the person collecting it required, would force them to bring her to the bank."

"Good thinking, it might work. In the meantime, before she goes to the bank, concentrate your search for this man, Fasido, in Ghana, see what you can find out. We need to be in a position to find him very quickly, if Sherry doesn't come to the branch."

"I'm on it as we speak, Karen. I will keep you abreast of all that's happening."

"Very well, let's keep our fingers crossed that we can extract her."

"So how is your holiday going then?"

"You were right, it's doing me good, Stanley. I didn't realise just how much the last weeks have taken out on me. I'm up to my twenty lengths again with ease. Spent lots of time in the gym. Even the bruising has all but gone and I've a tan again. The injury to my wrist is virtually healed as well."

"This all sounds positive, Karen. How about your social life? Are you finding people to spend time with?"

"I've made a few friends on board and joined up with two girls. We've been on a couple of excursions. To tell you the truth, Stanley, I've shied away from any sort of relationship. The last operation took a lot out of me, so I just want to chill and I'm happy with my own company. Oh, the CIA are here as well. You didn't tell them I was coming to the US did you?"

"No, but they would pick up your name, along with your visa on their computer. So I'm not surprised. How do you know it's them?"

"Believe me, Stanley, I know when I'm being followed by government personnel. I've even spoken to one three times now, he always seems to be around the pool when I go for an early swim. To tell you the truth, it's quite comforting. I'm not armed, and don't have any means of protection, so I'm not put out by them being around."

"Well, so long as you are happy with that, I'll leave you to it. If you're in your cabin at eight tonight, I'll update you. If I miss you, call me when you're free."

"The ship's on New Orleans time, Stanley, I'm six hours behind so it's five o'clock in the morning now. Can you call at seven, your time, I'll be back in here from lunch?"

"Sorry Karen, that was my mistake. I'll let you sleep."

After he cut off, Karen lay there for a while. She felt relieved; at least they had a location for Sherry. Ghana was one country they would never have thought of her ending up in. Turning over, she closed her eyes; her morning swim might be a little late today, if she didn't wake up. That would confuse the CIA.

Chapter 35

Baba came into Sherry's room. She was sitting on the side of the bed, combing her hair.

"You have heard back from your friend, I hear?"

"Yes, I called last night, while the man who was on the computer listened in. He nodded his agreement to the arrangement."

"And what is this arrangement?"

"She told me she'd been able to arrange the money, but the bank wanted ID. They have agreed after discussion, that a photo and a sample of my signature would be faxed to the bank. If the photo and the signature match, they will hand me the draft."

"I see. When will this draft be there?"

"Tomorrow, so I was told."

"Then we will leave in the morning. You are a lucky girl. After Fasido rejected you, if you'd not offered money to him for your release, you'd be working now."

"I know, I've my family to thank for leaving me the money."

"Then get some rest, you will be woken at five."

***

The journey to Kumasi was slow. The roads were packed with lorries and carts, often pulled by men, or donkeys. Inside their vehicle, the air conditioning was no longer working, so the heat was unbearable.

Finally, they arrived; Baba pulled into the courtyard of a house. "We eat here. Come with me, speak only if you're spoken to directly."

Sherry was surprised - inside, the place was

packed. Men were sitting around, some with plates of food in front of them, others smoking and talking between themselves.

A man came up to Baba with his arms outstretched. "Baba, welcome to my house. Please come this way."

"It is good of you to invite me, Dillo. This is the girl I called you about. You have somewhere for her to eat, so you and I may talk in private?"

"Of course. I will show you to your table, then I will take her."

After Sherry had been taken into a back room and given food, Dillo rejoined Baba.

"How is Fasido, we haven't seen him at the sales for some time?" Dillo asked, sitting down himself.

"He's busy, demand for cocaine has reached very high levels. It is fuelled by a percentage being intercepted. The dealers are taking the hit. Of course, it doesn't affect our profits."

"Yes, I can understand. In a way I presume it is good so much is found?"

Baba lowered his voice. "Essential. While the authorities are congratulating themselves on finding a small amount, the larger shipments running alongside are completely missed."

"The girl you have brought, what time will she be available for sale?"

"We have an appointment first. She will be back here at five tonight. Is that in order?"

"It is, and gives me enough time to prepare her for the final sale of the day."

"The payment, that will be ready when I come?"

261

"Of course."

At that moment two women brought the food.

"Ah, at last, it is time to eat," Dillo exclaimed, spreading his hands slightly in a gesture appreciation.

***

Sherry was back in the car with Baba.

"You enjoyed your food?" he asked.

"Yes, thank you. It was really nice."

"I have arranged we stay overnight with Dillo, after you've been to the bank. I suggest I take you to the British Embassy when they open in the morning. They will, I presume, arrange all the necessary documentation for you to leave the country."

"That's good of you, Baba. Thank you. I don't suppose you could give me a little money, I've nothing and I'd like something in my pocket?"

"I will make sure you have sufficient, providing you tell the embassy that you don't know where you were taken, or the names of your abductors. I'll remind you we have extensive contacts in the UK. Start opening your mouth, it will get back to us and we will send someone to shut you up."

"I just want to go home and live a normal life. I'm not interested in making complaints, or being a witness in any trial."

"Very wise, put it down to experience."

The roads around the bank's location were very busy, with Baba having difficulty in finding a parking place. Eventually, fifteen minutes late for the appointment, they were inside the bank. After introducing herself, Sherry, followed by Baba, was taken into a small office.

The manager opened a DHL package, taking out a photograph of Sherry and a sheet of paper. He looked at Sherry for a moment. Satisfied it was her, he made a note in his diary.

"Perhaps, Miss West you can sign your name on this piece of paper?" he asked, sliding a plain sheet across to her. The name Sam, short for Samantha West had been given her to use, rather than Malloy, just in case the trafficker holding Karen had made the connection.

Sherry signed it, passing the sheet back to him.

Again he compared it to the signature on the sheet that had come with the photograph of her.

"This all seems in order. You just need to give me the name of the recipient and sign for the bank draft, then you are finished," he told her.

Minutes later, they left the bank.

"I couldn't believe it was so easy," Sherry commented, after Baba had taken the draft off her, once they left the bank. "So I'm free now?"

"Of course. Once back at Dillo's, I'll call Fasido, tell him you have paid and tomorrow we go our own ways."

However, Sherry was confused. Where was Karen, or even Unit T? They must know she was here and needed help? All the time she'd been at the bank, then outside afterwards, she'd expected them to step in and rescue her. But there were no soldiers inside the bank, or around outside it, that she'd recognised from the unit.

Baba had told Dillo earlier, he'd be back by five, and it was only a little after that time that they turned back into the courtyard.

Dillo was waiting, opening Sherry's door. "Come with me, I expect you'd like a shower and clean clothes, after today?" he told her.

"I would, thank you for offering," she replied, still more than confused as to why the car hadn't been stopped.

Minutes later Sherry was in a back room. While she was under the shower, unknown to her, someone came in and took her clothes. The water wasn't hot, just lukewarm, but she was glad to get the dust from the journey out of her hair. Coming out, Sherry stood there with a towel around her, confused as to why her clothes had been taken. However, a man came in, grabbed her arm and pulled her out of the room, Sherry stumbling after him. Soon she was in an office of sorts, with Dillo sitting behind the desk.

"You were naive, believing that handing money over to Baba would buy you your freedom. It doesn't, girl, he's sold you to me. Shortly you will be taken to the main lounge and put up for sale. Hold your head up high, show yourself off and maybe a single buyer looking for a companion will make a bid. Don't take my advice and it will be a brothel working you fifteen hours a day, seven days a week. Take her away, she's the sixth one on."

Sherry had no time to object or comment, again being dragged out of the office and into another room where a number of women were standing in a line. The man who brought her, took the towel Sherry had wrapped around her, leaving her naked, and left. Another man was already in the room, he held a short whip.

"You – get behind the last woman, or you'll feel my whip across your back," he shouted at Sherry, cracking the whip in the air to reinforce his demand.

Sherry stood quietly, tears trickling down her face. With no one coming, she could only assume they had missed her, or because of the heavy and chaotic traffic, the followers had lost sight of Baba's car? Neither thought was any comfort, although the last thing she expected was Dillo to be conducting people sales. She had all the time believed she'd be taken back to the compound and given to the workers, once Fasido was convinced he had drained her of all her savings, but she had been confident Karen would not let her down. Now that was not going to happen and she could end up anywhere.

Two more women had been brought in and were standing behind her, by the time she was first in the queue. Suddenly she heard clapping, then less than a minute later, she was taken through. Immediately weighed on small scales and pushed to the centre of a circle.

Buyers were invited to inspect her before bidding began. Then, just as they closed in around Sherry, everyone stopped what they were doing, unsure what was happening with shouting and the sound of whistles coming from outside; seconds later, police burst into the room, via its two entrances. Buyers were handcuffed and made to lie face down on the floor, even Dillo and Baba were brought in, they too were told to lie flat on the floor. A policeman gave Sherry a blanket to cover herself with.

Lieutenant Marsh of Unit T entered and came up to Sherry. "Are you alright, Sherry?"

She grinned. "I am. God, I thought you'd missed me?"

"No, we hadn't missed you, we couldn't go in at

the bank, it was too difficult. Karen had a change of plan after talking to the authorities and agreed to let the police handle it. Even so, we were right behind you. It suited the police to let Baba bring you back here. I agreed, it was an easier place to storm."

"Was that the only reason?" she asked.

"No. The authorities had been after Dillo for some time, but couldn't catch him running an actual auction. Now, with four buyers who had left with their purchases arrested, and you on the sale floor, they have enough to convict him. As for Baba, he will be charged with kidnapping, extortion and trafficking. He's been searched and the draft found in his pocket. He has no way out."

Sherry walked over to Baba and knelt down. "Just to let you know, Baba. I'm a Unit T soldier, they come for their own, no matter where they are in the world. Your own greed has brought you down. I'll also tell you this. No bank would hand over such a large amount of money the way they did with me, unless they had been told to by Unit T. Then, with a statement as to what happened to me, you can be very certain that you will be facing a considerable amount of time in prison."

He said nothing and Sherry walked away.

Chapter 36

Karen replaced the telephone handset onto its cradle on the bedside table. Stanley had just called to tell her Sherry was safe and on her way back to the unit. She had also told Stanley that Sherry was never to go on a covert operation again, no matter what the reason was. He of course agreed.

He then broached the subject of Ally. "The girl is absolutely devastated, Karen. The school's told me she can't work or concentrate and spends a great deal of time alone, wandering in the forest," he told her.

"I'm sorry, Stanley, but that's not my problem anymore. Ally needs to have a little more loyalty and know when to keep her mouth shut. Not listen to stupid remarks by other children, even more believe them. God knows what she's been saying to Hazel's parents to have them offer her a place to stay, without them even contacting me. So, talk to the trauma personnel we use for the girls brought in, they will have to sort her out. I can't."

With those cold words, Karen dismissed more conversation about Ally and the call was brought to an end.

**

Tonight was the gala dinner night. Karen had decided to go to the main dining room. She was wearing the only evening dress she had with her, Karen wandered into the dining room, however the seat she'd been allocated was now occupied.

A waiter came up to her. "You look lost Madam."

"Not lost exactly, someone's in my seat."

He frowned, a little confused, and asked for her

room number, taking her back to the entrance to look at the allocation list.

"Ah yes, Miss Marshall from room 203," he began in a voice that sounded as if he was talking to a naughty child. "You haven't been to the dining groom since you decided not to stay for dinner on your first night."

"Would you, stuck in a seat being pushed all the time by waiters rushing to serve their tables. Besides having your order forgotten and nearly got someone's dinner spilt all over you?"

"I think perhaps that is a little bit of an exaggeration, madam. The person who has your seat hasn't complained of such things happening to them. As it is, with you not coming to dinner it left two empty spaces, so a couple has been moved from the early to late dining. There is no seat for you, the sitting is full."

Karen shrugged. "That's not my problem, it's yours. I'm entitled to a seat, even if I don't use it every day. Besides, you had no right to give it to someone else without at least asking," she told him in no uncertain words.

"Please wait here, madam," he answered.

At that moment Todd, along with Johnny entered the dining room. "Karen, you've decided to abandon the Lido tonight then?"

"I did, but it seems I'm back there again. They gave my seat away," she said, then smiled. "Mind you, the way I'm being talked to by the waiter, if I got a seat he'd probably pour the soup over me."

"We'll see about that," he said.

"Todd, forget it, I'm perfectly happy with the

Lido, believe me."

"Don't you move. In fact, Johnny, make sure she doesn't. If a guest all the way from England chooses to be waited on for a change and gets refused, I'll have something to say." Leaving Karen with Johnny, he went directly to the head waiter, who was talking to the waiter who'd told Karen there was no space. They talked for a short time, then the head waiter came over to Karen.

"I'm sorry, madam. The waiter was incorrect, it is our policy to accommodate all our guests' preference in dining. If you give me a moment, I will take you to your table."

Karen glanced at Todd, who just gave her a hint of a smile, before he turned and made for his own table.

"Would you come this way, madam," the head waiter asked, quickly returning.

The next minute she was standing at a table hosted by an officer, where a place had been hastily laid out.

"Welcome, please join us," the officer said, standing and embracing Karen, kissing her on each cheek.

Karen gave him a weak smile, she'd not expected to be sitting at an officers table. Already embarrassed over the way she was dressed. What she was wearing, she'd just thrown into her case from her wardrobe, not really intending to use it. Even her hair, although nicely styled and put up, was not how she'd have wanted to do it when sitting at this table, particularly after seeing the other eight guests, the women among them dressed to kill.

"Come and sit down, may I pour you some wine?" the officer asked.

Karen found herself seated by the side of the

officer, being introduced to all the guests using their Christian names. Karen also asked if they would use hers.

After small talk, where she found the officer was head of engineering, the conversation at the table was directed more towards her.

"So, Karen, why don't you enlighten us all as to what you do for a living and of course, where you live?" the officer asked.

She smiled slightly and sighed. "I think you already know who I am and what I do. Maybe after your head waiter talked to Todd?"

He didn't flinch, remaining in control. "You of course are correct, we had no idea such a famous and important person was on-board our ship. That was remiss of us and I apologise for not acknowledging you sooner. May I introduce you officially?"

The rest of the guests were now looking at Karen, wondering who this missing guest really was.

"I don't have a problem with that," Karen replied. After all, with one day left at sea, arriving in New Orleans the following morning, Karen no longer considered her holiday to have any risk.

"Then my fellow guests, we are very fortunate to have with us tonight, Lady Karen Harris, Commander of Unit T in Europe."

"You're Lady Harris?" a lady asked, confused. "Why didn't you recognise her Malcolm? You were telling us only yesterday how well you knew her?"

Karen could see how embarrassed Malcolm was becoming. She knew he didn't know her and was typically doing what people do, maybe to boost their standing among a number of others, by claiming he knew famous people.

"I asked Malcolm not to mention I was on board. It's for my security. I'm entitled to a holiday like everyone else, so I often go under the radar so to speak, and become the same as every other traveller. I'd also be more than happy if you carried on calling me Karen tonight and not by my title."

Everyone seemed satisfied with this explanation, now curtailed when the first course arrived.

Following dinner, the party retired to reserve tables in the main lounge, for the floor show to come a little later.

Malcolm, the man she'd saved from embarrassment, took the seat next to Karen, his voice low. "I really appreciate what you did for me Karen. It was stupid and I should have been exposed for what I'd said. Mother, warned me only last week, lies can often bite you in the bum. It very nearly did for me tonight."

"Don't worry about it, Malcolm. I'd already noticed a few of them are quite snobbish, more interested in one-upmanship. I bet it was nice to pull them down a little?"

"It was, believe me. After ten days in the company of that lot you were like a breath of fresh air. So how did you end up on our table?"

"I'd been using the self-service, rather than the dining room, so they'd given my seat away. Was the officer with you all the time?"

"No, he like you, only joined us tonight. But you must join me for a drink in the nightclub later as a thank

271

you? It's very nearly the end of the cruise, you should let your hair down."

She looked at Malcolm for a moment. He looked around thirty-five, slightly overweight, with black hair and steely grey eyes. Karen smiled. "You're right, why not, I'd love to join you. When this floor show is over, I'll go and change into something more appropriate and be there around twelve."

At quarter to twelve, Karen was in her cabin. She had got rid of her stockings and changed into tight trousers, slightly flared at the bottom, and a light open-top blouse, finishing off with high heeled shoes.

***

By half past one in the morning. Karen and Malcolm had spent most of their time together on the dance floor. They got on well; he could also dance, his enthusiasm washing over onto her. Now they had left the club and were making their way back to the cabins along the deck. He was holding her hand, which Karen didn't object to. There were a few couples doing the same thing.

Malcolm stopped, leaning on the rail, slipping his arm around her waist.

"I wish I'd met you at the beginning of this cruise, you are fun to be with, Karen. I've enjoyed tonight."

"That's a holiday for you, Malcolm. At least this way we've had a good end to the cruise."

"You are right, besides, you'd have been very frustrated with me, having my mother around all the time, if we'd met sooner."

They fell silent, then he pulled her closer; she turned to face him, they looked at each other in the light of the moon for a moment, then he kissed her on the lips. Karen lifted her arms and put them around him, they kissed long and passionately.

They broke away. "You're cold, Karen, I can feel you shivering. I'll take you back to your cabin."

She didn't refuse, it was cold with a strong breeze. Soon they were both standing outside her door.

He kissed her gently once more. "Thank you for a great night. I won't forget it for a long time."

Karen hesitated, Why not ask him in, she thought? After all, it was her holiday and she was pretty fed up. "You don't have to go. I've a mini bar inside, it's still very full, well, unused really."

"I'd like that," he replied softly.

They both went inside, he sat down, while Karen opened the small cabinet. "I can do all the spirits, or beer if you want it?"

"Vodka with any mixer would be good," he replied as he sat on the settee.

Karen joined him. She carried two tiny bottles of vodka, a can of orange and two glasses. While he held the glasses, she filled them up.

Malcolm took a sip, placed the glass on the side table and moved his arm around her. In minutes the drinks were forgotten, they were in a tight embrace, kissing passionately.

Karen pulled away. "I'll get out of these clothes, before I ruin them."

Once inside the bathroom, Karen stood for a moment, realising by telling him she was getting changed, she'd virtually invited him to stay. This was not what she'd have done in the past with any man on the first night. But Karen no longer cared about that. What little dignity she had left, had been well and truly knocked out of her. The values, she'd tried to live with, no longer seemed to matter, when she'd been forced to welcome to her bed any number of men. At least with Malcolm, it was her decision, no one was making money from it and she wanted him there.

Stripping quickly, she applied lubrication as if she was working in a brothel once more, before pulling tiny knickers on and her nightdress, which finished only slightly below her knickers. Karen tied her hair back, took a condom out her wash bag, then returned to the bedroom.

Malcolm, while Karen was in the bathroom, had looked around. He was surprised this famous and important woman could only afford the lowest grade cabin. Looking inside the wardrobe, he now understood why she was eating in the Lido during the cruise. The only items of clothing in the wardrobe consisted of the dress she'd worn for dinner, shorts and two pairs of jeans, apart from what she had on now for the nightclub. The stories in the paper talking about a jet-setting woman with a private aircraft began to seem a little hollow. Karen was obviously broke, had reverted to the only way she knew to make ends meet and was keeping up a cardboard facade that all was well. Except if she wanted him to keep her secret, she'd have to work for her supper.

He was leaning against the cabin wall, holding his drink when she came back in.

"That's better, have you finished your drink? There's plenty in the mini bar," she said.

274

"I've had enough, come here," he answered, putting down his drink.

As she came over to him, he put his arms around her waist, pulling Karen closer, before dropping them to her bottom. "You really look very sexy, Karen, dressed as you are. But a nightdress! Maybe later when you want to close your eyes; before that, why not show me just what you are capable of? I warn you, I'm demanding, very well endowed, expecting and getting a great deal out a woman," he said, at the same time grasping the hem of her nightdress, before drawing it up over her head. It left her standing there in her knickers.

Karen gave a hint of a smile. "I'm a little rusty on that side. I think I should be able to keep up with you, but I insist you use a condom," she said, pushing it into his hand. "As it is, I'm getting cold standing around virtually naked. What are you going to do about it?" she mocked.

He grinned. "Then I'll warm you up, first of all, with a good spanking."

"You wouldn't dare," she came back at him.

"I wouldn't, would I?" he answered, immediately grabbing her wrist, pulling her protesting, but weakly, to the bed. Sitting down on the edge, he was already urging her to bend over his knees. The next moment, he had her knickers clear of her bottom and was slapping her, not hard but in a playful way. Finally, happy she was more relaxed, he pushed her away, pulling his own t-shirt off and removing his trousers.

"Come on Karen, why are you still standing there? I suspect your claim that you're rusty is far from the truth? I've already noticed you've greased around your back entry. So it seems like you're wanting to be fucked both ways, are you? I'll not disappoint. Down on your knees and put the condom on for me and let's see how you perform, shall we?"

She never objected, in fact following what she'd done so many times, under duress; the light smacking of her bottom, making her relaxed, prepared to do all he wanted of her.

***

By the time Malcolm had finished and was collecting his clothes together, he had taken Karen in a number of positions, finishing up her backside, enjoying her objections when he forced himself up inside her. Karen, for her part, felt deflated, he'd treated her as if she was nothing, with no real affection and as he'd warned, demanding in everything he wanted, not letting her stop. This for Karen was like she'd known so many times with a man, when she'd been dumped in brothels, or raped by a captor. It was not the loving and affectionate experience she'd hoped it would be.

Now Malcolm was dressed, Karen still on the bed, her body covered with the sheet. He looked across at her. "You're not a bad fuck and know how to please a man. That's apart from a few lax habits that let you down. But it's obvious, in such a cabin, with a wardrobe with so little inside it, you've hit on hard times. It must be difficult, Karen, to have to revert to what you've fought against for so long, just to make ends meet, but you backed me at the dinning table, so your secret's safe with me." At the same time as he was talking, Malcolm had pulled out a bundle of notes, placing them on the side table. "I'm not short of a few bob, Karen. Maybe this is perhaps a little more than I'd usually pay, but I think you need it. You came up, the same as me, from nothing, we should stick together. If you're free tomorrow afternoon, call me on 6048 after breakfast. I'll book you for a two hour session. It'll be after lunch, I've plans for the night. Expect to work harder next time, I'm not in the habit of paying out my hard earned money, to a woman not prepared to give me all she's got, no matter who she is or her circumstances." Then he left the room.

Karen stared at the closed door, not knowing how to answer. He'd paid her for the sex, believing a woman who the papers claimed lived the life of a millionaire, being in this cabin, with few clothes, was in fact destitute and had reverted to prostitution to get by.

She climbed out of the bed in a daze, grabbed her nightdress off the floor, before going into the bathroom, washing herself down under the shower. Coming back into the bedroom, she picked the money up, counting the notes. He'd paid nearly three hundred pounds. Had she really fallen so far, that a man believed her invitation to come into her cabin was not because she liked him, it was because he believed she expected to be paid?

Karen lay in bed for over an hour, wide awake. She moved from indignation to laughter, even considering calling him tomorrow to see if he would pay her again. That didn't last long leaving her feeling embarrassed, dirty and very down, that she couldn't even have a night out with a man and finish off with a little sex, like thousands of women did, without the man thinking of her as a prostitute to be paid for.

Chapter 37

When Karen arrived home, the house was empty. The housekeeper had taken a few days off, not expecting her back; even Sherry wasn't there.

Leaving her bag in the bedroom, Karen wandered down to the kitchen, making coffee, taking it out to the pool with her. Changing in the changing room by the pool, Karen lay on a lounger in her bikini. She'd collected a document case from her office in the camp and brought it home; now settled, she began to go through the unit's current operations and their progress to date.

It was an hour later when she heard a car arrive, crunching on the gravel as it came up the drive.

Minutes later Sherry ran around the side of the house, flinging her arms around Karen.

"Did you have a great time on your hols?" she asked.

"Different, I can definitely say that. But it was a good rest, I needed it after the car crash, believe me."

"But did you get a holiday romance, sit under the stars gazing into each other's eyes, before making intense love?"

"I'm not sure that was my original intention, Sherry. Most of the holiday, I was still in pain, my body still pretty bruised. It took nearly all my holiday to look like I do now, after hours in the fitness and beauty centre."

"Well, you look your usual self now. Do you want a refill of your coffee cup? I'm going to fetch myself one after I've changed."

"Yes, thanks. Can you bring the biscuits? I'm

starving."

Once Sherry was back and settled, Karen wanted to know everything that had happened since she was taken by Tanny. After she'd finished, but avoiding admitting what she'd been forced to do on the ship, Karen said nothing for a time.

"You are sure he had a photo of me and said the Murphy's had a plan to take me?"

"Yes. He was pretty pissed off I'd been sent in your place. But to be rejected in preference to a woman he'd never met, and ten years older, I was pretty pissed off as well."

"It's my magnetic personality, Sherry. That's all I can say. Men want me. Well, not exactly want me, they want my body."

"I see - this woman everyone wants goes on a cruise, where all she's got to do all day is pose around, and doesn't even have an assignation. Hard to believe, Karen."

"Zip it, Sherry. As it is, you and I are going to fall out, if I hear that you are going behind my back, ignoring instructions to keep away from covert operations again. I don't want to hear excuses, like Foster had you covered all the way, or you believed I was in trouble and needed your help. You know from experience, the same as me, no matter how good the planning, it only takes one unforeseen action to wreck the plan completely. I really believed I'd lost you this time. In fact, if you'd not come up with what you did to alert us exactly where you were, Ghana would have been the last place we'd have looked."

"I'm sorry, it won't happen again," she answered

meekly.

"No, it won't and I mean that, Sherry. Anyway, it's forgotten, I'm having a swim, are you coming?"

"Course I am, that's the best thing about this house, you get to swim when you want."

***

Later the same night, after dinner, made by Sherry, they were sitting in the lounge. Sherry knew she had to broach the subject of Ally.

"What are you going to do about Ally, Karen?"

"Nothing, she's gone. The girl's sixteen and can do what she likes."

"You can't leave it at that."

"Leave it like what?" Karen asked.

"Except she's gone. You had a family, Karen. Didn't you argue with your mum and dad, maybe fight with your sister?"

"I suppose," she said, shrugging slightly with indifference.

"What's with the suppose? You bloody did, the same as every family has its ups and downs. They didn't throw you out on the street. They talked it through. Ally is our responsibility. You took her in, through good and bad. You don't stand over her and tell her to go, because you don't like what comes out of her mouth in times of stress."

"I don't think it's your place to tell me what I can and can't do in my own house, Sherry."

"Oh, I see. Because it's your house, I'm here under sufferance as well? Maybe finding myself homeless, like Ally, when I don't agree with what you do?"

"It's not the same. We often disagree, even fight.

280

I'm just saying it's not your place to comment on Ally and myself."

"We took Ally on together, Karen. Not you alone."

"Excuse me. I agreed to look after her until she was old enough to look after herself, not you. I also didn't agree to have someone tell me what I should and shouldn't do in my own house. It was the same as I did for you, when you had nowhere to go."

"You took me in?" she screamed at Karen. "Who the bloody hell do you think you are? I had a life, friends, enough money in the bank, even without what your charity obtained for me, to live without you, Karen. If you must know, I felt sorry for you, in fact, I put my life on hold to come here. You had nothing, no friends, a family that had virtually turned their backs on you. Face the bloody facts, Karen. Without me, without Ally and not even able to find yourself a man stupid enough to take you on, what have you got? Property, money? Big deal, you have nothing that matters in life and you know it."

Karen looked away, preferring to stare out through the conservatory windows, tears forming in her eyes. Neither girl said anything. Eventually Karen looked back at Sherry. "Well, at least I know now what you think of me. I thought we were friends, not that you were here just because you felt sorry for me. You may be prepared to live a lie, I'm not. I know I've very little in my life. I accept that. Even so, that is my personal business, not yours. You should find somewhere else to live. Take your time, I'll not be here. I'm going to London. From now on, our relationship must be that I'm your commander, nothing more."

"Then, once again, you want to run away and hide under a stone, not prepared to face reality?"

Karen was indignant at her suggestion. "Run away? I've nothing to run away from, nor hide under a stone for. This is me, my life. I'm not perfect and if I'm destined to be alone for the rest of my life, what can I do? I'm tired, my pathetic life played out so many times in my nightmares. You should have left me with the Nigerians and their memory destroying drug. Let them destroy my memories and give me a little peace. As it is, you didn't. So I still stumble from crisis to crisis, half the time not even knowing why I do it anymore. You asked if I had a man on the ship. Well, if you must know, I did. I liked him, we went back to my cabin and made love, that just turned out to be sex. Since when did I ever do that on a one-night stand? I used to have pride in myself. What little dignity I had is gone. Then to add insult to injury, he had the idea I was destitute, because all I could book at such short notice, was a cabin no one else wanted, after Ally refused to go with me." Karen hesitated. "He left nearly three hundred pounds on the dressing table, to pay me for the bloody sex we'd just had, believing I'd fallen so low that I needed to prostitute in order to survive. He even said he'd have me again the next day and left his cabin number."

Sherry grinned. "You took him up then, screwed another three hundred off the guy after such an insult?"

"No I bloody didn't. Neither did I go anywhere on the last night. I was hiding in my cabin, believing all the passengers saw me as a prostitute."

"Then you should have. Why don't you come

down finally from that pedestal you've put yourself on, become a real person once more, with all the warts."

"Yes, that's typical of you, wanting me to prostitute, so you can gloat. Well, I'm not and never will be one."

Sherry sniggered. "But you just said I should have left you with the Nigerians. They'd have given you nothing, at least this man paid you. Make your mind up, Karen, what you see yourself as. Like it or not, you took his money, did you give it back? If you didn't, then you are what you said you'd never be."

Karen said nothing, going over to the side table and pouring vodka into a glass. "You want a drink?"

"Providing it's not going on my final bill when I leave. Then why not."

Karen gave her a withering look. She filled two glasses and returned, handing Sherry her drink, then sat down again. "I'm bloody glad you're going. Since that degree you got, you think you're so bloody clever with your comments."

"Yes, well, at least I got a degree, you bailed school and never went on to university."

"I was abducted, if you'd forgotten?"

"You were, the same as me. How long was it, less than a month and you were home? The bloody school holidays hadn't even finished, what stopped you going on to college? I'll tell you, shall I? You came back to a press that placed you on a pedestal, believing you were some sort of female James Bond and you've never got off it. You look down on people like me. My mother an alcoholic, a prostitute, and I'm supposed to be grateful you gave me a roof over my head. Except never have I stooped so low as to actually accept money for sex and become like my mother."

"That wasn't very nice, I didn't ask, he just put it down and left. I even wanted to give it back, but bottled out when I finally found him. He was sitting with his mother."

"Maybe you're right, it wasn't. I'm sorry, Karen. You know both Ally and I love you for what we see you really are, not this pretend person. But even I know when it's time to let go. I'll look after Ally, believe me. I'll even knock the arrogance out of her, because like you, beneath this wall she's built around her, following the death of her parents and little sister, there is a thoughtful and loving girl trying to grow up alone, as I had to. I know what she's going through. I've often heard her cry herself to sleep at night, the same as I used to do. No one can comfort you, the memories don't go away. Alone at night, when the house is silent, your thoughts will take you back to the times you were happy. Then you want to die, not face another day without them. Ally can't take much more, if the people she trusts turn their backs on her. I for one won't, no matter what it costs me."

Karen stood, walking over to the window, carrying her drink. Sherry knew she always did that when she wanted to think.

Then she turned. "You're not going to look after Ally on your own. I was wrong, Sherry, I admit it. It was childish to take out my frustration about Foster placing you in danger, on a child - when it was obvious she was just as worried about you as I was, only showing it in a different way. Tell her to come home, we'll all sit down, sort out our differences and make this a better home."

"No, Karen. You will go and find her. You tell her she's still wanted and loved by us both. We're adults and will often argue, then make up. Ally isn't. She needs to feel you want her back, not have me go and collect her, telling her it's all sorted."

"But I have to go to London?" Karen said in her defence.

"No you don't, you want to go to London, there is a difference, Karen. You delay that; get down to the camp in the morning and find Ally. Because leave it to me and she won't come back. She'll be scared you'll throw her out again."

"Okay, I'll go, if that makes you feel better?"

"Why should I feel better? I'm not the one who threw her out. You did. Anyway, it's forgotten, but as you're standing, you can fill the glasses again."

***

At lunchtime the following day, Karen left her office at the camp, making her way over to the main dining room. Sherry told her this was the time Ally would be in there.

As usual, as she entered the dining room the soldiers came to attention, with the commander entering. Karen acknowledged them and they carried on, while the man in charge of the dining room approached.

"Good afternoon, Commander, are you dining?"

"Yes. Whatever the special is will be fine for me. Are the older children in their dining room yet?"

"No, the younger ones are just leaving, the older ones will be in shortly."

285

"When they come in, can you have Ally collect what she's having for dinner, then come and sit with me?"

"Of course. Your usual table is ready, I'll bring your dinner, you'd like a drink as well?"

"Coke, please."

Karen was part-way through her dinner when Ally approached nervously, carrying a tray with a burger, chips and a drink on it.

"I was told you wanted me to join you?" she said hesitantly.

"I do, Ally. Sit down, will you, we need to talk after you've finished your dinner."

Ally sat down, picking at her food.

"Ally, if you want to have junk food for dinner, the least you can do is eat it while it's hot. So is this what you're living on now?"

She nodded and carried on, eating faster.

Two apple pies and custard were brought, along with coffee for Karen, when they had both finished the main course.

"I don't really want apple pie," Alley said quietly.

"Well, I'd eat it if I were you. Sherry's cooking tonight, so don't build up your hopes of a full dinner. She never goes much more in depth than egg and chips."

Ally stared at Karen. "You're saying, you want me to come back?"

"Of course I do, Ally, the house seems empty without you. I'm sorry for what I said. It was stupid of me. I've no excuse, I'm supposed to be an adult and understand youngsters. I hold my hands up, I don't, treating them like adults, expecting maturity. As Sherry pointed out, families

286

argue, I did when I was your age, believing they were all against me, when I wanted my skirt shorter, not to take a coat, or be back by half ten. I wasn't shown the door. Grounded perhaps, with a cuff around the ear if I really got stroppy, but that was it. I want you to come home; let's start again and forget the last few days." She hesitated for a moment. "If you don't want to, I'll understand and accept your decision. Sherry has indicated she would find you both a house, so you can go with her, or return to England to stay with your grandparents. Sherry, unlike me, understands you more, you and her are on the same wavelength. You won't have to see me again."

Ally said nothing for a short time, fiddling with her sweet, taking a few mouthfuls. Then she looked at Karen. "Both Stanley and Sherry have told me I was wrong to speak like I did. I know that now and I'm deeply sorry if I hurt you. You've done a great deal for me and taken nothing in return," she looked down at her food. "I don't want to come back to your house, Karen. I'll always be the visitor, left wondering if the next time we argue, I'll be shown the door again. If Sherry will have me like you say she will, then that's what I want." She glanced at her watch. "I have to go back to the school," she added, and stood to walk away.

Karen followed, quickly standing and grasping Ally's arm. "Don't go just yet, Ally. You're with me, the school won't have a problem with that."

She looked at Karen. "That's my point. You have this belief you can break the rules when it's convenient for you, no one else. Why should you worry if my teacher is sitting ready to begin a lesson, but can't, because the great Karen Harris has deemed she should wait at your convenience, while you finished with her student? I could never understand why you let me stay. I couldn't decide if it was a token effort on your side to show you're doing your bit to house an orphan, or if I was a substitute for the loss of your sister. Not that it mattered, after showing me your true colours, reminding me I was in your house only while I towed the line and didn't rock the boat. So you live in your posh house, but don't expect me to ever go into it again. I hate it, the same as I hate you and all you stand for."

Karen sighed. "Then everything's my fault, is it? Maybe I'm not very good at showing my affection, Ally, the way I live has knocked most of that out of me. But believe this, I'd never have brought you into my home, if I didn't love you. Neither were you there as a sister substitute, or out of me having the need to show I was doing my bit, by taking in an orphan. I meet many girls and boys in the same or even worse situations than you. Most are destitute, living on the streets, often reverting to prostitution to survive. Their parents' dead, with no relatives to take them in. Yes, I take them off the streets, place them with a house mother, or in one of our many houses with others of the same age, but did I ever feel the need to bring them to my home? No, I didn't. You still had relatives who were prepared to give you a home. But when you stayed with me, while we sorted out you perpetrators, the house took on a new life with your youth, your enthusiasm. You made me want to come home, be a part of it, I'd even worry at times about you. Throw it in my face, convince yourself you were some sort of substitute, or it was all an ego trip on my part, if it makes you feel better, but don't place all the blame on me, it takes two to argue," she hesitated. "You'd better go, we can't have this teacher left waiting, can we, while you sort your life out. I bear no malice and like every child I help, I hope you find happiness in what you decide to do with your life," Karen added, then turned and walked away.

Ally watched her go. She'd already made her mind up to live with Sherry, convinced Karen couldn't be trusted to keep her word.

***

Sherry listened without comment while Karen told her what Ally had said. "That leaves you to decide on where you will go from here, Sherry, I can do no more," Karen finished.

"So you're just giving up. She's a child for god's sake, their emotions are all over the place, often just lashing out with no real thought."

Karen shrugged indifferently. "I don't think so. You didn't hear the way she spoke. The girl despises me. As it is, I've not got the time, or inclination to keep chasing after her. As far as I'm concerned, Ally is just another victim of the very real and dangerous game played out between myself and the traffickers. I have no interest in her anymore. Personally, I think you're a fool wanting to look after her. She has relatives, send her home. That girl will only throw it in your face when the going gets tough."

Sherry shrugged. "Even so, I must try."

"In that case, Ally has also managed to destroy our relationship. You can't live between two people who don't seem to be able to get on, Sherry. You've made your choice, so it's best you leave and find a place for you both. I've logged a flight plan for London, leaving at four this afternoon, and don't expect to be back until the end of the month. You should know by now that I'm not one for long goodbyes. So please don't be here when I return. It's better that way."

"What about my job as your personal assistant?"

"I'll have you re-assigned to a Dark Angel unit. It's probably best, you operate far better in a team."

"Then that's it? Will we still be friends?"

"We'll always be friends, Sherry. But will we socialise together, go to the coast and pose on the beach? Hardly, I'm getting too old for that sort of thing anyway, I no longer turn heads, even if I wanted to, which I don't. Besides, this is the army. You know an officer does not mix with the lower ranks, it can lead to discipline problems."

"What sort of friendship is that? By the way you're talking, it's hollow, pushing me away, the same as Ally."

Karen sighed. "Just what do you expect me to do, Sherry? I'm the bloody commanding officer. Like it or not, while I hold that rank, I don't have choices afforded to the lower ranks. I send people out that may never come back. I have to discipline people, the same as Lieutenant Foster, my second in command. It's bloody hard at the top, thankless and lonely. We managed to work within the rules and kept together, looking after each other. That can no longer happen. You and I must go our own way, you follow orders given by your senior officers. I oversee, can't have favourites. It's a game I play. A dangerous game. Where people get killed."

"If I can convince Ally, she's wrong and we should

try again, would you accept that?"

Karen stood, looking down at Sherry. She could see the hurt in her eyes, torn both ways. "I'll tell you what. You're suspended, pending my inquiries into the ill-conceived operation. I'll give you two months. Rent, buy a house, whatever and move in with Ally. At the end of the two months, we'll all sit down again and see if there is any future for us all. Personally, I think Ally will have what she wants with you, Sherry. A girl closer to her own age, away from me. Why should she compromise, it wouldn't make sense?"

Chapter 38

After a meeting with Stanley and her senior officers, where Karen had agreed a plan directed at taking down the Murphy gang, she flew to London, parked her aircraft, then took a scheduled flight to Dublin. On arrival, she took a taxi from outside the airport to a one star hotel close to Leeson Street. This area was well known for illegal brothels, shady massage parlours and street walkers. The main player controlling these operations, being the Murphy's. Karen intended to remain in the area and meet Odette Boyer, with a view to joining up with her in a covert operation.

Odette, for the operation, now called herself, Emily Sibley, complete with a new hairstyle as well as going blonde, heavier make-up and a deeply tanned body. She looked very different to the Odette who was here in Ireland before. However, although they were useful changes in her appearance that allowed her to be there and not be recognized, they would have little value to Karen. Odette's real strengths were in her skills of self-defence and combat. Along with these important parts of her training, she had an array of communication methods, with expertise in installing not only sophisticated listening devices, but also secret cameras. All this came about after being tricked by the Murphy gang into coming to Dublin on the pretext of a job, only to be forced into prostitution, before finally escaping, having shot Simon Murphy. She hated Mace, was determined to make her pay for what she had done to her. Karen accepted this, from her own time after she was first abducted, she too had a determination to bring down the people who had taken and abused her.

Now Odette, following her training in Unit T, was under cover, back in Dublin and had stumbled on an operation that involved girls as young as twelve. Karen's meeting at Unit T over her report now gave them the opportunity to take the gang down, providing they could tie the Murphy's directly to using girls of that age. Without that, and with prostitution legal in Ireland, the chances of finding women trafficked, as Odette was, would be very difficult and need an extensive covert operation. With this in mind, Karen decided she too would go in covertly to help Odette.

Once in the hotel, Karen, already with her hair dyed blonde, made her face up with long eyelashes and heavy eyeshadow, besides a slightly deeper shade of red lipstick than she'd normally use, and inserted brown contact lenses. For the times she went covert, often leading her into prostitution to keep her cover, even being captured at times and forced to prostitute, disguise made sense. Although, she hated the very thought of becoming what she'd fought against for so long. But to continue with the way she collected evidence, by infiltrating trafficker operations, she had to accept a prostitutes way of life, or walk away. Karen was not one to walk away, besides, what would she do, she'd no friends, no social life, in reality, no future that she could see beyond Unit T and the often twilight life of the covert operations she led. Completing her look with skimpy underwear, high heels and a dress that was tight, buttoned up the front and finished eight inches above the knee, Karen was ready. Pulling on a light coat slightly longer than her dress, she left the hotel.

This was an area she needed to blend in. So a short distance from the hotel, she unbuttoned her coat, revealing the sexy and short dress she wore, which was typical of the streetwalkers.

Entering a coffee bar, she looked around before seeing Odette, with a sandwich and coffee in front of her, sitting on her own.

"Emily," Karen called across the café.

Odette looked up, grinning from ear to ear. "Zoe, Dieu, je ne pensait qu'à vous et vous voici," (*Zoe, God I was only thinking about you and here you are)* she shouted back, but in French. At the same time she stood quickly and ran over to Karen, hugging her tightly. "Venez vous asseoir, laissez-moi vous prendre un café" (*Come and sit down, let me get you a coffee*), she said.

Karen took her coat off and sat down. Odette collected a coffee and came back to the table. Their conversation remained in French. They had no idea if they were being watched, so with them supposedly being French and Karen her friend from France, it was logical to speak the language they'd usually use, when together.

"I got your text to say you were coming, but didn't expect you until the end of the month," Odette said, carrying on with her sandwich.

"It was quiet in Paris, I got bored so I thought, what the hell, I may as well come and see what you're up to."

"Busy, I can tell you. Nothing like Paris, around a third of the money, but they don't expect, or get much."

"When you've finished, we should leave and you can show me around," Karen told her.

Once outside the cafe and walking the conversation changed, from casual - if anyone was listening and understood the language - to the operation.

"I like the look, Karen, you'll fit in well. As it is, besides me stumbling on them using schoolchildren in a back room of the illegal brothel where Eric Harper, my pimp, has me working, there's something else going on. They seem to be in a panic and already one girl has left. A man known as Bile is meeting with each girl, I'm going to see him later today."

"This meeting sounds interesting, he's Mace's sidekick, so he'll not be wasting his time seeing girls for nothing. How can I tag along?"

"I'll take you with me. When I see Bile, you sit around waiting for me. If anyone asks I'll say after Bile has seen me, we're going out. They'll not say anything, it's my night off."

"That makes sense."

Odette came to a halt and turned to Karen. "Eric already knows you're looking to move from Paris and wanting to work in with me. If it's anything like when I came for the job, he'll want you to check you over and probably put you to work till the end of the week. If he's happy, you're in. Take care, if he does want to check you, don't be difficult, he can get quite aggressive."

"I don't have a problem with any of that. In fact, it would be expected."

She openly sighed with relief. "Thank god, I was really worried, when I was told you were coming. With you being who you are, I wasn't sure how you'd react."

Karen smiled. "I've been in this position on and

295

off since I was eighteen, Odette. I've never looked at myself as a prostitute, for me it's a job, a means to an end. That's how I get through it."

"That's the same with me, my target is Mace. If I have to work the street, or in one of her brothel's, to get at her, I will."

Arriving at a large house in a row of terrace houses, Karen followed Odette in. They went up two flights of stairs and into a room with two doors off. Inside the room was a wardrobe, a large double bed and a settee. Alongside the bed was a kitchen chair. The room was clean and tidy.

"Though there's the bathroom, the other door leads into my kitchen. This is where I work, eat and sleep, so at times you'll need to wait in the kitchen, or go for a walk. Downstairs in the cellar is a bar. Customers enter it from behind the house. They're the ones who've not made an appointment, they're just looking for a quick shag. Eric's married to one of Mace's grandchildren, Helen. I don't see him much, he leaves a list on the bed each day. It gives me times of clients that have made appointments. They ring the bell at the front door and you buzz them up. You have to work around those fixed appointments with the ones from the bar. He expects you to do at least twenty a day, most times the number is made up from clients downstairs in the bar. With them, it's a five minute shag, sixty quid in your hand and he's gone. Most clients sent by Eric demand more, like blow jobs, or up your backside to finish. A few like to see a strip first. What you get up to depends on the time Eric has arranged with the client," she grinned. "Except when he's paid for half an hour and he's come in five minutes, it gets a little difficult to know what to do with him. Are you okay with all this?"

"If necessary, not that I like them going up my backside, but I will put up with it."

"I'm the same, I try to avoid it."

"How did you stumble on the younger girls being used?"

"Come with me," she told Karen, going through to the kitchen." The room was small, with a boarded up window. "This window looks onto the back. I made a tiny hole for one of my covert cameras, to watch the back. Let me show you what it picked up yesterday afternoon."

Switching her iPad on, she selected an app and entered a password. Soon the iPad was showing a video. It kept freezing, then would start again when movement happened, like a person coming into view of the camera. Karen watched, in between clients making their way to the bar, three girls, all in school uniform, came through the back separately, but always accompanied by the same lad, not much older than them. Watching the activation times of each clip, it seemed the girls would be inside for around an hour, then leave alone.

"Have you any idea which rooms they would be taken to?"

Odette thought for a moment. "This floor and the next one down are all working girls. Only the one next to me is empty, but they didn't go in there. I'd have heard them. The walls around here are really thin, there's not much that you don't hear. On the ground floor, there are four doors. They aren't the original doors like the one leading into the small lounge. They look more modern, as if one of the original rooms downstairs had been partitioned off to make smaller ones. They must be using those."

"That's a good observation, Odette. Have you any plans as to how we check?"

"Yes. Late tonight, I'm planning to plant a camera in the ground floor corridor. There's an old electrical box above the cellar door. It's covered in paint, but partly open. I don't think it's used, in the cellar on the way to the room converted into a bar, there's a completely new board with lots of wires coming from it."

"Then we do that together tonight. As it's your night off, I'll come back with you and stay here overnight."

At that moment there was a hard knock on the door.

"Who is it?" Odette shouted, turning off her iPad, before coming out of the kitchen, with Karen following.

"Eric, open the fucking door."

Odette glanced at Karen. "Wonder what he wants?" she commented, releasing the lock on the door.

He pushed his way in. "You're seeing Bile early," he began, then saw Karen. "Who the fuck are you?"

"This is my friend, Zoe, she lives in Paris, we used to work together. I did mention she was coming to look around and maybe join me," Odette answered for Karen.

Eric was Karen's height, looked close to forty, broad, rugged in looks with brown hair. He walked up to Karen, "So you worked with Emily then?"

"Yes, both of us worked the hotels in Paris."

"How many clients did you get through, we expect at least twenty a day."

"We could do similar."

Eric looked at Odette. "Fuck off, while I talk to Zoe," he told her.

Odette looked towards Karen, who just nodded very slightly. Then Odette left the room.

"You look a lot older than Emily. How long have you been working the streets?" Eric asked.

"Over ten years."

"A long time, are you branded?"

"No."

"What about drugs, are you a user?"

"No, I don't do drugs."

"Both are easily checked, strip, then face me arms at your sides," Eric demanded.

Karen unbuttoned the dress, slipped it off her arms, laying it on the bed, followed by her underclothes. Standing in front of him as he wanted. She had expected this after Odette's warning, more so with him mentioning her age and maybe owned by a cartel. In the past, she'd been checked for an ownership brand. If she had been branded, and once came very close to be branded, a pimp wouldn't take her, or would call the owner of the brand, to collect her, that's if he knew them.

Eric stood back, looking over her, before taking each arm and looking along the arms for needle marks. Satisfied, he came closer, pulled her head back by her hair and looked up her nose for signs of her snorting cocaine. Following this, he let go of the hair and gently rubbed a hand over each of her breasts, bringing the nipples up. Again he stepped back, before walking around to the back of Karen.

"Face the bed and bend down, hands on the

mattress," he demanded.

As she bent down, he gripped her buttocks, parting them to look at her back passage. This was followed by him having her stand up straight once more and raise her arms above her head. As soon as she did that, he reached around her body, taking her breasts in his hands, squeezing them until she gasped with the pain, before he released.

Karen was beginning to get nervous, confused at what was an excessive inspection for a woman not up for sale, just to work for him. But worse was to come.

"Lay on your back over the side of the bed, legs well apart."

"Why?" she asked, feeling disgust at what he was asking.

"You don't ask the questions. You tell me you've been opening your legs twenty times a day for men, so you get on the fucking bed, open them wide, or fuck off," he shouted at her.

Karen sighed, there was no way she could leave, she had to stay with Odette, lying on the bed as he demanded, her legs well apart.

He came up to her, running his hands over the inside of her thighs, looking carefully at her vagina, before reaching down and parting her entrance, pushing his fingers inside, feeling around. Karen flinched, although he was taking little care and hurting her, all she could do was put up with the abuse.

Eric pulled his hand away. "You can stand, but don't dress," he told her, before walking through to the bathroom, rinsing his hands.

Soon he was back, drying his hands on a towel,

which he threw to the floor. "Do you know what I look for in a prostitute, claiming she was servicing ten to twenty men a day?" he asked coming up to Karen.

Karen, was not sure why he should ask such a question. Then Eric's inspection of her showed he was no fool, when it came to women working as prostitutes, she was certain of that, but decided to play dumb.

"An ownership brand?" she answered as meekly as she could.

"Besides that."

"Then I've no idea."

"You want to be enlightened?"

Karen nodded.

"I look closely at her body. Particularly the tits, for signs of bruising, soreness around the nipples. A bruised backside, with an arse inflamed around the entry, from cocks pushed up regularly, besides an enlarged cunt, swollen from constant fucking." He fell silent, still looking at her. "Simple checks don't you think? How about I bring one of the working girls here, have her strip and show you what twenty to thirty clients a day has done to her body? Then Emily tells me you worked with her and your claim you've been doing at least ten, maybe twenty a day. Yet when I look and feel your tits, I find they're firm, not bruised, the nipples sharp when erect with no signs of soreness. I see no bruising to the buttocks, caused by a clients grip to make you work harder, or from regular smacking, besides an arse that isn't inflamed, or even red around the entrance. You've got rid of the pubic hair, most women do that anyway, yet when I look at your cunt, I can see no swelling, or enlargement. All I find is a slit, with firm and slightly rounded lips either side, typical of any young woman. The inside of your cunt, is tight, with little or no inflammation. Add to that, I see a body bronzed from the sun."

Without even waiting for an explanation, he suddenly moved very close to Karen, grabbed her hair, to hold her, before punching her hard in the stomach.

Karen doubled up in pain, gasping for breath, feeling sick and faint.

But he didn't give her time to catch her breath, yanking her head back by her hair, his face inches from hers. "Who the fuck are you? Where have you come from, because believe me, the only cock that's been up your cunt recently is some man you've picked up off the beach, where you got that tan. You've certainly not been on your back, in a place like this, being shagged twenty times a fucking day."

"You're right, I've not worked for some time," she stuttered, between heavy breaths. "The girls in Paris are younger, most not even eighteen, men didn't want me, unless there was no one else. I was desperate, even thumbed a lift to the coast and tried off the beach. The police kicked me out the resort for prostituting, so I came here, I couldn't tell Emily how desperate I'd become." Karen was still reeling from the blow, she couldn't get her breath, hoping her explanation would hold together.

Eric had let go of her hair while she answered, at the same time releasing the thick leather belt around his jeans. now he'd pulled it out from the loops.

Karen, even after her explanation, still disoriented and breathing hard from being hit in her stomach, saw what he was doing and began backing away as he pulled the belt out, terrified as to what was to come. But Eric had controlled women for some years and very experienced. The punch to the stomach had been intentional, to partially disable her, making it very difficult for Karen to fight back, when the next moment he'd grabbed her, turned her around, pushing her face down over the side of the bed. Immediately raising the belt bringing it down across her back, stunning her for a moment, before he stood and followed with another across her bottom and the last across the top of her legs, both with far greater force. For Karen, with it happening so fast, then the shock of feeling the belt, left her screaming, the pain intense.

Moving closer, he dragged her up, again by the hair. "A woman who lied to me in the past, I strung up and let the lads use her as a punching bag. Believe me, by the end of the day, she could only crawl, with nearly every fucking bone in her body broken." He hesitated allowing it to sink in, then looked directly into her eyes. "If another lie comes out your mouth, I'll have you strung up. Understand?"

"Yes, I'll never lie again. If you give me a chance, I'll show you I can get the clients," Karen answered, tears streaming down her face, desperately holding herself back from giving Eric a taste of what he'd just done to her.

He released her and pushed her away. "You use next door, I want to see you working your arse off, for the rest of the week. I take seventy percent of your earnings, to pay your accommodation, you keep the rest. Less than thirty a day, you'll feel my belt across your bottom for each client short, then you add them to the next day's quota. Do you have a problem in that?"

"I don't need telling how to work with a pimp. Thank you for giving me a chance. I'll work hard and show you I can meet your demands."

"Then you will begin work at twelve tomorrow and don't fucking stop till the bar closes."

"I'll be here."

"You'd better be, or expect another good thrashing when I find you. While you under this roof, you do everything I say, without question." Then he left the room.

Karen ran into the bathroom after he left, throwing up in the toilet. His description of a working prostitute, the way he'd expected her body to look handling twenty a day, had hit home, very hard. This was the reality of what she was turning herself into, voluntarily. She felt disgusted with herself, that she'd calmly agreed to take so many to her bed. Karen knew she needed to sort this brothel out very quickly. Only once was she forced to work at that level, but never again, even if it left her open to a good strapping at the end of every day she didn't meet the target.

By the time Odette came back into the room. Karen had dressed and was sitting on the side of the bed, with a glass of water.

"I'm sorry about that, he didn't hit you, did he?" Odette asked.

"He had doubts I'd been prostituting, which of course I hadn't, so I got a thrashing because I lied." Karen shrugged indifferently. "I've had far worse, believe me, so it's not a big deal. As it is, I'm in, he's given me the room next door and wants thirty a day for the rest of the week.

I'm alright with that for the few days before we bring him down," Karen lied; no matter what Odette wanted with Mace, she intended to close this place down in hours rather than days.

Odette shook her head. "He's bloody handy with that belt of his, I was getting it regular at first, because I was short on clients. So is this how you operate all the time - get yourself abused, raped and even forced to prostitute?"

"As you've found out, Odette, sometimes it's the only way of getting inside and finding out what's going on."

"How long have you been doing it?"

"In covert operations, the last ten years. Before then, I'd be abused, stripped and often raped, but only once in the many brothels I've been in, was I servicing thirty men a day."

"And you still carry on? After this operation I'm out of here."

Karen shrugged. "I can't have children, I've no family, they're dead. I've never really had a boyfriend, not one that's survived, that is. My life's pretty pathetic, don't you think?"

"But you have money, you can go where you want. You're attractive, men would want to be with you."

"Yes, I've had that said to me a number of times. But they find out who I am, what I do, and don't stay. I even tried to make a family life with a girl who's lost her parents. She threw it in my face and walked out." Karen hesitated. "Now I've nothing, I go home to an empty house, no one to talk to. I may as well be here. At least

I get to talk to people, even if they are only there for one thing and will walk away after they've had it." Then she seemed to buck up a little. "There is one achievement in all this, Odette."

"What is that?"

"I've saved well over five thousand trafficked girls, given a new life to over a thousand, and taken down so many trafficker operations I've lost count." Karen lowered her voice slightly. "One day, I'll have to stand in front of my God and have to answer for what I've done. My head will be held high. Even if, with what I've achieved in my life and the way I achieved it, he won't let me into heaven."

Odette gave Karen a short hug. "He'll let you in. God will know what you've gone through to get there."

"Thanks for your confidence in him to forgive me, I just wish I could believe it sometimes," Karen replied, with obvious resignation in her voice.

"You give the impression you're very religious?"

"I was brought up a Catholic and went to a Catholic school. They were strict and in a way ruled by the fear of God sending you to hell, if you strayed. I don't go much, I'm too frightened to face him, I suppose fear that is deeply entrenched, drummed into you at a vulnerable age, it never leaves you."

"I'm glad I never went then," Odette commented, at the same time glancing at her watch. "I'd better go and see this Bile, before Eric's back shouting abuse."

"I'm coming as well."

Chapter 39

Mace came into the bar of the brothel where Odette was working, it was currently closed, not opening until later.

She walked over to Bile looking annoyed. "This is a bloody farce, Bile. Is he delivering or not?" she asked.

"He told me he'd had a far better offer and we'd have to wait till next month. The original girls for us had been sold."

"Crustkin will pay dearly for leaving us in the lurch like this. How many of our girls have you got to send to London?"

"One, the others are shit. Most can hardly speak without every other word being a swear word, and then, some are obviously on drugs. I'm hoping the girls we have in this brothel will be better than the one we've just been to."

Eric walked in. He was surprised to see Mace as well as Bile. "Mace, it's been a long time, how are you?"

"I could be better, Eric. But time's money, where are your girls?"

"I've three still with clients. Emily, who has a day off, is going out, so I've brought her forward. She's a nice girl and can speak French."

"So where is she, we're not here all night?" Bile cut in.

"I'll call her, she was following me down."

Minutes later Odette came in, along with Karen.

She came up to Bile and Mace. "I hope you don't mind my friend being with me, she's come from Paris to see me and is looking for work, we're out later for the night."

"So long as she's quiet, I've no issues," Mace said. "How long have you been with us Emily?"

"Two weeks."

"You came from Paris as well as your friend?"

"Yes."

"Take your clothes off down to your knickers, leave the high heels on, then walk up and down the room," Bile cut in.

Odette knew you don't object to anything Mace or Bile told you to do, if you didn't want to feel a strap on your back. So she removed her clothes and walked up and down as she was told to do.

Bile stopped her and came closer, looking along her arms and into her mouth, before tilting her head back and shining a small torch he'd pulled from a pocket, up her nose. Then he sat back down again.

Odette stood there, not knowing if she should dress, but decided against it.

"The clients in Paris, were they off the streets?" Bile asked.

"No, I worked the hotels. Sometimes, if you were lucky, you'd get all night with a client. Most were businessmen and pretty rich?"

"Why are you in Ireland then?"

"Have you heard of a military unit, called Unit T?"

"We have, what about them?"

"The Madam, I worked for was taken down big time. She had twelve of us, but also dealt with underage girls and boys. She is awaiting sentencing, according to my friend here, and will get up to twenty years. She owed us all money; without such a person in Paris, you don't work. I was virtually broke, so with prostitution in Ireland legal, I came here and met Eric. He looks after me now."

"Get yourself dressed, Emily, then go and sit down," Bile told her. "Eric, a word," he said.

Eric came over.

"How do you find her work?" Bile asked.

"She's good, looks after her clients and I never get any complaints."

"What of the girl with her?" Mace asked.

"She came today. Been at it over ten years, but lied to me as to how much she was doing in Paris, so she's already had a taste of my strap and told in no uncertain terms what to expect if she lies again while she works here."

"Very wise. Sort out the others we're to see," Mace told him.

After he'd gone, Mace looked at Bile. "Personally, I think Emily's perfect. I heard about the hit on Chanter's operation by Unit T. The woman didn't have a chance and has lost everything, her house, her bank accounts, they have been impounded. Just for being caught with one child. I think we should use Emily."

"I agree we take her. What about the girl she's with? She's obviously older, but if she was doing the same as Emily was in Paris, she could be suitable."

"Bring her over."

Bile stood and walked over to Karen.

"What's your name?"

"Zoe."

"Mace would like a word."

Karen shrugged. "Okay, who is she then?"

"Emily works for her, in fact, you don't work in this area unless you work for Mace. So if you are here looking for work, you'd better make a good impression."

He walked back with Karen following.

"You worked the same as Emily did in Paris?" Mace asked.

"I did, in fact for the same Madam. I was lucky, I had a few clients who'd get in touch with me, so I looked after them. But it's getting harder, the young girls are taking all the clients, so I'm looking for something more stable. That's why Emily told me to come over and look around."

"Eric said you lied to him. Why was that?"

"I always did up to twenty a day and told him so. But not that it had dropped off to virtually nothing. He found me out and I was punished for the lie. I accept my punishment, but I need work and can meet his demands if the clients are there."

"How old are you?" Bile asked.

"Twenty-eight."

"What languages do you speak?"

"English, French, German and I can get by in Arabic."

"We may have a more lucrative position for you, rather than here. Remove your dress and walk up and down the room," Bile told her.

Karen took the dress off, leaving her bra and knickers on, including the shoes, walking up and down, one foot in front of the other, swinging her hips slightly and keeping her back straight. Again Bile stopped her and checked for drug taking, before telling Karen to stand in front of them.

"You can dress. Are you around for the week?" Bile asked.

"Yes, I intended to get a ferry on Saturday morning if Eric won't take me," Karen said, at the same time fastening up her dress.

"If we decide to use you, you'd leave before the end of the week, maybe sooner."

"Where would I be going, if you gave me the job?"

"London. You must be settled in our house there and prepared for starting Saturday. We already have bookings."

"I could do that with ease, but sometime soon I'd need to go back to Paris. I've all my clothes there, besides still paying for a flat."

"We would sort that out, if we take you. Now you may go."

After Karen and Odette left the bar, Eric returned, with two girls.

The girls were interviewed like Odette and Karen. Then the final girl came.

"What's your thoughts, Mace, now we've seen them all?" Bile asked.

"For me, I'd only use Emily and her friend Zoe. The others are good for what they do here, but with businessmen paying us a grand a time they are expecting conversation and intelligence, the last three fall very short. Marlene couldn't even get beyond 'you know' after every sentence."

"I agree, we take Zoe and Emily. Get them on a

flight tomorrow, so we've at least three girls for Saturday."

"Arrange it with Eric. Zoe's alright, but Emily needs her hair cut to give it some style, before she goes."

Chapter 40

By twelve the following day. Karen and Odette were sitting in the kitchen of Odette's room, eating takeaways. They had gone out the night before drinking in a few of the local bars. By midnight they had been back. Odette had taken Karen down to the bar, at the same time she'd pointed out the electrical cupboard where she intended to place the camera. Karen agreed it was the best place and they planned to go back later. They did so at close to three in the morning. Karen kept watch, at the same checking that the signal from the camera could be seen on the iPad, telling Odette when it was correctly set.

Eric barged into the room. "You're both leaving tonight for London. Get yourself down to the hairdressers and sort your hair out, Emily. This is fucking up my bookings." He handed Karen a piece of paper. "Zoe you go to the room next door and work through that list of Emily's clients who've already got appointments. All are half hour sessions, with quarter of an hour between each."

"What about my bags at the hotel, I need to collect them?" Karen asked.

"Fuck, you'd better go when Emily gets back from the hairdressers, she can take over the clients. When you're back, find your clients from the bar till it's time for you to leave."

"I don't want to go to London, Eric. I want to stay here," Emily cut in. She was in Ireland to take Mace down, not to be hundreds of miles away.

"It's not possible, something about the girls being late coming. When they finally do arrive, you can come

313

back."

"So long as you promise, then I'll go."

He gave her a hug. "I promise, Emily, you're one of my favourite girls." Then he looked at Karen. "Why are you still sitting there, fuck off and get yourself ready. Have you condoms?"

"No."

"Give her some Emily, then you move your arse as well."

With that, he left the room.

"What do we do now?" Odette asked.

"Let me think about it. We'll talk a little later."

She sighed. "Okay, you'll find everything in the bathroom cupboard you want. I'll be off. God knows if I can get in anywhere."

After Odette left, Karen took a few condoms from the cupboard and went into the room next to Emily's. She'd accepted there was no way of getting out of a few clients, but was relieved that the need to find upwards of thirty clients in the bar downstairs had gone. That was something she had been dreading.

***

Karen had already been with one man. After tidying herself up and dressing again, she was sitting in the kitchen watching the covert camera looking down the hall on the ground floor. She had seen a number of men being taken through by the girls from the cellar bar. Eric was also on camera, going into a room off the hall. The next shot showed him coming out. Leaving the picture on the iPad, Karen filled a glass with water sipping it slowly, looking down at the screen. She was hoping that the school girls would show up, so she could bring to an end the abuse she was having to put up with.

At that moment the buzzer in the bedroom went twice. She sighed and walked through, pressing a release button on a pad by the side of the door. "It's open, come up, room six, second floor," she said.

Minutes later a man came into the bedroom.

"Hi, I'm Zoe, Emily's not well, so I'm looking after you," she said, giving him a smile.

"So long as you fuck, I couldn't care less. Get your clothes off and lie on the bed."

"That's fine, you must use a condom, they are on the side table," Karen answered, unfastening the buttons down her dress. Slipping it off, she laid it on the chair, followed by her bra and thong. All the time watching him as he removed his trousers and pulled the condom on. Almost immediately he was on top of her, pushing himself inside. "Get your fucking arms above your head," he demanded, going at her for all he was worth.

Karen just lay there indifferently, giving the odd gasp, telling him he was making her come and to go faster. In reality, she was feeling nothing, just wanting it finished.

Suddenly he stopped. "Over on your face, I'm finishing up your arse."

"In that case, you need to give me a minute, to grease my backside. You also change the condom."

"I know what to do, I'm here every freaking week. Just slap the grease on, I'm here to fuck you, not stand around, I'm back to work in fifteen minutes."

Karen slipped off the bed, going through to the kitchen, where she'd left her bag. Pulling a tube out, she squirted some up her rectum. Putting the cap back on, she glanced over to the table. She stared for a minute; she had left the iPad running and displayed on the screen was a girl in a school uniform. Eric was with her, in fact, he was holding her hand. Karen watched as he took her into one of the rooms off the hall. She backed the clip up to the start. It showed the school girl coming out the door leading down to the cellar with Eric.

Switching off the iPad, she placed it into her handbag. Coming through to the bedroom carrying her bag, Karen pressed the button of her watch three times. She'd the intention of getting rid of the man and dressing, before the unit stormed the building.

On the client's part, he was fed up waiting and was behind the door as she came through. Immediately he grabbed her arm, cuffing her across the head with the other. "Where the fuck have you been? I said I didn't have much time and you're pissing me about," he shouted at her, at the same time dragging her across the room, ripping the handbag out of her hand, before pushing her face down on the bed and climbing on top of her. The next moment he was forcing himself up her back passage, gripping her hips, preventing her from getting out from under him.

He was hurting her, but determined not to give him the satisfaction of knowing that, so all she could do was relax, allowing him entry, it would be over in minutes and he'd be gone.

Chapter 41

Bile burst the flimsy lock as he forced the door open of the room Karen was in. He looked at her, lying face down on the bed, the client on top, going at her as hard as he could.

"Piss off, wait your turn, I've still got time left yet," he shouted at Bile, gripping Karen's hips, pulling her body up tight to his own, determined to carry on.

Bile was not for waiting around while the man finished with Karen, he lashed out at him, sending him sprawling onto the floor. "Get lost, the fucking place is being raided, I need this woman out now," he shouted at him, at the same time grabbing Karen's arm and dragging her off the bed.

"My clothes, my bag," she protested.

"No time, you come as you are. We need you in London, not in a cell."

"I must have my handbag, it's got my passport inside," Karen told him. In fact the bag not only had a passport in the name of Zoe, it also had a tracker in the lining.

Bile picked it up, then left the room, gripping Karen's arm with his other hand as she stumbled after him naked, with only enough time to grab the thong she'd been wearing. He went into a room at the end of the corridor, shutting the door, before moving the bed away from the wall.

Karen took that opportunity to pull the thong on. It didn't hide much and she hated wearing them, but it was better than nothing.

Opening a small panel behind it, he looked up at

her. "Get inside."

Karen knelt down and crawled into the opening, which led into a passage. The passage was narrow and so low, you could only move along inside on your hands and knees. Bile also climbed in, but before following, he reached out to the bed, dragging it back into place, shutting the panel.

"Keep going forward, it will end at another panel, there's a bolt, slide it and get out," he urged her.

After minutes of crawling, Karen released the bolt, pushing the panel open. She was in a small room. It was empty. The only light was from a roof light in the ceiling.

Bile followed, then went to the door, pulling a key from his pocket, opened it, and looked out.

"It's clear, come on," he said, grasping her hand, virtually dragging her out of the room.

They went down the stairs towards the front door. Karen pulled back, realising where he was heading. "I thought I was just moving to another room? There's no way I'm going out on the street wearing a thong, I may as well be naked."

Immediately, Bile hit Karen across the head, sending her reeling. "I couldn't give a fuck if you were naked. The car's only outside, so like it or not, you're coming with me."

With Bile being a big man, gripping her tightly, her head still reeling from his blow, he had no trouble dragging her, still protesting, outside and along the pavement. Bile's 'just outside' was closer to twenty cars further down the road. With him, gripping one of her arms, her trying, but failing, to cover her breasts with the other, she stumbled

318

after him. Acutely embarrassed as drivers gave a honk when they passed, pedestrians looking on with interest, some obviously shocked to see a virtually naked woman being dragged along. But this was an area well known for its prostitutes, so no one was that interested as to why the woman was being dragged down the street like this. Soon she was pushed into the back of a car, Bile climbed in the front and they sped away. Karen pressed her watch winder twice. She suspected they would be going to another house belonging to Mace's gang. If that was the case, no matter how she felt about being forced down the street as she had been, this was an operation and as such, the more locations taken down the better.

"Well, we gave the people something to talk about today," he said, with a laugh.

"Maybe for them, I was bloody embarrassed," she retorted.

"Don't give me that shit, you're a prostitute, spending half your life naked with different men, what's your beef if a few more see you? Is it because you're upset they didn't pay for the privilege? Anyway, wipe the grease off your bottom. I don't want it getting all over my car seats," he said, passing her a small packet of tissues from the glove box.

"Where are we going?" Karen asked, pulling the thong down and wiping not only between her legs, but her backside. With being dragged out of the room and having no time to clean herself, she was glad of the tissues.

"We have a house not far from here. You can stay there until it's time to leave for the UK."

"Why did they raid you, I thought it was legal to

prostitute in Ireland?"

"It is, but not to run a brothel. As it is, we'll be back up and running by morning. We've friends in the police, they'll sort it out."

"So it happens a lot?"

"No, it's never happened before. We need to find out what went wrong and why we weren't warned. But it's not a problem for you, you have a place to work."

He turned into a car park at the front of a large house. Bile didn't stop at the front, but drove round to the back of the house, coming to a halt at a door. Climbing out, he opened the back door.

"Come on, let's get you inside, maybe they will find you something to wear?"

"That's bloody big of you, I had the impression for a time I was going to London like this."

He grinned, grasping her arm and pulling her out of the car. "Good idea, at least customs would know you had nothing to declare. As it is, you'll not need the clothes before you leave anyway."

"Why?" she demanded, coming to a halt.

"You're here for at least five hours, so you'll have time to make up for what you lost, having to get you out the other place. Here, it's more intense. The girls can get through five an hour. At that rate you'll be constantly shagging and not have time to dress. Then, at thirty Euro a pop, you can earn yourself around three hundred, after our cut, before you leave for the airport."

Karen's heart sank, this was fast becoming her worst nightmare. There was no way she intended to be used at that level. She pressed her watch button three times.

Bile was just going to knock on the door, when he heard the screeching of vehicle tyres turning off the road. He let go of her and ran to the corner of the house. "Fuck, they're here as well. Get back into the car," he shouted at Karen.

She did as he asked, not relishing standing around outside wearing only a thong with a raid going on. At least in the car, she could maintain some dignity. Bile also got back in the car.

"You may as well give up, we can't escape," Karen commented.

"Shut up, put the seat belt on," he shouted back at her, then started the engine, turning towards the lawn. The next moment they were bouncing over the lawn, crashing through a wooden fence panel at the bottom, into an area with rubbish bins, before coming out on a service road running along the back of the houses. Again Karen pressed her watch button twice and leaned back. She would really be enjoying this, if she'd been dressed. As it was, already embarrassed about running naked down the street, she was now shivering with the cold.

"So where now?" Karen asked.

"That's none of your business," he retorted. Then his mobile began to ring. He answered it.

"Where are you Bile? I'm still sitting here waiting?" Mace said.

"We've had a raid, I'd managed to get Zoe out, couldn't find Emily. Then I took her to our other place, but the bloody police turned up there as well. I'm on my way to collect you now."

"I've had no warning from Rupert about this. After it settles down, you will go and sort him out. I don't pay good money not to know what's going on."

"I agree, Mace. I'll be there in ten minutes."

Ten minutes later he stopped outside a row of houses on a busy road. "We're here, let's go," he told Karen, at the same time opening his door.

"Just a minute, this is a main road, where are we going?" Karen demanded.

Bile didn't answer, just came around to the passenger side, pulling open her door. "You coming, or am I dragging you? The fucking door is only there."

"Then open it and I'll follow you. I'm hardly going to run down the road like this."

He grinned. "You really are shy then. You should look at it as advertising. Let potentials see what's on offer."

"I may be a prostitute, but I do have some dignity left, particularly in public. So you get something to cover me, or I don't move."

He sighed. "Maybe you're right, this is not the place to attract attention. I'll find something, you stay here."

"You can be sure of that," she came back at him.

Karen watched him go up to the front door, using a key to get inside. Minutes later he was out, carrying a blanket.

"Here, put this around you and let's get inside."

Karen pulled the blanket around her and followed him, carrying her handbag. As she got to the door, she again pressed the watch button once before going inside. The house stank of body odour. She was taken through to the lounge where a man was standing, leaning against the wall. Mace was at the table with a few papers in front of her.

"Mark, take Zoe upstairs," she told the man.

Mark grasped her arm. "Come on," he told Karen.

She followed him out the room and up two flights of stairs to an attic room. He pulled a key from his pocket and opened a door, urging her inside. Inside the room was a double bed, no blankets, just a towel laid on top of a mattress. There was also a kitchen chair and a sink in the corner. Above the sink was a shelf with a few condoms and a small tub.

"This room's not really for one of the girls, it's got no bathroom. But you're only here for the afternoon, if you need a piss tell me. You can shower before you leave with Bile later."

"May I have a drink and something to wear, please?" Karen asked.

"I'll see what I can do, in the meantime, don't leave this room."

"You can be certain I won't," she answered.

Mark returned downstairs, coming directly into the lounge where Mace was.

She looked over at him, "What do you want?" she demanded.

"We're really busy, Mace, the woman who came with Bile, can I use her?" he asked.

Mace looked at Bile. "When does she leave?"

"Eight, I need to get her to the airport, the plane goes at eleven."

"Then yes, so long as she's ready to leave when

Bile wants to go."

Mark nodded, leaving the room, collecting a glass of lemonade from the kitchen and a client waiting for the next available woman. Going back upstairs, he stopped the client outside the door of the room Karen was in.

"Give me a minute with her, then you can go in," he told the client.

Karen was sitting on the bed, with the blanket wrapped around her, when Mark returned.

He handed her the lemonade. "This will have to do for now," he said, taking hold of her left hand slipping the watch off her wrist, and ring from a finger, putting them into her handbag. "I'll look after these. Some of the clients here, would snap your finger off to get the ring. You can have them back when you leave."

"Excuse me, clients?" Karen asked. "Bile didn't say I'd be working."

"Why shouldn't you, we're a fucking brothel and you're a prostitute. As it is, if Mace says you work, you work? Lubricant's in the tub and a few condoms. I'll fetch more condoms later. I've a client already waiting outside and more downstairs. We do a ten minute session, plenty of time for him to come and get yourself cleaned. After the ten minutes, I'll collect him and bring you your next."

"How many are you talking about?" Karen asked, already dreading the answer after he said he'd bring more condoms.

"Depends how many are waiting, only today we're behind, so expect to get through at least five an hour. All my girls are capable of that. If they give less, when we're busy, then they feel my belt across their bottom, you included. Get yourself ready, I'm earning nothing standing here talking." Taking her handbag he walked to the door, pulling it open. "She's ready for you," was all he said to the client waiting.

After the man came into the room, Mark left, slamming the door shut behind him. Karen also heard the key turn.

Karen was annoyed with herself, coming here, she'd indicated, by pressing her watch button once she was safe and they should watch and wait. With the intention to see the day through and go on to London, to take that brothel down. She would even have put up with a few clients to do that. But at least five an hour, with no idea how many hours she'd be here and the threat of a beating if she didn't manage it, made her feel sick inside. However, she'd no time to dwell on her dilemma, the man was unfastening his jeans, telling her to bend over the side of the bed.

***

Downstairs, Mace had been on the mobile for the last thirty minutes, calling a number of different people, trying to find out just what had happened. Eventually she managed to reach someone in the police force they used. "What do you mean, the raids aren't by the police? Who the fuck are these people?" she shouted down the phone. Then she listened. "Well fucking find out and call me. We've lost two important locations because of this."

Bile was listening, alarm bells were starting to ring. He stood quickly. "Put the phone down and let's get out, Mace. If it's not the police, it can only be military. That's got to be Unit T. They must be working on information, maybe from inside. They could have a list of locations. You can't afford to be here, all the girls in this house are trafficked and we don't know how much Unit T has found out."

She stared at him. "You're right, we should leave," she said, quickly standing and hurrying through into the hall.

"We'll use the cellar link to the house next door and not come out the front," Bile told her.

"Good idea, get Zoe. We've already lost Carol and Emily, we still need girls for London, Bile."

"Then you go down, I'll follow."

Bile ran upstairs, going into every room, looking for Karen. Coming out the last room, he saw Mark with a man. "Where the fuck's that woman I came in with? Mace wants her out now," Bile demanded.

"Attic, we had nowhere else. I've just taken in her third client, the women's really going through them, after I threatened her with the strap, if she couldn't do five an hour. I'll get six, maybe seven out of her at this rate. She'll be finished in ten minutes."

"Fuck that, give him to someone else, I'm not waiting around while he fucks her," Bile came back at him, running up the next flight, turning the key in the lock and pushing the door open.

A man was sitting on the edge of the bed, his pants at his ankles. Karen knelt down in front of him, putting his condom on. She pulled away, looking up towards Bile.

"We go," was all he said to Karen, then he looked at the man. "Sorry mate, Mark will give you another woman, on the house. This one's needed."

Karen wasn't going to argue, if he wanted her out of here, she'd go, relieved it had come to an abrupt end. Grabbing her thong, she quickly slipped it on, before picking the blanket up.

"This is getting to be a habit, Bile," Karen said, as she struggled to keep up with him along the corridor and down the stairs.

"What are you on about?"

"You keep coming in and stopping me working. Is it going to be the norm for me, not to finish? Because if it is, I want my money in advance. I've already lost out twice today," she commented. Trying to complain like she believed a prostitute would, after having her clients taken away.

"Fucking comedian, aren't you? As it is, with what we've got lined up, you'll soon be working your arse off, without interruption."

Once in the cellar, Karen pulled back. "You're not leaving me in this cellar, I'm bloody freezing, it's like a fridge down here?" she asked.

"No, you're going through to another house."

"In that case Mark's got my bag with my passport inside. I'll need it."

"I'll get your fucking bag. You stay here."

Karen sniggered. "I'm going nowhere like this. Just hurry up, then at least I can go to somewhere warmer."

***

When Mace left Bile to collect Karen, she made her way down into the cellar. At the far end of the passage, was a door. It was obviously new, with the surround of the door unfinished in rough brick, where the builder had cut the opening.

Using a key from her bag, she unlocked the door and went through, locking it behind her. This door always had to remain locked, Bile like her, would have a key when he came through. Now in the next house, Mace made her way towards the cellar steps along a similar passage as the other cellar, leading upstairs.

At that moment, she stopped dead, hearing a sound coming from one of the rooms off the passage. Going to investigate, she saw a figure dropping down onto the floor, through what used to be a coal hatch years ago.

"What the fucks going on here?" she demanded.

The figure spun round, stared for a moment at Mace, then pulled a gun. It was a girl.

Mace looked at her standing there, in jeans and a jumper. A gun with a silencer attached, held firmly in both hands. She grinned. "Well, if it's not Emily. Bile missed you at the brothel, he only got Zoe out. Where were you, then why are you here holding a gun? Do you even know how to use one?"

"I've used guns since I was eleven, so yes, I do know how to use them. As it is, I came back to the brothel, after getting my hair done to see Bile pushing Zoe down the bloody road naked. I decided to follow, so I commandeered a car. I think the driver may have been a bit pissed off, having a gun pushed in his face. But hey, needs must. Then to see Bile come to this house after doing his off road jaunt to escape from a Unit T raid, was interesting to say the least."

Mace frowned, confused. "You say 'this house' as if you know about it? How?"

"Oh, I know all about this house. I was brought here when I first came to Ireland for a so-called job that never existed. Simon Murphy forced me into prostitution, after beating me until I could take no more, to be fucked thirty times a day. At night taken to hotels, by day led through this passage to service five men every hour in the house next door. I blew his fucking kneecaps off for that and promised myself I would come back for you. I can't believe my luck, actually seeing you standing there."

"So Emily, is in fact Odette?" Mace said with interest. "Very clever disguise, Odette, I'll give you that, it even fooled me. Mind you, I've only seen you the once apart from photos. But coming to this house was a grave mistake and a foolish one. Mark, who runs the houses, will certainly recognise you. You owe Simon big time for crippling him, so expect your punishment to be strung up and used as a punch bag. Believe me girl, you won't survive."

She shrugged indifferently. "They're too late. With stumbling on to you, my work here in Ireland is very nearly done. I won't be hanging around, or coming back."

"What are you talking about, your work's done?" Mace asked confused.

"You don't get it, do you. Are you that stupid, or just so full of your own self-importance that it makes you blind? You wrecked my life, turned me into a prostitute, for your own gain. Unit T took me in, trained me. I went along with it, because I had my own agenda."

"What Agenda?" Mace demanded.

"It's very simple. I experienced first-hand what you do to girls like me, who believe you offer them a new life, only to be raped day after day and beaten if they refuse. You have no idea what it's like to have every bit of pride and dignity you have in yourself, knocked out of you, in order to line someone else's pocket, not even your own. To stand in a dock, followed by prison, like everyone wants for you is too good. You'd still carry on from inside, threatening, intimidating. The world can do without people like you. My agenda, you ask? That's very simple, I intend to kill you."

Mace raised her stick, waving it in the air at her. "No one threatens to kill Mace Murphy, especially a fucking prostitute. I run Ireland, north and south of the border. Go home little girl, if I ever see you again, you will regret it."

"Believe me, I'm going. But you run nothing from now on, the Murphy's are finished. Unit T will mop up." Odette squeezed the trigger of her gun, sending Mace crashing to the floor in agony. Walking up to her, Odette looked down with indifference. Mace stared up at her in disbelief and terror. "Die, Mace Murphy, die for all the victims you've pushed into a living hell. Answer to your maker, for your crimes against children, the vulnerable, the same as we all must do one day." Then she fired a bullet into her head, before unscrewing the silencer and pocketing it.

At that moment she heard a key being put into the lock of the door Mace had come through, before it was pulled open. Going to the door of the room she was in, Odette pushed it virtually closed. Moving into the shadows, her gun held tightly. With no idea who, or how many may be coming through, confrontation was to be avoided if possible.

***

While Karen waited for Bile to return, she was already trying to piece together what was happening. For Bile to move her, yet again, he must have the belief Unit T was on its way. That would mean they really did need women to go to London. Fortunately, she wasn't here as a prisoner, but one of their working prostitutes. Because of this, she offered no threat to him. Now she was left with a dilemma. She remembered Odette's statement of where she'd been held. She had talked of a house she lived in, where during the day she would be taken through the cellar into another house to work. Could this be the house? Then she'd noticed the rooms, like the one she'd been in, all had keys in the door, meaning they too could well be locked, pointing to the fact that the girls here were working against their will. With Unit T close behind her, they would already know of this house, so it didn't make sense, yet again, to end the operation. By carrying on they would have even more of their houses, including the London house. Karen decided to see it through and move on. Today, Bile had unwittingly saved her from hours of constant abuse. He'd embarrassed her being forced out on the street naked, yes, but she had to live with that. This covert operation, to take down the Murphy's, was increasing in pace. Every brothel they had, including their new venture into London, must be closed, squeezing them financially and destroying their hold, besides their reputation as the most powerful gang in Ireland. Mace would be annoyed, make mistake as she tried to keep everything together. Then she'd go down. Except Karen also had a more personal reason to move

331

on. By her leaving, she wouldn't have the indignity of having to admit what they'd had her doing here.

Bile was back in the cellar with Mark, who was carrying Karen's handbag.

He handed the bag to Karen. "Pity you have to leave, you know how to make them come quickly and were doing well upstairs."

Karen just gave a weak smile, the last thing she wanted was to be complimented on her efforts to prevent a strapping by acting as a prostitute.

"Come on, let's go," Bile told Karen, pushing past to unlock the door.

After Bile and Karen were through, Mark closed the door and locked it.

Making their way down the corridor to the stairs leading up into the hall, Bile wasn't interested in looking into any of the rooms, unaware that Odette was hiding in one and Mace lay dead on the floor.

Once out of the cellar and into the hall of the next house, Bile took Karen through to the kitchen. A man was sitting at the table, he looked up when Bile came in.

"Why are you here, Benny, where's Mace?" Bile asked.

"Carl's sent me to fetch another woman, to take to a private party that a local business has laid on for its clients over from Italy. I've brought one back, she's thrown up twice and seems pretty ill to me. Frances has just taken her upstairs and is sorting another one out. But I've not seen Mace. Mind you, I've been in the backyard for a smoke, so she could have gone out the front."

"Probably, anyway, show Zoe where the storeroom

is. Sort some clothes to wear from in there, Zoe. While you do that, I'll find Frances and check if she's spoken to Mace."

Running upstairs, he found Frances coming out of a room, carrying a pile of soiled clothes. "Have you seen Mace?" Bile asked.

She shook her head. "No, not today. I think she's next door."

"I left her coming through to here."

"If she did, she didn't come upstairs. I've been with Colette and have just put her to bed. The girl's got some sort of virus, so I'm changing her for Sonia, she's all that's left, although Mark's going be put out, he wants her after she's finished her dinner."

Bile thought for a moment. "I need to find Mace, I've got a woman with me, she's going to London later tonight. Mace doesn't want her in this house, so give her to Benny to take to the party, I'll call him later about where she's to be delivered to. She's far better there earning for us, rather than trailing after me all day."

"Are you certain, especially if she's going to London? They can get a bit wild, these parties, if last time was anything to go by. Is she a prostitute, or a newbie?"

"The women's a prostitute, nearly thirty, been at it at least ten years in Paris. She'll have had her fair share of wild parties I would think and know how to handle drunks. Besides, she's not here under duress, she's already working for us."

"Then she's ideal. I'll tell Mark he can have Sonia after all."

"Her name's Zoe and she's downstairs with

Benny, Tell Benny to hold onto her handbag while she works, it's got her passport in it. Make sure he gives it back to her when she leaves. With Mace not here, she must have left through the front door. So if you want me, I'll be with Mace," Bile said, leaving Frances to put the soiled clothes she was carrying in a basket, before he ran back downstairs and out of the front door.

Frances came into the kitchen, Karen was sitting at the table with Benny. She'd found a pair of jeans that fitted, besides a jumper, and trainers. Karen had also retrieved her watch and ring from the handbag. The watch, of course, being essential to summon held if she needed it.

"You must be Zoe? Bile tells me you're going with Benny this afternoon to join another girl at a party. Come with me and we'll find more suitable clothes for you to wear."

"Bile said I was going to London. Has that changed?" Karen asked, realising just how little women were thought of by this gang, taking every opportunity to keep the girls earning for them. Now she was faced with a party of men, in unknown numbers, with just another girl, leaving her open to being raped multiple times."

"No, you're still going to London. But he has things to do today and you can't stay here, so let's get you ready, shall we?" Frances replied.

Karen followed her back to the room, Benny had taken her to sort out clothes to wear. Karen also carried her handbag. Already she'd decided that entertaining men all afternoon was going too far, just to take out a new brothel location, which wasn't even operating yet. As one of Mace's working prostitutes, she'd not be secured.

Then, the girl already at the party could well be there under duress, so deserved her help. She would have this house raided when she left. Then, once at the party, bring that to an end as well.

Frances opened a cupboard removing underwear, suspender set and sheer nylons, handing them to Karen. Then began looking through the rails. Pulling out a red blouse and waistcoat, with a short, black dress.

"If you follow me, Zoe, you can have a quick shower. Have you make-up with you?"

"Yes a little."

"That's good, when you're ready come down."

Soon Karen was ready, dressed in the clothes Frances had given her to wear, covered with a light coat.

As they left the house, Karen pressed the button of her watch three times. Delayed until she was in Benny's car, then pressed the watch button twice. She leaned back in the seat. Unit T would now go into the brothel, with her press of the button three times. Then her delay before two more presses, indicated she was leaving and they had to track her. This was made all the easier, with her having the handbag. In the lining were two trackers. Karen was more than happy to be finally cutting the operation short. She'd had enough, after the embarrassment of being dragged down a street naked, before being put to work for the rest of the day.

Chapter 42

Karen was with Sir Peter Parker in his office at New Scotland Yard.

"It was a good move to call for a raid on the house where Mace was found dead in the cellar of the property next door," Peter began, after looking at the report from Ireland."In both houses, all the women inside were trafficked, locked in rooms and being forced to work. Then Eric Harper has been arrested and charged with not only running an illegal brothel, but using underage girls for the purpose of sex. He'll go down for ten, maybe fifteen years. Bile and a number of other men in Mace's gang are facing at least ten years. We also obtained a warrant for the house Mace lived in and have taken away documents. One lists a number of prominent people, including police, as being in her pay. The woman was meticulous in logging how she distributed her bribes. You've done, Karen, what many couldn't, and pulled her down."

"The Murphy's deserve all they get. They ruled by intimidation, stooping as low as their own children, forcing girls as young as twelve into prostitution. I only saw a little bit of it, believe me it opened my eyes as to what they were getting up to."

"I must agree. The statements from the schoolgirls found in the brothel, besides the ones caught on camera being taken there by a sixteen year old son of one of the Murphy's, have shaken many officers now investigating. Although we are no closer to finding out who actually killed Mace."

"I'm not surprised, if a list was made, it'd fill a

book. As it is, we had nothing to do with it, we wanted her to go down. So don't have them look our way, we only found her."

"We won't. So what are your plans now, Karen?"

"I'm giving fieldwork up, Peter. For me it's getting harder, my age is against me and I can no longer continue being part of a covert team. It's time to pass the baton on. One girl I have in mind will soon be leading the covert operations, the same as I always have."

"Will she be as ruthless as you, Karen?"

"I think so, not that she knows it yet."

He smiled, this was just like Karen. "Will we know who she is?"

Karen shook her head slightly. "No, no one will know who this girl is. Gone are the parallel worlds I've had to live in. I'll always have informers, undercover workers, but when she goes in, it will be the same as my own intentions always were, to bring them down."

"Then this is the beginning of a new era in the fight against people trafficking?"

"Yes, Peter, a new era as you say. I wish I had my time again. With the backup I have now. Maybe, then I'd not have made so many errors, risked my life, often unnecessarily, lost people who were close to me, including my family."

"I believe we can all say that in hindsight, Karen. You did a good job, girl. Forced a change in the law, gave so many a chance of a new life and restored their dignity. But somehow, I don't think the world has seen the last of Karen Harris. I believe while there are traffickers, you will be there, spearheading the fight."

"We shall see, Peter. How about lunch? I leave for France in the morning, in an effort to start some bridge-building. Then tonight I actually have a long awaited date, with a booking at a very posh restaurant."

"This all sounds very positive, Karen. You are actually suggesting having two meals in one day, going on a date and stepping down, allowing others to take up the baton."

She smiled. "Why not? I'm fed up with being skinny all the time. Besides, I've missed such a lot in my life. I've a few pounds saved, it's time to spend a little of it and enjoy myself."

***

Karen, wearing a long evening dress, slipped her coat on and left the London flat. Waiting outside was a taxi. It was no ordinary taxi, this was a Unit T taxi, driven by a unit soldier.

"I like the dress, Colonel, it suits you," the driver commented.

"Thank you, to tell you the truth, it makes a change to go out, away from unit business."

"I can understand that. We all look forward to leave, just to let off a little steam."

As they worked their way through the typical London traffic, Karen checked her watch for a signal. She depressed the winder a number of times to watch the response on a radio receiver on the seat at the side of the driver. Satisfied, she checked the locator signal coming from the transmitters embedded in her clothing.

"Everything's working alright. I might go on to a nightclub after dinner. I'll call you as my taxi as usual."

"That's fine, the unit surveillance and support vehicle has just come up behind us," he answered, glancing in the mirror. "Are you expecting trouble tonight?"

"God, I hope not. I just want a night out. But La Figeroes is a top restaurant with dinner falling not much below a hundred and fifty pounds, even without wine. Besides, to get in, it's more who you know, not by a casual telephone call from Dominick. I might be miles off the mark and he might know someone, but until I'm sure, we treat it as a potential threat."

"I must agree with you there, it's out of character on a security man's wage. Have you been there before yourself?"

"No, so it will be an experience if nothing else."

At that moment they turned into the street where the restaurant was located. As the taxi drew up, the driver turned around, before the doorman of the restaurant opened the door.

"Take no risks, Karen, just have a good-time, but even the slightest inconsistency, call us. We'll be less than a minute away from you at any time."

"Thanks Frank," she answered, handing a ten pound note across to him, just as the cab door was pulled open. It was important to remain in character, even details as simple as not paying could ring alarm bells to someone watching.

As she entered the restaurant a man dressed in a lounge suit approached.

"Good evening, madam, you have a reservation?"

"Yes, the name's Lady Harris, I'm meeting Mr Fehr."

"Of course, Lady Harris, Mr Fehr is in our lounge, may I take your coat?"

Karen went through into the small lounge, where Dominick was sitting at the bar.

He saw her enter and quickly got up, coming over to kiss her on each cheek. "Karen, you look stunning. Can I get you a drink?"

"Thank you, Dominick, I'd like a Manhattan, please."

Soon they were sitting alone on lounge seats, both holding menus, after the waiter had given them the specialities of the evening.

Dominick was looking at the menu, most of it was in French, which he was very weak on, and then, the waiter hadn't been much help, half speaking French in his descriptions of the specials.

"You choose for us, Karen. This is your night, I've really missed you and had hoped to see you sooner after our meeting in Regent's Park."

"I'm sorry, Dominick, sometimes my work has me jumping from one country to the next. This is the first time I've been back in London for some weeks." Then she smiled. "I'm going to be in London for the foreseeable. I've a lot of work surrounding my charity. So if you want, we can get together quite regularly?"

"I'd love to. Now we need to select from the menu. What do you suggest?"

The dinner went well, the food was good and their conversation just general, apart from covering their time together in Switzerland. With the dinner finished, they were back in the lounge, brandy and coffee in front of them. Even so, Dominick was getting agitated, he'd expected Bile to be here by now.

Karen had excused herself and gone to the ladies.

Dominick took the opportunity to speak to the waiter. "Has Bile arrived yet?"

"You are talking about Bile Murphy?"

"Yes, he was supposed to meet us here.

The waiter shook his head. "I believe Mr Murphy was booked in for nine, but is no longer coming."

"Well, he could have called me. He said he'd made arrangements to cover the bill"

The waiter looked confused. "I will speak to the owner, Sir."

Minutes later the same man who had met Karen at the door came over.

"I understand you had made an arrangement with Mr. Murphy? I know him, of course, but I'm afraid he has said nothing to me about this. Perhaps you would prefer to settle up before your guest returns?" he said, handing Dominick the bill.

Dominick looked at the bill and went cold. It was two hundred and forty pounds

"I can't, I've only a hundred and fifty pounds on me."

"Perhaps a credit card, Sir?"

Dominick shook his head. "They haven't given me one yet."

"Then, short of our calling the police, you must talk to Lady Harris. She of course is well known and with a nod from her, we would be happy to allow you time to pay."

341

"I'll talk to Karen," he answered with resignation.

Karen returned, taking the seat opposite him. "Can we move on to a club, Dominick, or would you rather go somewhere quieter?" she asked, sipping her brandy.

"I've a confession to make, Karen. It's really embarrassing but I need to tell you."

She gave a hint of a smile. "You've overstretched yourself?"

"How did you know?"

"Dominick, I know what a restaurant like this costs to dine at, you forget the circle I live in, I'm often taken to these places. Why did you do it, I'd have been just as happy in a pizza place, or even a steak house?"

"I won't lie to you, Karen, and try to cover-up. I would never have come, I couldn't afford it, but for a reporter called Bile Murphy."

Her mood changed a little. "What has Bile got to do with us being here?"

"He told me he was working with the reporter Archie Pelar. He said Archie was dead and he'd taken over his series of articles about you. He said he just wanted to ask you a few questions, before he went to print, so as to at least give you the opportunity to correct any assumptions Archie had drawn. He told me to come here and he'd bring his girlfriend and just recognise you. Then ask you the questions. I thought it reasonable and I wanted you to be shown in your best light in their article by correcting any wrong assumptions they may have had. After all, you've done such a lot for so many people caught up in trafficking."

"So he was going to cover the bill, in return for

this so-called interview, Dominick?"

"Yes, but I'll pay, it's just that to do that I need to get more money. They won't let me leave unless you tell them I can."

Karen felt sick inside, every man who she liked and got herself involved with always seemed to let her down.

"Go home, Dominick. I'll sort the bill. I need a man at my side, I can trust. A man who would come to me and tell me that he'd been approached, so that we could work out what to do together. That's not a lot to ask, be it a reporter looking for a story, or maybe a real threat on my life."

Dominick gasped. "No one was going to threaten your life, I'd never put you in such a position. I knew Archie, he got us together and it seemed reasonable to let his partner make sure they didn't damage your reputation, by checking on a few facts. He told me to come here because he knew the owners, that they'd give us a good meal and as a thank you, he'd cover the bill."

"Yes, so you said. So let me enlighten you as to who this man really is? Bile Murphy is part of the notorious Irish gang tied up in prostitution, drugs, extortion and kidnapping. I was investigating them, they wanted me out of the picture, you lured me to my possible death. Except, for your information, Bile Murphy is in prison awaiting trial. He couldn't have come here, unless it was in a police van. So like I said Dominick, just go, will you?"

After Dominick left, the owner approached Karen. "I understand from the gentleman who's just left, you are going to settle the bill, Lady Harris?"

343

She looked at him for a moment. "It was interesting that you were able to accommodate us, given the difficulty in getting a reservation here normally. Then, for a stranger to get a booking so easily, points to you dropping in popularity, or strings being pulled. Which is it?"

"You're correct, we're always fully booked, however, for a favour, I obliged one of our most important clients."

"Yes, a client who rarely comes to London, a client who has just been arrested and faces charges that will keep him in prison for quite a number of years. Collusion with such a man to entice me here, leaves a person open to arrest. Tell me, is Mace, or even Bile, the real owner of this restaurant, or your partner?"

Already obviously uncomfortable, he gave a weak smile. "Bile is my brother. I've only just heard that he's been arrested. If I'd known earlier, we would have cancelled the reservation. As it is, I wouldn't take penny of your money, so tell your lapdog he owes us nothing."

Karen stood and moved closer to him, her mood, the tone of her voice changed, far more intimidating. "Unit T, now have you in our sights. We never go away, if I hear even a whisper about this place, that it is not what it seems, we'll be back. Then it won't be to dine, it will be to arrest, or maybe kill you. Have we an understanding?"

He looked back at her. "You may have put some of my family in prison, Harris, but we Murphy's don't go away as well. Your time will come."

She moved away, picking up her bag, pressing her watch button twice to tell her surveillance she was leaving and wanted a cab. Then looked back at him watching her.

"Thank you for the dinner, but if I'd known it was on the Murphy's I'd not have come. As it is, I also don't take kindly to being threatened, be it meaningful or just in idle comment. It brings out the very worst in me." Then she walked away.

***

The following morning Karen left her London flat for the airport. Already the flight plan, via Paris, had been lodged to Unit T. By the time Karen had parked her car and gone through security, her aircraft was fuelled and ready to go. As usual, she walked around the aircraft, satisfying herself all seemed well and climbing aboard, pressing the button to bring up the steps and shut the door. Going into the cockpit, the co-pilot's seat was already occupied.

"No problems getting aboard, Odette?" Karen asked, taking the pilot's seat and adjusting her position.

"No, it was a breeze with the pass you sent me. I even had a nice man carry my bag."

Karen smiled, slipping on the headphones and calling the tower. Minutes later, after starting the engines, they were soon waiting behind two similar sized aircraft for their turn to take-off.

"I'll have one of these one day," Odette said, with confidence.

"Perhaps, you never can tell the future."

Once in the air and on autopilot, Karen leaned back. "The gun you used on Mace, it is destroyed?"

"Bottom of the Irish sea."

"That's good. So what now, have you thought about my proposal? And more importantly the risks involved, now you've actually experienced an operation?"

Karen asked.

Odette remained silent for a short time, Karen saying nothing, spending time checking her instruments.

"I have thought about it, Karen. After Mace, I really believed that was it and I'd go back to the life I had before. Then I asked myself, what life? Dad's dead, mum's virtually a vegetable. I have sufficient money now to be able to buy back the family home and shop, but it all seems pointless alone. What about you?"

"I'd love to carry on, Odette. I really would and I'd be the first one to come in and back you, like in Ireland. Except being there made me realise I was just the alternative, the one to make up the numbers when they were busy, not the preferred one. Whoever goes in must be the one they want, the one they can sell. On that basis, can I compete with eighteen to twenty year olds? No, I can't. I can hold my own in a one-to-one as an escort, but that's not the world we're in, when it comes to traffickers."

"So at times, you and I will be a team?"

Karen grinned. "You'd better believe it. If necessary, I'll be at your side, Odette; I'll not shy away."

"In that case, I loved working with you, so I'm in, what's next?"

"I've arranged for you to spend time with the French DGSI. They will build on your initial training with Unit T, besides learning a great deal about how to use intelligence you gain in covert operations to your advantage. Once out in the field. I've contacts all over Europe, you will receive help, weapons and anything else you need, through a fully manned contact number, on any covert operation. Once you leave there you will move around various cities in Europe, get temporary jobs bars, so you can bail at a moment's notice."

"Will we meet socially at times?"

"We will. I'll not look like Karen Harris, the same as I didn't in Ireland."

"Then I'll look forward to it."

***

After leaving Odette in Paris, Karen was soon landing at Unit T's headquarters. A car was waiting to take her home. It had been a long day, already meetings had been set-up for tomorrow, lasting all day, to piece together the Irish operation and how it impacted on operations still running in Europe. Particularly Crustkin's operation, who Karen had every intention of targeting. In the past he'd made a fool out of her, taken her for a ride and very nearly got away with millions in drugs. Karen didn't like that, but tonight, she just wanted a long soak in the bath and to sleep in her own bed.

The housekeeper met her at the door. "Good evening, Lady Harris, the office informed me you were on your way, dinner is ready when you are."

"Thank you, is half an hour okay, I'll just get changed?"

"Half an hour it is," she answered with a smile, before returning to the kitchen.

Karen remained standing there. The house was so quiet it made her shiver a little. Was this to be her life, forever alone, passing on to Odette what had kept her alive and given her some purpose since she was eighteen? She sighed, making her way upstairs and into her room. After a wash and a change of clothes, Karen sat in front of the mirror, combing her hair, listening to the messages on her personal answer phone. Five were from Sherry, wanting her to call when she arrived home. Karen knew she must talk to Sherry sometime, but decided to eat first. There were also three messages from a girl she knew as Ross. They had got on well, and spent time together in Karen's London flat, before Ross was relocated to Spain. Although, they still kept in touch and regularly spoke. However, Ross's call wasn't just to chat. She was in Paris the following week, on behalf of the company she worked for, and was asking if they could meet and perhaps spend a few days together.

Finishing off her hair, Karen placed the brush back on the dressing table. She looked at the answerphone for a moment, then picked up the handset, dialling Ross's number.

"Finally Karen, I'd nearly given up, can we get together then?" Ross asked, once they were connected.

"I've been a bit busy Ross, but I've a few days leave due, so yes, I'd love to meet you in Paris."

"Great, I've got to go, the taxi's here and girls are already jumping up and down wanting me to come."

"Where are you off to then?"

"Janet, my flat mate, has some of her old school friends over from England, so they roped me into doing the rounds of the local clubs."

"Then you should go. We'll talk later in the week and firm up the arrangements."

"Will do, love you, Karen."

"I love you as well, Ross, take care."

Karen replaced the handset. Ross would never be

any different, living life to the fullest, after the years she'd been kept as virtually a prisoner by a trafficker. But she really liked the girl and enjoyed being with her.

***

Following dinner, Karen went to her office in the house and called Sherry.

"Hi, Karen, I hear there's congregations in order."

"In what way?"

"You took the Murphy gang down."

"It's what we do Sherry, you of all people should know that. Anyway, you wanted to speak to me?"

"I do, but I'd have rather we met face to face."

"Is this unit business, because I'm in the office tomorrow, or is it personal?"

"A bit of both."

"Just tell me what's on your mind, Sherry."

"If you want. Since you've been gone, it's given me time to think, besides talk to Ally. All of us said some very harsh and hurtful words to each other, at a time when we were all under real stress."

"Excuse me, Sherry. Not all of us, I'm the victim here, with not only Ally, throwing all I've done for the girl in my face and you backing her. So, is this an apology and you both want to come home?"

"It is an apology, but neither of us are coming back. I considered the new arrangement we talked about, before you left for London and decided for me, at least, it wouldn't work, so it's best I go. In fact, I've already resigned from Unit T and I am returning to the UK with Ally next week. There's to be a farewell party and we'd like you to come."

If Sherry had been in front of Karen, she'd have seen the tears trickling down her face. But she couldn't and Karen voice gave nothing away. "I did tell you she'd not come back, Sherry. I'll not say I won't miss you both, you in particular, because I will. I always believed we were good together and more like a family. Then, like any family that have arguments, I had the hope we'd find common ground. It seems that is not to be the case, so all I can do is wish you both well. As for your leaving do, I'm sorry, I've already made arrangements and will be in Paris. Maybe it's for the best, the last week's been particularly bad for me, on a personal level, so I'd not be good at a party."

"So after all we've been through, you're not prepared to delay your departure to see us off?"

Karen swallowed hard, taking a deep breath. "What do you think I am, Sherry? I'm only human with feelings as well you know. How can you ask me to stand there with a smile on my face and watch you both walk out of my life, the same as my sister did to me? I can't do it. In fact, I won't do it. Goodbye Sherry, we shouldn't speak again."

Placing the handset back on its cradle, Karen sat there, looking down at the telephone. Never had she felt as alone as she did tonight.

Titles by the Same Author

Action Adventure

     The People Traders
     The People Trafficker
     Unit T Special Forces
     Goin Goin Sold
     The Royal Grandchild
     Nigerian Connection
     Russian Connection
     Italian Connection
     Romanian Connection
     English Connection
     Irish Connection
     Girl in a Web

Romance

     Gemmas WhiteCliff
     Catwalk Supermodel

Fantasy

     Tall Ship Magic
     Plagarma
     The Timeless Chamber

Fairy Stories

     Sparkle and the Insect Collector
     Sparkle and the Whirlwind
     Sparkle and the Hole in the Ground
     Sparkle and the Lost Bees

Paranormal

     Ghost Diamonds

Audio Titles

     Nigerian Connection
     Russian Connection
     Italian Connection
     Romanian Connection

Full information at: www.keithhoare.com